ALSO AVAILABLE
FROM BITTER LEMON PRESS
BY POL KOUTSAKIS

*Athenian Blues*

# BABY BLUE

## Pol Koutsakis

Translated by Anne-Marie Stanton-Ife

**BITTER LEMON PRESS**
**LONDON**

BITTER LEMON PRESS

First published in the United Kingdom in 2018 by
Bitter Lemon Press, 47 Wilmington Square, London WC1X 0ET

www.bitterlemonpress.com

First published in Greek as *Baby Blue*,
Patakis Publications, Athens, 2015
© Pol Koutsakis, 2015

English translation © Anne-Marie Stanton-Ife, 2018

A CIP record for this book is available from the British Library

ISBN 978–1–908524–91-1
eBook ISBN: 978–1–908524–92–8

Typeset by Tetragon, London
Printed and bound by CPI Books (UK) Ltd, Croydon, CR0 4YY

Bitter Lemon Press gratefully acknowledges the
support of the Arts Council of England.

*For the Tramp and his girl, for that night in Florence.*
*You moved D so much – I was jealous. I owed you one.*

# 1

"Evening, Stratos." This was a voice I hadn't heard for a while, a voice so authoritative that anyone hearing it for the first time would never imagine its owner was homeless.

"Angelino," I replied, looking at my screen and noticing that he had changed his number yet again. Angelino never phones unless I've asked him to get me some information, the kind of information only Angelino can dig up. But this time I hadn't asked.

"You did say if I ever needed anything ..." he said.

I sat back down on the bed. "When do you want to meet?"

"In an hour?"

Any minute now Maria would be coming down to my room. We hadn't seen each other for days; her wishes, not mine. And I felt the need to be with her and far away from other people more strongly than ever.

"See you then," I said, my phone wedged between my ear and my shoulder as I tried to get a head start on the unpredictable Athenian traffic by dressing as I talked.

We always let down those we love most. And we always take the gamble that they'll understand. I told Maria something urgent had come up. When you've been with the same person since you were teenagers, you don't need a great many words to communicate; sometimes you don't need them at all. Her belly was already beginning to swell – she had just entered the third month, but her baby seemed to be in a hurry to get out and spend time with us. I refer to it mentally as "her baby" because I didn't know, and didn't dare ask, if it was mine. There were two reasons for this: first, even if it wasn't mine, I would love it as my own; the second reason was that I thought about the possibility of it being mine every single day and felt that happiness such as this was beyond my grasp, and I didn't know how to handle it. Maybe I just didn't deserve it.

I got into the Peugeot and set off for the Ambelokipi metro station. I have made a mental note of all the side streets round all the stations in a thirty-minute radius of my flat where it is possible to park. I use different stations all the time so I don't become an easy target. In my line of work, being able to move around unnoticed is a major advantage, and standing at six foot three and weighing in at slightly over two hundred and twenty pounds, almost all of it muscle, I'm automatically at a disadvantage. Fortunately, most people who use the metro look straight down. And only down. It's as though they've had all curiosity for the world erased by the financial crisis.

I'm a caretaker – that's my job. I cater to such dark desires that a good many of my clients look shocked as they listen to themselves articulate those desires. Not so shocked, though, as when they try to convince me that their target deserves to be taken down. Years ago, one very rich lady, who tried to hire me to take care of her business partner, called me a "maverick" when I explained to her that my investigation showed that everything she'd told me about him was a lie and that I would keep the deposit as agreed but wouldn't be going ahead with the job. Most people who hire me don't really believe I'm serious about my terms and conditions.

In a way they are right; they pay a lot of money and expect their instructions to be followed and their victims taken care of, no questions asked. But not by me.

When you're the best, you can afford to be a maverick.

# 2

This was not my city. It was something else, something sick trying to look, sound and smell like Athens. But it was failing and it knew it, just like the old juggler I used to see around this time of day in the middle of the square. He would lose track of one ball after another but always bent down, picked them up and kept going. Because there was nothing else he could do.

The good thing about Omonia Square was that it had not waited for the devastation of the last three years to go to seed. The state it was in surprised no one. It had managed to descend into darkness much earlier than that, as though it had seen the crisis coming and the path the country would take and wanted to get ahead of the game. Any neighbourhood you walked through in Athens, there'd be a surprise waiting for you: where there had been a shop you were greeted by a sturdy lock; where you'd once seen the postman inserting letters into the individual letter boxes that line the entrance halls of every block of flats in the city, you now saw the mail piled high on the floor by the main door, next to the outstretched body of some homeless person wrapped in a blanket, resting on the front steps of the building. But in Omonia this sort of thing came as no surprise to anyone. They were familiar sights and had been for a while. Omonia had become the only part of Athens where you knew what to expect, morning, noon and at night – especially night. Certainty can be very reassuring, if depressing, especially when everything unexpected that happens in the city seems to force reality further into a downward spiral. But in Omonia, as the old song goes, "you can't get any lower than this".

It was almost 9.30 p.m. It was completely dark and conditions that spring night in February were close to perfect for all types of vampires to come out – both those that drink their own blood, scouring their legs for a vein to stick the needle into, and for those who go round exploiting the needs of others. The escalator took me out of the station next to a hoarding advertising a new department opening inside the Hondos Center department store, where customers would unlock all the secrets of chocolate. On the pavement outside the shop, a dark-skinned Asian man was kneeling down, sobbing, with jets of blood spurting out of his cheek. He'd been stabbed; a friend was trying to help stem the flow with a piece of paper. Like most people, I walked on.

For most of the last twelve years, Angelino had lived right there on the square with Hector, his very sweet, very large geriatric German Shepherd, who walked with great difficulty. Hector had disappeared one night last winter. Angelino explained at the time that very loyal dogs take themselves off when their time has come, to spare their owners the sight of them dying. Their owner is their family, and their family must not be made vulnerable by their death. The next time I saw Angelino, he was all alone in his usual spot on the square, and I asked him why he didn't get another dog. "If I did, it would mean that Hector was replaceable," he answered.

We weren't meeting at Angelino's usual spot. He'd moved. I was walking quickly, not just to make sure I got there on time, but to escape the stench from the side streets, which had been turned into public conveniences and sites of infection. I passed kiosks groaning under the weight of porn mags; Nigerians selling knock-off designer handbags and watches; Chinese people selling energy bracelets and ointments promising to heal all wounds and cure all cancers; Georgians on the corner of Agiou Konstantinou Street, asking me if I "wanted some"; Kurds magicking cartons of contraband cigarettes out of nowhere; girls and boys of all nationalities offering up any and every part of their bodies for between ten and forty euros to any sex-starved passer-by, and multicoloured used condoms left behind after each quickie; dilapidated buildings with people piled ten high into studio flats of no more than three hundred square feet. If instead of the ten olive trees the municipality had planted to symbolize the ten tribes of ancient Athens they had planted one tree for every race living in modern-day Omonia Square, they would have created a lung of green for the city. But then again, that would not serve the interests of those who'd been buying up the most central building plots in the city for a pittance in recent years.

I kept on going down Agiou Konstantinou, keeping a close eye on the pavement so that I wouldn't fall down one of the manholes that no longer had grilles over them. It seemed that local gangs had run out of statues to steal after the violent reaction of residents who had been furious about the destruction of these monuments. Instead they had turned their focus back to stealing metal grilles and manhole covers and melting them down. Copper is quick and easy money and nobody gets emotional about sewers, not even the police, seeing as the owners of the city's two biggest furnaces were the money behind so many Athenian MPs – at least according to an independent website, which had been mysteriously shut down the day after it went up. When I wasn't looking down at the ground, I looked at the few shop windows left untouched by the riots that regularly took place round here. They were fortified, waiting for the next attack.

Before I got as far as the National Theatre I turned right, and was walking down Chateaubriand Street two hundred yards later. I felt like I had suddenly been teleported to another city, to a time that merged past with future and had given up on the ugliness of the present. I stared a while at the aristocratic listed building housing the Cultural Center and the historic Musicians' Coffee House opposite before ringing the bell of the neoclassical building next door, which seemed by some miracle to have escaped the graffiti and the slogans denouncing the police and the bankers gracing the wider neighbourhood.

Truth was, it was no miracle. When the first slogans went up, Angelino's men had gone out and painted over the walls and the door and stood guard outside for forty-eight hours, making sure that whoever was doing this would see them and get the picture of who they were dealing with. In the words of Lieutenant DeGarmot in *The Lady in the Lake* (Bogart should definitely have played Marlowe), "you stick your nose into my business, and you'll wake up in an alley with the cats looking at you." And because Angelino had friends in the National Intelligence Service whom he had helped out in the past when they needed it, the entire block was clear of CCTV cameras, so there was no chance of anything being recorded that could prove awkward for him and his associates.

An unfamiliar voice answered the intercom, wanting to know who I was. I gave my name – my given name, not the one on my ID card – and heard the usual buzz of the door opening.

The bulk waiting behind the door was called Jimmy, and for the last couple of years had been Angelino's main bodyguard. If his chest had been just that little bit wider, he could have been on the cover of *Steroids and You*. Or *Penthouse*. Jimmy didn't like me much. To be precise, he didn't like me at all. He felt uncomfortable whenever we were in the same place, in Omonia and now here in this impressive neoclassical building. He said nothing, just motioned to me to go inside. While there's a lot to be said for keeping conversation to a minimum, I prefer it when it's a matter of choice rather than forced by someone who can only communicate in snarls.

I went into the sitting room and looked around at everybody there – about twenty people, I reckoned. I thought to myself that the black jeans and old grey sweater I was wearing made me by far the worst-dressed person in the room. I didn't have time to think about much else because my gaze was following the gaze of the other guests, all of them looking in the same direction.

I asked myself if my eyes were really seeing what I saw.

# 3

In the middle of the room was a stunningly beautiful young girl. She was wearing a black jacket, black shirt and white trousers and couldn't have been more than sixteen, but for some reason her formal clothes did not seem out of place on her. Her long chestnut hair was pinned back in a ponytail, emphasizing her high cheekbones and soft blue eyes – baby blue, as the Americans call it – which remained devoid of expression as she held us all spellbound.

She was sitting at a round table, completely motionless, and seemed to be listening to the soft, hypnotic lounge music coming out of the speakers while waiting patiently for one of the guests to shuffle and cut a deck of cards, choose two cards at random and hold them up for everyone to see. It was the eight of diamonds and the six of clubs. The girl took the cards out of his hands, let everyone see them again, and put them down on the table, placing her hands over them, rather like a poker player who is worried that the other players will see what cards he has. After a while, she took away her hands to reveal two bright red aces. She stood up quickly but not abruptly, placed one ace in each palm, turned her hands over in the air, and the aces metamorphosed into kings. An exclamation escaped the mouth of the heavily built fifty-year-old blonde woman standing next to me, her fur stole struggling to balance itself across her jewellery-laden throat. After another flick of the hands, the kings became queens. Then jacks, tens, nines, eights until, with one more flick of the wrist, which resembled the way you might accompany your lover in a passionate tango, her hands magically produced two aces, only this time they were the two black aces from the deck. I felt the urge to clap, but the girl had not finished. She set the aces down on the table, leaned over and started to blow on them. She blew them as though she was trying to animate them. Then, still silent, she turned them over and motioned to the guests that one of them should step forward. The large woman next to me volunteered. The girl pointed to the cards without touching them, prompting her to turn them over. As the eight of diamonds and the six of clubs reappeared before her, my neighbour let out an even louder exclamation.

But none of this was either as impressive or unsettling as the sight of the girl herself, serious and completely absorbed in her art. Because those wonderful baby-blue eyes, perpetually devoid of expression, never blinking, were looking at nothing and everything.

Because the girl who had enchanted us was blind.

# 4

The loud applause, even the whistling from the less restrained guests, seemed to make no impression on the girl, who did not so much as smile. She bowed three times and without any assistance walked past the fireplace with the marble columns and Minoan murals and disappeared into another room.

"Emma's amazing, isn't she? Do you know how many people in the world can pull off seven card changes in a row in the air?" came Angelino's voice in my ear.

I turned round and almost didn't recognize him. When you get used to the way someone who lives on the street looks, it can be hard to recognize them in a different context. I read somewhere that our brain does not record as many faces as it does styles and situations connected with particular faces. That night Angelino was dressed like a prince: gold cufflinks, a blue tailored suit that looked like it had been sewn straight onto his slight frame, a salmon-coloured shirt and discreet tortoiseshell glasses. He seemed to inhabit a planet far away from Omonia and his sweatshirts, army fatigues and dark-brown overcoat. The only thing that was completely unaltered was his expression, which belonged not to a forty-five-year-old but to an Athenian from the days of Pericles, the face of a man who had seen everything and had a crystal-clear view of everything that happened, nothing of which seemed to surprise him. Nothing, that is, apart from Emma.

"I'll be ditching the look – it's just for tonight. Maybe for tomorrow night, too," he said almost apologetically as he registered my confused look.

"Tonight? Why?" I asked.

"For them," he whispered, pointing with a slight movement of his head towards the people standing round drinking punch and discussing the girl's incredible talents.

Angelino explained that the performance had started earlier and I had only seen the last part of it.

"Who's 'them'?"

"Investors," he said with a faint smile, leaving a sense of mystery hanging in the air.

Angelino likes to give half answers, and he likes to keep the other half of the answer to himself. But tonight he'd called on me for help, and I for my part like to deal with full explanations.

"I'll need more than that," I said.

He gave in, accepting defeat. A lock of grey hair – his hair had been grey for the twenty-odd years I'd known him – fell across his forehead. His scent was particularly strong, a mixture of mint and basil, but this was not part of the new look. Angelino had a thing about fragrances, and whenever he discovered a new one he liked he would literally douse himself in it, possibly to mask the stench of the square that clung to him.

"Emma is going to take part in the Magic Olympics in Helsinki in six months' time," he told me.

"Never heard of it."

"Oh, it's big business. The winners appear in Vegas, New York, amusement parks in California, with amazing takings every night. By 'magic' they mean legerdemain, of course, but I'm not always convinced that what Emma does is not magic. She doesn't explain most of her tricks to me. She shuts herself away in her room for days on end and comes out when she has perfected another unbelievable trick. There are two categories: stage magic and close-up magic, which happens right beneath your nose. That's the one that Emma's going to compete in."

"So everyone here is smelling the money?"

"That's why we've brought them."

"Have they got a strong sense of smell?"

"I hope so. There'll be more tomorrow, they've all been individually selected on the basis of their wallets. If they sponsor Emma in her campaign, we both stand to profit."

"When you say 'campaign'...?"

"We have to travel to festivals, network, show off some of her tricks – but not her best ones – all so that she can get onto TV shows abroad, generate interest, make a name for herself. Everything she does on tour has to be completely different from what she pulls out in the competition itself."

"Who will be travelling with her?"

"Her agent, who lives in England, and me, her manager."

"So you *will* be sticking with the look."

"Maybe for a bit longer, then."

"What if she doesn't win anything at the Olympics? If she doesn't do well at all, what's in it for the investors?"

"Nothing. But that's the wrong question. Only insecure people consider the worst-case scenario. The sort of people who even when they're winning never stand out, never do anything exceptional. The sort of people who only play because they don't want to lose. The right question is the one I asked you earlier: how many people in the world can do seven card changes in a row in the air?"

"Not many, I suspect."

"Nobody can even do six. And I'm not even talking about right now. It's *never* been done before. And she can do seven in the air plus another two on the table, before and after. I've brought in gurus from Europe and America – and they all tell me that Emma is the kind of talent that only comes up once in fifty years. Ah! I'm so happy you could make it," said Angelino, suddenly changing tone.

He had turned in the direction of a well-turned-out sixty-year-old investor who was approaching him with a smile so sardonic that if his eyes were to start blinking out dollars in the way they do in the comics, it would not have struck me as anything other than completely normal.

# 5

While Angelino was charming the investors, I decided to tour the building. Each room of the four on that floor was larger and more impressive than the last, with their painted ceilings with different designs giving them a distinct character and the heavy drapes, chandeliers and ornate mirrors completing the picture. All the floors were marble just like the staircase, which was broad enough to hold a large family on each of its steps. The main sitting room was different: its cream-coloured walls matched the deep-pile rugs, the antique clocks and long white curtains. In all the other rooms, the main colour was blue – even the paintings were inspired by the sea, or by Emma's eyes. Unlike the eyes of most blind people I've seen, they weren't unsettling. The only emotion they provoked was deep sadness at the misfortune in front of you.

I was on one of the back balconies, looking down at the apricot, peach and palm trees in the back garden, when I heard footsteps behind me. I turned and saw Angelino and Emma. He was holding her hand.

"You must be Stratos," she said, looking straight at me.

"Good evening. Nice show."

"Great show," said Angelino, correcting me.

"It was OK. I still need to work on a couple of details," she replied.

Her voice was serious and a bit nasal. She had already changed and was now in jeans and T-shirt underneath a white cardigan. Her hair was loose and she had cleaned off her make-up, which left her looking completely natural and as such, even more beautiful. The more I looked at her, the more convinced I was that I knew her from somewhere – but I couldn't put my finger on it.

"We've been looking for you," said Angelino. "Emma insists on telling you everything herself; she doesn't want you to hear it all from me. Do you want to stay here, or shall we go to my office?"

"Have the … left?" I didn't want to say "the investors" because I wasn't sure how the girl would take it.

"The investors?" She supplied the missing word for me. Maybe she wasn't especially sensitive to language.

"Yes, I saw the last one out a little while ago," said Angelino.

"We'll be fine here; we don't need to go to the office," Emma reassured him.

She let go of Angelino's hand and made for one of the three chairs in the room, completely independently. She knew the space off by heart, which meant that the hand-holding was less a sign of dependence and more a sign of affection.

I moved closer and sat down opposite her.

"How did you know where I was when you walked in? Can you see?"

"I haven't seen a thing since I was eight years old. Up till then I could make out a few colours."

"Then how?"

"I sensed there was another presence in the room, and Angelino had told me that you were wandering around up here. I guessed your position from your smell, I mean your lack of smell. I couldn't smell you, which meant that you had to be quite far away from the door, so logically, you would have been on the balcony."

"A rough guess, then."

"When you can't see, you're forced to guess a lot of things based on probability, and hope that you're right."

I thought to myself that that's pretty much how it works when you can see.

"Do you want me to stay?" asked Angelino.

"If Stratos doesn't mind being alone with me, I'd prefer it if you left us for a while."

*If Stratos doesn't mind being alone with me.* I found this so funny, coming from a teenage girl. I had to smile.

"Just make sure you don't make him disappear like those aces," said Angelino and walked noiselessly out of the room, closing the door behind him.

A homeless businessman with a sense of humour. A sense of humour that Emma did not appear to share. She remained serious, silent, almost frozen. I couldn't tell whether this was because of a sudden drop in adrenalin now that the performance was over or whether this iciness was a permanent accessory.

I don't generally mind silence. The fact that I don't say much probably encourages it. But silence can help you see how the other person looks at you. You can gauge the temperature and the light of their gaze. But with Emma I couldn't do that. Silence, I discovered, when you're sitting opposite a blind person, was the definition of awkwardness.

"I'm all ears," I said after a minute or so had passed.

"Sorry about the silence. I just wanted to test your patience. Most people when they're around me feel the need to say something right away so that they don't feel uncomfortable."

"I didn't know I was going to have to pass a test."

"Don't take it too seriously. Angelino tells me that you're the only person who can help us. But this is an old case, and if you take it on, you will need a lot of patience."

"What case?"

"Tell me, is it true what Angelino's told me about you?"

"Only the bad stuff."

"He told me he trusts you completely. I've never heard him say that about anyone."

I didn't have an answer to that, so I kept quiet.

"Are you still here?"

"I'm not going anywhere until you've finished."

"How come?"

"Angelino and I have been through a lot. I owe him. We're not friends, if that's what you're asking. But he's right; he can trust me completely."

"Good. I'll give you the short version now and the details later. Stop me at any point if you want to ask me something. Agreed?"

It felt like I was talking to a forty-year-old CEO, someone who had learnt that every second counts in business and that nothing else is of any interest.

I nodded, before realizing she couldn't see me. I would have to do more talking than usual.

"Agreed," I said.

"Three years ago, my dad was murdered. He wasn't my real father, but he rescued me from the orphanage. He just turned up and took me away – I was three and already struggling with my eyesight. He brought me up, so he was my actual dad. He was found full of bullet holes. They tortured him before they killed him."

She kept a steady voice the whole time. Her tone was like that of a TV presenter, trying to relay the bare facts without any emotion. She was so controlled that she reminded me of my younger self when I had to talk to the social workers who would turn up suddenly at our house and had to hide from them the fact that my mentally ill mother had disappeared once more into the streets of Athens. I listened to the perfect balance in her voice, which never faltered, but I could hear the cracks inside her.

"I'm so sorry," I said. Because there was nothing better to say. Because there never is when somebody has lost someone.

"I want you to find out who killed him. And I'll pay you; I have money. And I'll get more."

"Aren't you getting ahead of yourself? I haven't agreed to anything yet. What you're asking me to do is police work."

"The cops couldn't care less about us."

"Us?"

"We were living on the streets. We were homeless after Themis – my dad – left his job. Cops don't care about street people. 'One less to worry about' is what they think, and what they say. Once I saw a homeless man ask them where he was supposed to go when they kicked him off the park bench he was sleeping on. They told him to go to hell."

"They're not all like that," I said. I knew one who really did care. But apart from him, I couldn't come up with many other examples.

"It's been three years now, but they closed the case after only a few days. They're all the same. They only take an interest if they want to catch you."

"Did Angelino try to help?"

"Angelino has been taking care of me for over two years. Like family. The only family I've had since Dad. He takes me to doctors, shrinks, he sits and talks to me for hours whenever I ask him to, even though I know he would rather be out on the square. He took on this building to make a home for me, so I'd be comfortable and have somewhere to work on my tricks. And he buys me DVDs of American magicians I can listen to ... He did everything he could to track down the killer. But he didn't find him."

Angelino's network covered the entire city. If he couldn't find out who did this, this was going to be tough. And the fact that three years had passed would make it twice as hard. And the fact that Emma's dad was home-less – with no fixed points of reference – made the whole case look like a joke.

"I think there's been some kind of misunderstanding here. I don't think Angelino has told you what kind of work it is that I do."

"He's told me exactly what kind of work you do."

"Then you'll know that I don't —"

"You owe him," she interrupted. "You said so yourself."

The forty-year-old CEO was steering the conversation once more. I was glad she was, because she stopped me from getting carried away by the sympathy this young girl provoked in me.

"I see. And how long were you living on the streets?"

"Five years. From when I was six. From when Dad left his job till I was eleven and they murdered him."

Which meant that she was now fourteen. Even younger than I had first thought.

"How did you get by?"

"We had this act we would perform around various squares. Chaplin's Tramp."

That's where I knew her from. She was the girl I'd seen so often in Omonia, Syntagma and other squares in the city, performing comic and dramatic sketches in the style of the Tramp. All their acts attracted big crowds and were inspired by *The Kid* – a film I loved for its melancholy spirit, despite the fact that it wasn't noir. Of course, the "kid" of the title is a boy, so Emma had her hair cut short then, and it had been really hard to tell that she was a girl. I remembered now that all the other parts were played by the Tramp character and Emma had played the adopted son who was always having to run away from the police and everyone else who was trying to separate them. I couldn't get over how much she had grown up. Nor that the child, who even did acrobatics with the Tramp, was blind and nobody in their audiences had had the slightest clue.

"I've seen it," I told her.

"Yes. Dad said we drew big crowds. I sensed it from the sound of the applause. Dad had a thing about that film; he really loved it."

"Those acts would have been tough for any kid to pull off; how did you —"

"That's not important. We're here now so that I can give you whatever information you need about the murder."

"You don't know what information might be useful to me. Neither do I. That's why I'll ask the questions, so I can see what I can use. *If* I decide to get involved, that is."

"OK," she said in that disdainful way teenagers have.

I decided not to repeat the question for the time being. I'd get back to it at some other point.

"So where did you usually stay?"

"At different shelters, and in the time just before the murder, on Filopappou. There are lots of homeless people living up there on the hill. It's a small community for anyone who wants to join it."

"Any idea if he had any enemies?"

"No enemies. No friends. It was just the two of us. We were a team. 'The pack', he used to call us. We'd have the occasional conversation with other homeless people so that we could see how we could help each other out with everyday stuff. But that was it. We were never really true members of the community there."

"When he was murdered …"

"I found him." Her perfectly composed voice was suddenly thrown off balance, so I didn't insist on details. Angelino would be able to fill me in. There was no reason to make her cry in front of me.

"You mentioned that he left his job eight years ago. What did he do?"

"He was a journalist. Newspaper and TV reporter. He wanted to change the world," she said, full of pride, the balance in her voice now restored. That's what pride does; it helps you forget. For a while.

"Where did he work?"

She gave me the names of some of the best-known newspapers and TV channels.

"What about the orphanage? Did he take you from there alone? Wasn't he married?"

"He'd come to report on it. The orphanage was not funded properly and was in danger of closing. The management was trying to raise awareness through a TV programme. As soon as he turned up, the other children started doing what the nurses there had trained them to do. They threw themselves down on the floor and started shouting, 'Daddy! Daddy!' They told us to do that whenever anyone arrived, and that was the trick to get a home and some parents. I didn't do it. I didn't like asking for things. I'd already had a bad experience when I was younger the one time I had done it and the other children had thrown me down and pushed me to the side so that they could get a better position. Dad was aware of the trick and didn't fall for it. He was struck by this child who held back, playing alone. He started talking to me, came back the next day, and the next, asked about me, wasn't put off by my problem and eventually abducted me."

"He *abducted* you from the orphanage?"

"Yes."

"Without causing a commotion?"

"He had a friend there, Hara, the social worker. It was Hara who called him about the funding. Hara supposedly made a home visit and saw how happy he was with his fiancée. He didn't have a fiancée, of course, so they put down a false name and some signatures on the form and reported that the house was perfect for bringing up a child in. She also put in her report that Dad had started to learn Braille so that he could teach me how to read and write. That part was true. It's one of the hardest things to learn, especially for an adult, but he did it. For me."

For the first time she smiled. I couldn't tell whether I felt more relieved that I had confirmation that she could smile, or that her smile was so bright that it seemed that it was trying to balance out the endless, definitive darkness inside her eyes.

"Through some of his connections, it all went through the courts quite quickly and in just six months he had officially adopted me. It usually takes over a year; some children wait as long as two years with all the delays. They can't go to live with the parents who want them, so the parents have to keep coming to the orphanage to see them and say goodbye again when they leave in the evening, when both the children and the parents burst into tears. But he left with me on the first day. I never had to go back."

I noticed how she said "they have to keep coming to the orphanage". Present tense. As though a part of her was still there.

"Do you know why he left his job?"

"He said it didn't fulfil him any longer. Too much dirt everywhere."

"But you said he wanted to change the world."

"Yes. I don't know. I think he realized he couldn't."

He realized he couldn't. Just like in Fritz Lang's *Clash by Night*, when Mae Doyle says to her brother, "What do you want, my life's history? Here it is in four words: big ideas, small results."

"Did he try to get another job, or did you go straight onto the streets?"

"I don't think so. I was very young and I don't really remember. And then afterwards we never talked about it because we were having such a good time."

"On the streets?"

"*Yes.*"

A calm, full, abrupt "yes". The tone we reserve for things we refuse to discuss. Things that are a given. A reporter working for a big newspaper and TV channel deciding to give it all up and become a vagrant. After all, what could be more normal than that?

"When you were performing, especially in the early days, didn't people recognize him, people who'd seen him on TV?"

"I can't remember. I don't remember anyone saying anything to him. I imagine that when he was dressed as the Tramp they wouldn't have recognized him."

"So what do you want now? You want to find the murderer and see him put behind bars? Is it justice you want?"

"I'm only out for revenge. Justice disappeared the moment he died."

Not fourteen. Not forty. When you have seized on such a basic truth as that and are still standing, you are ageless. Forgetting myself again, I nodded.

"All right," I said.

I was the man for the job.

# 6

Emma directed me to Angelino's office on the floor above, but before I even got as far as the staircase, I saw Jimmy's chest flash past, closely followed by Jimmy himself. He threw me a quick sideways glance and turned to his boss, who had just reached the top of the staircase.

"Shall I get the others?" he asked, opening his mouth and appearing to shriek more than speak.

"Yes. Give me a couple of minutes with Stratos first," replied Angelino and Jimmy disappeared.

Angelino came down the stairs quickly. Inside his now buttoned-up jacket I saw a pistol resting inside a shoulder holster. I'd never seen him carrying a weapon before; the ability to get hold of information, however deeply buried, had always been Angelino's weapon.

"I'm sorry, but we'll have to do this some other time. A friend of mine has been hurt and is in hospital. Did you and Emma talk?"

I nodded. It was a relief to be able to revert to gestures again.

"Good. Anything else you want, we'll talk again later tonight – or maybe better the same time tomorrow – there are some things I need to tell you. I'll be here all day. We're expecting a second round of investors."

I said goodbye, and as I was walking towards the door I found myself face to face with Jimmy again, who was standing smack in front of me, blocking my exit as though he wanted a confrontation.

"I've heard a lot about you," he said. At least that's what I thought he said, but I couldn't be sure.

"Then you'll know who you're dealing with," I answered and waited patiently for him to step aside.

He stayed there for a while, giving me hostile stares. He was trying to communicate something with his expression, and perhaps he thought he had managed it. Maybe he felt vindicated – but while Jimmy was standing there feeling better about himself, I was standing there thinking what a massive idiot he was. But he did know a thing or two about professional orientation. He had found the perfect fit between his talents and his chosen line of work.

I made it onto the last train, got back to my car at 12.30 and rushed home to see Maria, hoping she'd still be awake. Her days as a night owl were long gone, and with the pregnancy she was usually in bed before midnight.

The pregnancy had changed everything.

By the time I'd turned into my street in Psychiko I was already on my second cigarette. About thirty yards in front of me, I spotted a very familiar black Nissan parked. The tall, thin, fair-haired guy in the driver's seat, posing as its owner even though he was still trying to pay it off, happened to be the most competent cop in the Athens

Homicide division. His name was Kostas Dragas, but ever since our schooldays everyone had called him Drag. He was my closest friend.

It looked like this really wasn't the night for me and Maria to talk.

I jumped into Drag's car. I saw at once that the weather had forced him to leave the tragic, ancient white trench coat he loved so much at home. But when I looked closer I saw that this had not in any way improved his dress sense. The khaki trousers and the electric-blue shirt did not work together, not even in the wildest dreams of the most perverted designer, and the fact that both garments looked like they'd only ever had the very loosest relationship with an iron didn't do anything to improve his image. And the man wondered why he had no social life.

For a while we just sat there, without him even looking up from his Scandi detective novel.

"Excuse me, sir, this is a patrol car," he said, eventually deigning to acknowledge me.

"Papi's? My shout?"

"In view of your generosity, the car is at your service."

In the last crime novel he'd read, the main character had been an English aristocrat, and it looked like Drag's admiration for its hero was having a worrying influence on the way he spoke.

"I've just come back from —" I started.

"Shh … I was listening to that!" he said and turned up the volume on the radio, releasing the horrible, impulsive voice of a young singer, who was being marketed as *laïkos* because nobody in the country knew how to tell good popular folk music from tragi-kitsch rubbish any more. He was already a headline act at some nightclub in the city, and, judging by the frequency with which I saw his face on the Net, took every opportunity to make profound statements to the media.

"Tell me you fancy this," I said.

"Of course I do. I keep changing stations to catch him."

"You – fancy – this."

"Worship him."

"That *thing*."

"When someone with such a bad voice can sing something as terrible as that with so much passion, you've got to admit that's pretty remarkable. You have to admire him – for his self-confidence, if nothing else."

"Back to the question I wanted to ask you."

"The chorus – the chorus. Listen!"

I spent the next few seconds filling my thoughts with Maria. I had promised to be back as soon as I could and had left again before I'd even got back inside the house. Maria's house – my studio flat is in the semi-basement of her house. I imagined her waiting up for me in the kitchen, struggling to keep her eyes open so that we could talk. Her divorce from Sotiris was very recent and very painful, so much so that she'd said we shouldn't see each other for a while, just while she worked out how she was feeling.

But Drag would have been waiting for me for a reason. Even if he wasn't, I couldn't just leave him and go inside; and I couldn't ask him in, either. I should have, but couldn't. It's a bit awkward when your best friend happens to be the love of your lover's life. When you don't know which one of you is the baby's father, since Sotiris couldn't be, given his condition. And when your best friend has no clue that Maria is pregnant.

Drag seemed satisfied with the song, turned the volume back down and turned to face me again.

"Now I'm listening."

"What are you doing outside my house?"

"Waiting for you."

"Why didn't you call me to see where I was?"

"I was really getting into my novel."

"What if I had been home? What if I'd been out and wasn't coming back till the morning?"

"Maria might have come out. Or I might notice some suspicious movement around the house and check on it. The worst thing that could have happened was that I would have got to the end of my novel and had a kip in the car. All those options are more attractive than the shitty case I took on yesterday."

"Really?"

"Yeah," he said, shaking his head in disappointment.

Drag approaches every murder case like a falcon in relentless pursuit till it spots its prey and swoops down on it without any inhibitions and without mercy. He will go to any lengths to catch a perpetrator, and neither the letter nor the spirit of any law can hold him back. It was this drive that had led to a conviction rate greater than that of any other policeman in the capital and had earned him minor celebrity status, which irritated many in the force immensely – not least himself. I'd given him a hand with some of the cases his fame had been built on. And in one of them, a year ago, we had come closer than ever to death. So had Maria; and Teri, our other close friend from school.

The most recent case that had revived the media interest in Drag had all been his own work: the successful arrest of eight Bulgarian lifers who had escaped from prison in Thessaloniki and spread death and terror across the whole of the north of Greece for a whole month was justly credited to my friend. He had installed himself up there and spent days studying their movements on the map, along with all the evidence from the six young officers, the best around, that he had recruited to his team. They were the only people he trusted in the entire force. Whenever a colleague asked him what they should do, he would answer, "Shut up! I'm thinking," and would argue with his superiors both in Athens and Thessaloniki, who believed that the lifers would keep going north-east so they could cross the border back into the fatherland.

Drag threatened to walk if things weren't done his way. He put up a roadblock and thermal-imaging cameras in the Pindos National Park, convinced that the fugitives were heading for Albania instead. The following day five of them were caught by special forces in the forest. The other three were following a different path; they had crossed the Arkoudorema gorge three times and were climbing up to the Valia Kalda, hoping to get to the lakes on Mount Flega. That's where they bumped into Drag, who had worked out that it was the only possible escape route for anyone who had the balls to make the journey through the blizzard at the time, but he didn't really expect them to make it. Drag told me that "Valia Kalda" was Vlach for "Warm Valley", and that the place had either been named by someone with a keen sense of irony in view of the horrendously low night-time temperatures or by someone who had only visited it during the day, in summer, when it is hot. When I asked him how he knew all this and how he knew so much about the geography of the area, he complained that he had spoken to me about it a long time ago – this mountaineers' oasis inhabited by imperial eagles, Lanner falcons and all kinds of rare birds and animals. His brain is basically a database of useless information picked up on his various adventures, which he is very keen to share in great detail with his friends. Unfortunately, he is not as keen on sharing the details of the adventures themselves, like the one up in Grevena. As I discovered from the news websites, the three escaped convicts were found with their Kalashnikovs and hand grenades on the ground beside them; they hadn't had time to fire a single bullet.

The opposition party probably struggled to believe that Drag was so fast and accurate – in the parliament café where they sit around eating and drinking, they'd never seen him pull a gun. They demanded a full official inquiry on humanitarian grounds, to satisfy themselves that Drag had given the Bulgarians a chance to turn themselves in. Some journalists (sworn enemies of his ever since they had worked out that he deliberately fed them misinformation so they in turn would mislead the suspects in various difficult cases) jumped at the chance to cause him embarrassment and got their own back by writing some inflammatory articles. The inquiry took place, Drag refused to turn up to give evidence and the matter was closed after the government promised the opposition that Drag would not be made assistant chief of police. When the minister broke it to him, sugaring it with a great many apologies, and statements to the effect that "you are amazing, you are our strength, and we have such faith in you, but you know how it is," Drag asked him if he could recommend any good pet shops. The minister, an animal lover, immediately reeled off the names of three or four, and told him to feel free to mention his name to the owners so he would get better service and a fifty per cent discount. After that, he asked what kind of pet he was looking to buy.

"A crocodile, so you can shed your tears together," Drag replied.

Even in those rare cases my friend hasn't been able to solve, he still maintains the same dogged approach, and never stops chewing over them even while he is reading his favourite crime thrillers. There are very few serious crimes that Drag doesn't think are within his competence. And unfortunately for him, he'd just taken on a whole job lot of them.

"The new chief – that short stumpy one – he can't stand me. He knew I didn't want this case. That's why he's put me on it."

"Drag, your last chief – the one who was six foot five – couldn't stand you either. Nor could the one before that."

"That's because I'm ridiculously handsome. They're jealous."

"That must be it," I said. And we drove on as far as Papi's, searching through the stations for some decent music.

All in vain.

# 7

It's a relief to know that you can jump in your car and in three minutes be in a place that resists the stranglehold of cacophonous commercial radio. The music at Papi's never lets you down, whether it comes out of the sound system or out of the grey Seeburg M100B Select-O-Matic, the sixty-something-year-old jukebox he bought online and watches like a hawk. On this occasion the only thing playing was a selection of film soundtracks picked by Papi himself.

It is a relief that we came close to losing, last year. Papi had a heart attack while reading the newspaper in the bar at five in the morning when the place was empty. Fortunately, I had been struggling to get to sleep that night after an evening with Maria and decided to pop down to Papi's for breakfast. If I hadn't, our friend would have been history. While Papi was fighting for his life, Drag was back in the neighbourhood like one possessed, hunting down some kids who had attacked Papi the day before because they didn't like the colour of his skin. They had backed him up against the outside wall of the bar and told him to close up and leave the country, otherwise they would close down the bar for him. Papi told us later that he didn't turn the Glock 26 he always carried for protection on them because those kids were so wet around the ears that he was embarrassed to: "Whatever they did to me, they've got their whole lives ahead of them to regret it, unlike me." Those kids, with their whole lives ahead of them, had spat at him, kicked him, thrown him to the ground, ripped his shirt and carved the letter N for "nigger" into his shoulder. When Papi came round in hospital, he told Drag it was nothing – that he'd lived through things that were ten times worse as an adolescent in the Congo. In 1959 supporters of Youlou had cornered him and forced him to shout out that he loved the French occupiers. He reassured Drag that the heart attack had nothing to do with the other attack.

"Then what *did* cause it?"

"I had a bet with a friend of mine to see who could eat the most," replied Papi.

"I don't suppose the fact that you live in the bar and never sleep has got anything to do with it?" I asked.

Papi frowned, emphasizing the wrinkles in his forehead.

"But of course not," he answered in his impeccable Gallo-Greek accent.

As soon as we walked into the bar, Papi handed each of us an American nickel from 1950 for the jukebox, just like he does to all his customers. He then disappeared for ten minutes to be discreet, before coming back to take our order. He does this even to us, his oldest customers. In that ten-minute slot, Drag used his nickel to listen to "Angel

Eyes" by his beloved Ella Fitzgerald. I told him I didn't much like the song. We wasted three minutes arguing about it and calling each other "ignorant" and "pitiful" at every opportunity. After that I told him everything about Emma and Angelino.

"Do you want me to pull all the information we've got on …"

"Raptas. Themis Raptas. I thought you'd have done that already. Are you getting old and losing your touch?"

While Drag was on the phone chasing this up, I went over to the jukebox and picked a song. On the way back to my seat I passed two clapped-out sofas and matching velvet armchairs and noticed once again the oil paintings and sketches on the walls of jungle scenes, gorillas and elephants from the Congo. The faded carpets and the wooden fireplace at the back were a perfect fit for the walls, which were yellowed with smoke, but less so with the mural behind the bar of a blonde mermaid with a half-open mouth, leaning forward so that she could show off the scorpion tattoo on her left shoulder.

I went past Papi too, who, standing at just four feet nine, looked like he was sitting down. He hadn't taken his white hair to the barber's for ages, and it was sticking out in different directions as though searching for an escape route. As soon as the intro was over, he winked at me, satisfied. After a minute and half of pure music, the voice of Billie Holiday, long before it collapsed, began to caress the notes alternating between piano and sax in "Pennies from Heaven". I closed my eyes and imagined I was in a Harlem club in 1936, listening to her singing about how every time it rains, it rains pennies from heaven, about how those in love shouldn't run under trees when they hear it thunder. This is the biggest pleasure that Papi's has to offer; it makes you feel like it exists beyond time and you can belong to any era you like when you're there.

"That's not fair. We agreed that there's no competition as far as Billie Holiday is concerned," said Drag as the song came to an end. I'd seen him come off the phone very suddenly and sit down to enjoy the song.

"Drag, not everything's a competition. I just wanted to hear that particular song."

"Oh, OK."

"You shouldn't feel bad just because your choice was so inferior to mine," I smiled.

Before Drag had time to get annoyed, Papi came smiling up to the table to take our order. He told us about a new cocktail made with rum, rosemary and chillies he was expecting to be a hit with the customers. When he heard this, Drag looked round and saw that, apart from us, there were just two dogs in the bar: Papi's Bullitt, who had even whiter hair than his master, and a female dog that Bullitt had recently installed and was not in a mood to leave alone. Papi did not seem to be able to read Drag's expression and I was hoping that my friend would be able to restrain himself just this once, keep his mouth shut, and not say out loud whatever it was that was going through his head. Just this once – I wasn't asking for much. I shot him a look, hoping to make him understand.

"What customers?" he said, dashing my hopes yet again.

"The ones who are going to come," replied Papi, with the sober certainty that had been typical of him since the first time we met him. He disappeared to make our drinks.

Papi's had been struggling to get people through the door for a long time now. In the past, couples of all ages used to come here, especially in the early hours, and also for morning coffee. The crisis had sent these couples back indoors, but you could never tell what might happen in the future. This new cocktail might do the trick. I ordered it, hoping that Papi would still be able to remember the order when he got back to the bar. Every time he serves you it's a surprise, a game of chance; each order is made more to make Papi feel good about himself than anything else. I wasn't sure that this helped keep customer numbers up.

"They'll be sending everything we've got on Raptas through to my phone in a minute."

"Tell me about this case you're on. The stuff I don't get from the news."

"OK," he said, remaining silent.

"No developments?"

"Journalists have got so many sources in the force that we get to hear things at about the same time they do – if not *after* they do."

"In other words, you haven't got a clue."

"None. No idea who the perpetrator could be, or whether there was another motive, apart from the obvious. The worst part is I don't give a damn what his motive was. Whatever it was, I'm sure he had a good reason. And if he finished someone off who he shouldn't have, then yes, I would look into it."

About six months before, a small private TV station had started broadcasting a weekly show called *Among Us*, whose purpose was to expose paedophiles. The presenter got information from police files and was naming and shaming them on-air, complete with full names, photographs, details of their activities as well as updates on the progress of all their trials: the delays, who had got off because of insufficient evidence, and details of the personal lives of those still facing charges as well as of those who had done their time. They would then send reporters after them with hidden cameras, pretending that they wanted to speak to them about some job or other – a different one each time – and then they would ask how they felt about the children they had raped. Some would play the innocent, some would curse, some would burst into tears and ask for forgiveness and others would swiftly take off, with the reporter and cameraman hotfooting it breathlessly after them. The broadcasting authority and the data protection people were very slow to pick up on the show and therefore slow to put a stop to it, and when they finally did, it was too late. *Among Us* was hotly debated all over the country. Videos from the show got the most views on YouTube – several million each, with thousands of comments underneath, all of them baying for the blood of the child molesters. The presenter made a big deal about the social function the show was fulfilling by alerting parents to the fact that their neighbour was an animal and enabling them to protect their children. "When the police won't do anything about the animals living among us, somebody has to do something, don't they?" she would ask, trying her best not to smirk triumphantly before she got to the end of her sentence.

The judges who ruled on the interim measures requesting the immediate suspension of the channel's licence, sought by three government ministries, decided that the public had a right to be informed as this was a matter of child protection. The TV station enjoyed ratings it had never dared dream of, and advertisers were queueing up for those crucial spots during the show. It was obviously in its interest to keep broadcasting and just pay the first, the second and the third fine without a quibble even if all the noise around it started to ease off.

It never did.

That was because the wishes of all those people posting comments on YouTube for the past month or so had started to become reality. The paedophiles who had been featured on the show were starting to turn up dead, about one a week, with the same MO: ten bullets at close range, the corpses covered in bruises and cigarette burns. The Avenger, as the media had baptized him, had already got rid of three of them, and the only piece of evidence the police had was that the perpetrator had used a lock-picking gun to force a swift entry. That was it. No notes left next to the bodies, no online announcements. He hunted them, found them wherever they were – one had been in Athens, one in Halkida and the third in Thessaloniki – and executed them. The publicity brought in massive sums of money for the channel, which at this stage was broadcasting exclusively on YouTube through subscriptions. People were paying to watch this and to speculate about who the next victim would be. With all the noise it was making, it wouldn't be surprising if people started placing bets on it.

"One thing's for sure – it's a very professional job. Sure the Avenger's not you?" Drag asked me.

"He's that good, is he?"

"Yes, he is. I mean, he's not bad," he said without smiling, but then again, Drag doesn't smile much.

"If it was me, wouldn't you know?"

"You might have decided to do it for free, and then be too embarrassed to tell me."

"If I was doing it for free, that would mean that nobody else cared enough to sort it out."

"You mean enough to pay?"

"That's the only way that genuine interest in anything is ever shown. In payment – either money or effort."

"It seems that someone does care – and not just some angry random type. This one's been trained. Doesn't put a foot wrong. No witnesses, no evidence, nothing."

"Not bad, then."

"Well … the question is, did someone hire him or is he acting on his own? They did some experiments recently in Switzerland to show that most people, given the opportunity to take revenge, take it. Brain scans showed that when they do, the area of the brain associated with rewards is activated. We are wired to feel pleasure when we take revenge."

"Amazing conclusion. If this hadn't come from Swiss scientists, I never would have believed it," I said.

"Swiss gravitas is important."

"Crucial."

"Definitive."

"Serious."

"Of the utmost seriousness."

"Nothing better came to mind," Drag said.

"So that's why you were hanging around outside my house."

"What do you mean?"

"Because the work of the Avenger looks professional, your ego is pushing you to try to find him and arrest him. Prove that you're better than him. But all that conflicts with something you believe to be right: the paedo witch-hunt. There's a part of you that doesn't want to get in his way. So you want to stay up with me to see if we can work out what the best thing to do is."

"I just wanted a drink," said Drag defensively. When he saw I wasn't responding, he carried on. "But if we come to a conclusion, I'd be fine with that too."

Whenever we came to Papi's we ended up talking about whatever was on our minds and we were never entirely happy with our conclusions. Just happy talking things through. Maybe there aren't any conclusions that are completely satisfactory, completely clear. Perhaps the only thing that is clear is the feeling you get from spending time with a close friend.

Papi brought my cocktail over. In a moment of rare inspiration he had come up with a name: Papi's Cocktail. He also had some draught beer for Drag, who had ordered scotch on the rocks, but we said nothing. We clinked our glasses and drank under Papi's watchful eye as he waited anxiously for the verdict.

"Very nice," I said.

"Honestly?" asked Drag once a delighted Papi was out of earshot.

"I've never tasted anything so terrible in my life. I think the roof of my mouth is burning off."

As I attempted to recover by downing a glass of water in one, Marlon Brando's voice was heard coming out of Drag's mobile, saying "I'm gonna make him an offer he can't refuse." That was his message alert. The message contained a link to Raptas' file. He opened it and started skimming through, and then gave me a look that was even more electrifying than Papi's cocktail. He turned the screen so that I could read it.

The first paragraph contained various details, details of the way the coroner's examination was carried out, the coroner's details, the victim's details. The second paragraph was where it started to get interesting. Emma told me that her father was found full of bullet holes and that before he was killed he'd been tortured. What she didn't tell me was that there were ten bullets, and that his body had been covered in bruises and cigarette burns.

Three years ago, Themis Raptas was murdered in exactly the same way as the paedophiles the Avenger was killing.

# 8

A barefoot chief coroner, Iakovos Martinos of the Forensic Science Division, was waiting for us in the tiny flat in Exarcheia he had converted into a studio. Iakovos was getting on for fifty, and it showed; at the end of each year it seemed he was twenty pounds heavier than the previous one. The last time Drag and I saw Martinos, I remember him saying, "When it's my turn to die, I want to give the coroner plenty to look at." Coroner humour.

His long hair, pulled back into a ponytail, had only recently begun to turn grey. He wore wedding rings on both hands without ever having been married. Drag had asked him once why he wore them, and Martinos had told him that he wore them to remember "the love affairs that almost made it". This time he welcomed us with a blue scarf round his neck, a pair of XXL shorts and a tight black T-shirt with a half-naked Amazonian warrior woman emblazoned across it. The air conditioning was on full blast as usual and the temperature inside the studio must have been edging thirty. The minute you stepped in, you started to dream of the moment you'd leave.

Martinos knew me as someone who worked with Drag, and had never shown any interest in finding out more about me. To be fair, he didn't really show any interest in anything apart from painting and the great talent he thought he had for it, if only he could find enough time to develop it. As soon as we came in, he walked us over to his latest creation – a swan in pink that was about to sink.

"What do you think? I call it *Painting as an Extension of Rhyme.*"

"Words fail me," I answered.

He told us once that his ambition was to produce a painting that would rival his favourite, Munch's *The Scream*, in value. Fortunately, Drag, who was capable of demolishing a man's dream in a single sentence without giving it a second thought, also believed in Martinos' talent. He genuinely did.

Zigzagging through the canvases, we made our way to the kitchen where Martinos kept his computer permanently hooked up to the coroner's office. He had to, because sometimes he took a break from his painting to assist in the arrest of murderers. The kitchen walls were painted black to go with the yellow of the main room, the colours of Martinos' favourite football team, AEK.

"I remembered the case as soon as I got your message," he said to Drag. "I remembered it because it was unbelievable the way that forensics messed the whole thing up."

"What do you mean?"

"OK. Let's say we find a body in the forest. We need to ask how it got there. We need details about the path the murderer followed; we examine the body, looking for soil, pollen, leaves – anything that's caught in the clothing – so we can compare it with the vegetation of the area the body's found in. They found Raptas' body up on Filopappou, where most of the trees have dried up but there are still a lot of bushes, as well as olive trees and cypresses and a bit of soil above the limestone. All things you can make use of. And if you can draw any conclusions about the path, you can then start looking for hairs, threads, anything that could have fallen from the murderer, any prints. And blood, of course, saliva, any kind of biological material."

"And they found nothing?"

"That would be a generous way of putting it. The body had been there for at least three days – apparently the other homeless people up there were too scared to call the police because they thought they would automatically become suspects and didn't want to be moved on. After three days, decomposition is well under way and the body leaves various fluids on the ground, a bit like fertilizer. The soil then changes its texture and colour, albeit a tiny bit. Some shrubs turn yellow in these circumstances and start to look like artificial plants. Nature tells you very clearly where to look. But you need to have the mind of a hunter who makes use of every single piece of evidence he sees to bring him closer to what he's look-ing for. The team that worked on this found nothing. Nothing at all. Unbelievable. They must have missed countless pieces of evidence. They worked like rookies – but they weren't."

"So what happened?" I asked.

"Maybe they weren't bothered. It happens in a lot of cases that seem to be unimportant. As if they were going to waste their time on some homeless guy. It was also about then that they started cutting salaries and everybody was miserable and not in the mood to get into a car and go and look at dead bodies. I was on leave, and by the time I read their report it was too late. Before I forget, they did find a lot of white hairs on him, but they were his own – we tested them. Raptas had gone completely white around the temples."

He pulled up some photos of the hairs. I looked at them closely and failed to come up with any profound conclusions that could lead me to the murderer.

"They also found two or three female hairs, but they were discounted as random, considering Raptas' lifestyle. When you live and sleep outdoors, all sorts of hairs can be found on your clothes; they could be from anywhere. If they're in insignificant numbers, we ignore them."

"May I remind you that on the phone you said you had something that would be of interest to me?" Drag said abruptly, with his usual discretion.

"Yes. I don't need to tell you that when you hold your weapon next to the skin and shoot, apart from the wound, the bullet is going to leave a circular burn mark around the opening in the flesh. The paedophiles had ten of these, one for each bullet, but only Raptas had three marks, looking like tattoos, around his gunshot wounds. That means that those three wounds were inflicted by shots fired from an approximate distance of between four inches and three feet; the murderer only subsequently planted the other seven in him, from close range."

"What about the bruising and the cigarette burns?"

"I wanted to talk to you about those too. While all the paedophiles were beaten and burned in the same places, Raptas' bruises and burns were on other parts of his body."

"So what you're telling us is —" began Drag.

"I'm not telling you anything. You're the ones who are investigating here. I'm just a simple artist," interrupted Martinos.

"Simple artist." He'd hit the jackpot with that. Zero out of two for self-knowledge.

What Martinos told us without actually saying as much was that there were two possible scenarios. The first was that the close similarities between Raptas' murder three years ago and the paedophile murders were coincidental. The second scenario was that we were dealing with a copycat crime; someone who knew how Raptas had died was deliberately taking out paedophiles in the same way, as though he was trying to tell us something.

# 9

Maria never managed to look as beautiful in my dreams as she did in reality. I was always aware that something was missing from my dreams as I lay there tossing and turning my way through the early hours. What was missing was the warmth of her green almond-shaped eyes when they suddenly came to rest on me after she had examined everything around her. At that moment I felt as though I was the centre of the universe and that it was very natural that I should; it was as though that had been my place for centuries but nobody had noticed until the moment I was illuminated by those eyes.

I had often thought about telling her that it was unfair that people couldn't enjoy their dreams, but I didn't. I let her take the lead to see if she just wanted to talk, or if she needed a hug or something more. I'd never really felt that she belonged completely to me, which is why I was quite happy playing a supporting role when I was with her. I didn't want to scare her by listing everything I felt. Better for her to understand how I felt without saying anything, even if it meant she didn't understand at all. It didn't really matter. A client once told me that the stronger partner in a relationship is the one that loves more deeply. And I wanted to believe this was true.

It was eight in the morning when I opened the door to let her into my flat, and once more the dream I'd been having only minutes earlier paled in comparison to the real thing. I hit the button that turns off the lights activated at the door by the sensors I had connected on each step. In my line of work, you have to know the exact position of everyone who comes down into your flat. Ignorance could kill.

I sat down next to her on the bed. "How's it going?" I asked, pointing at her belly, which for the first time in twenty years distorted her very athletic body. And it managed to make her even more beautiful.

From the moment I found out about the baby, the urge to stroke Maria's belly grew stronger and stronger every day. Should I tell her how much I'd been missing her these past few days when we hadn't seen each other? Every day I found myself hating the codes we used to communicate and everything that was left unsaid between us. But I have learnt to live by various codes. Without codes, there is no discipline, no method. Without method and discipline, you die. You die, someone you love dies, your relationships with other people die. If you just do what you feel like all the time, you end up blowing your life to pieces. Codes offer stability. I stuffed my left hand between the sheets to stop it from touching her.

"Great. I can't feel it kick yet, but the doctors say that in a first pregnancy it's normal not to in the first twenty-five weeks, so I'm not worried. All the tests show that everything's fine."

"Good," I said, failing in my happiness and awkwardness to think of anything else to say.

"For just this once today can you sit in the chair?" she said, and although she didn't move, I could feel her distance herself. I stood up, feeling like I'd been kicked in the gut.

"Let's hear it," I whispered as we sat facing each other. There couldn't have been more than a couple of feet between us, but it felt like an entire ocean.

"You know Sotiris and I broke up. He wasn't expecting it, the pregnancy. And he couldn't handle it. He'd been trying to come to terms with it for about a month to see if he could stay with me, but …"

"You weren't expecting it either."

"Yes, but he's innocent. The only innocent person in all this. For years he'd suspected that something was going on between us, but since he was happy with me and I was happy with him, he convinced himself he was wrong."

"So the definition of innocence is choosing to ignore reality?"

"Yes – if you're not responsible for that reality."

"No. The minute you pretend to be unaware of reality, you're no longer innocent."

"Don't try to make me feel better with your theories. That's not why I'm here."

"Don't you go blaming yourself for things that aren't your fault."

"It is my fault. It really is. I never dared broach the subject. It's called hypocrisy."

"And what exactly would you have told him, Maria?"

"The truth."

"And there's only one truth here, is there?"

"Yes."

I considered telling her that we were far too old to be buying into this fairy tale, but I didn't want the conversation to veer off course.

"There's only ever one," she repeated.

"And what is this one truth?"

"That yes, it's not reasonable to expect your partner to live without sex just because you can't offer her that personally. But we should have talked about it. That's why we were together in the first place, a couple, rather than two separate people. When I married him, I knew about the MS and that it would get worse. I'm the one who should have brought it up; what was he supposed to say to me: 'run along and find someone else'?"

"And what would you have said to him? 'I want to find someone because you're in a wheelchair'?"

She went on as though she hadn't heard me. "He knew that you and I have loved each other since we were kids and you're so close, right here downstairs from us. He suspected it but said nothing; if we didn't talk about it, it would go away."

I stretched out my hands. She held them and put hers between mine.

"Nothing ever goes away just because you don't talk about it, does it?" she said.

"It doesn't go away even when you do talk about it. It just gets easier. Sometimes."

"But at least if you talk about it, you're trying. Trying to make it go away."

"It's always the person who has the problem who brings it up – it's a sign of how much they care. If you had brought it up, it would have humiliated him even more."

"When I got pregnant, he felt that I'd been fooling him for a very long time. But I was just scared."

"Scared because he didn't have the guts to talk about it. He transferred his own fears and guilt to you."

The tears started flowing from her eyes and the only thing I could think of was that the baby shouldn't be distressed. Who cared about Sotiris anyway? Only the baby mattered. But I said nothing, and didn't even attempt to wipe away her tears. She was here to straighten things out.

"We'd often talked about adoption, but we kept putting it off. But now ... it's over." She spoke as though she wanted to believe it. As though she would quite like to learn how to say it without crying.

"Did you suggest …?" I asked after taking a deep breath.

"Suggest what?"

The deep breath proved pointless. I would need entire tankfuls of oxygen to get through this. I had come face to face with death many times in my life, but right now I couldn't find the courage to come out with the words that were boring through my head. They were that unbearable. Maria could see that I had no intention of carrying on, and decided to say it herself instead.

"Suggest that he should bring up the baby himself?" she said, touching her belly.

"Yes."

"How could I? How could I make decisions about the baby without consulting you?"

I said nothing.

"Well?" she asked.

"What?"

"You need to say something. Not about Sotiris. About us."

"What do you want to hear that you don't already know?"

"A lot. The baby changes everything."

"Before we go any further, there's something I need to know. There's no other way of asking, so I'll just come out with it."

If she stared hard enough, her eyes could demolish entire walls. Now she was staring at me. And there were no oxygen tanks visible on the horizon.

"Your answer won't change anything. I just want to know," I added.

"We said we'd talk frankly. Get to the point."

"Is there any way that Drag could be the father?"

Twenty years. From the age of sixteen to the thirty-six we were now. Twenty years together as friends, lovers, family, lovers again, and all that time she had never once hit me. Perhaps she'd been building up to it, something between a slap and a punch, which felt to me as if it had come from a different body, a furious wild animal which seemed to be punishing me for my insult. This incensed beast was looking at me with eyes I had never seen the like of. With eyes so very different from the ones I had fallen in love with. It seemed to relieve her anger and turn it into limitless sadness, a thousand times greater than her anger. A silent kind of sadness, a wave of enormous disappointment at what she was hearing. It felt like I was the one who had landed the punch rather than being on the receiving end of it. But the question was a fair one, not irrational – or at least I liked to think it wasn't. Drag, until we were thirty, had been the love of her life – after they split up they didn't speak to each other for five years, but the last three years they had become inseparable again. Drag and I never discussed his relationship with Maria, and we never talked to Maria about how she felt about either of us. Talking about things does show willing, as Maria said, but it can also make things a whole lot worse. We didn't want to do that.

"Stratos – Drag and I haven't been together in that way for eight years. I haven't even seen him for two months. We only talk on the phone. And when we do get together, all we do is meet for coffee, you know, to stay in touch. And yes, we do care about each other a lot, just like Teri and I care deeply about each other, just like we've all cared about each other since we were kids. Do you really think I could … with both of you? At the same time? Is that why you think I've come here – so you could humiliate me?"

"I …" I stopped. What could I say to her? That when the three of us were together I'd noticed her legs would turn slightly towards his under the table, and that every single analysis of human behaviour shows that we turn unconsciously towards the people we love or like most? If I did, she would have lost it and told me to go straight to hell, and to take all those analyses I read with me. She waited a while and then saw that I had no intention of finishing my sentence. I think this only deepened her sense of disappointment.

"We'll talk about this some other time," she said, using my desk to help herself up.

"Please …"

She walked towards the front door, pressed the wrong button to open it, pressed it furiously another three times, and eventually turned round and looked at me.

"Open the door! So you think I'm capable of sharing a bed with three men at the same time and playing games with you all about the paternity of the baby and who's going to step up and who I'm likely to saddle with it. Well, none of you need worry. I'm not going to saddle any of you with it."

"Maria, I couldn't care less who the father is!"

"It's you. You're the father! And you're making me feel like a whore!"

"I love you just the way you are, whatever you do, whoever you want to be with! I want this child so much that the mere idea of it paralyses me. It had never crossed my mind that I might become a father one day. I want it like crazy. There's nothing I want more. Apart from you, maybe." I had never said any of this to her. Ever. Not even when we were seventeen and first together. I saw how she stopped in her tracks when she heard it, and walked over to hug her, but she put her hand up to stop me.

"Not now. I need to be alone for a bit."

"I'm sorry about earlier. I want it more than anything. I've dreamed about what it will be like, a little girl like you."

"A little girl like me … You've got an opinion about the sex … Great. And we'd bring her up how? What job will we tell her that her father does? What do you want the child to call you – 'Stratos', or the one written on your ID? Will our home be surrounded by weapons and sensors? Are you going to frisk her friends and their parents before you let them into the house? Are we going to be living with the fear that someone who's after you could kidnap her or kill her at any moment in revenge? Or blow us all to pieces? Will she be able to walk as far as the school gates, or will you have to go with her to keep her safe? We'll be just another ordinary middle-class family, won't we? You'll disappear now and again for a few days to get rid of someone, and then you'll rush home so we can all visit the soft-play centre together. How are we going to explain it all to her? Explain to her that one day you might not come back, ever, and she might never find out what happened to you, and there might be no body to bury and mourn. Explain to her the odds that she'll be growing up without a father? Yes, I did think about raising the child with Sotiris. I didn't say anything to him. But I did think about it. But not here, of course, living literally on top of you. We would have to move far away from you and all the dangers around you. And never let the child know you. Where you would be invisible and non-existent. But Sotiris has left and I have to make my decisions. Open the door," she repeated. Only this time there was a calm in her voice. The calm that comes with desperation.

# 10

I spent most of the day staring at the ceiling. *Where you would be invisible and non-existent.* Some words go together perfectly. So perfectly that they don't just form phrases but bombs that explode inside your head. I tried to get up twice to drink some water and then a third time to do some exercises, hoping that the latter would provide some temporary relief. The trick is always to concentrate on something else, to force your brain down a different route to avoid the collision it's heading for in its terror to escape everything. But it turned out that squats and thrusts were not the antidote to misery. For years now I had been hiding behind the security that her marriage brought us all: the sense of stability that I could never offer. And now when things were tough I had fallen short. I gave the impression I didn't trust her and had no answers about the future. How could I? The kind of work I do defines who I am. Who I am defines the kind of work that I do. I am my work. It gives my life meaning. I clear the world of filth and get paid for it. I didn't ever want, didn't know, didn't think about doing anything else – and probably couldn't. If I wanted to be with her, I would have to change my job. Change my life. Become someone else. And neither she nor I would be able to recognize this someone else. I wondered whether life would be different if I could just cry. The ceiling had nothing to say about this, even when I shouted at it after downing three vodkas.

While I was thinking about Maria and the pregnancy, my mind blocked out all other problems, as though it was aware of them but just didn't care. As though I wanted to believe that I would find out that the baby wasn't mine after all. Or that because what was happening to us was so unbelievably amazing, everything would work itself out. Denial.

Somehow the time went past. One hour passed the baton on to the next, recognizing that they could not stay on a minute longer and disturb the smooth flow of events. Perhaps I should find Sotiris and talk to him, explain how much Maria loved him and persuade him to raise the child, and having talked him round, disappear. Become *invisible and non-existent*. To be like time, once my time was up, pass the baton to the right person.

I threw on some clothes and went up the steps to the front door. I didn't look to see if Maria was in her bedroom. If you can't find an answer, at least don't become a pain in the arse for somebody who *is* searching for one. Out on the street, my first thought was to escape that thankless ceiling; my second was to drink myself to the point where I wouldn't be able to remember my own name. That wouldn't be difficult. In any case, Stratos Gazis has been officially dead for years, and my ID is in a completely different name, as Maria had pointed out. After walking for a while, a short distance past the primary school and a bit before Agia Sofia Square, where I intended to get wasted at the café bar that I liked there, I suddenly felt the need to sit down. Perhaps the vodkas had numbered more than three. I had a vague recollection of a bottle and someone breaking it in the sink, cutting his hand on it and then looking at his bloodied self in the mirror, threatening it with the broken bottle.

I sat down. As there were no benches on this stretch of Seferis Street, I had to sit down on the ground. This was an excellent second choice. That's the nature of second choices. They're very appealing when no third choice exists. And for years I'd felt like a very appealing second choice for Maria. How could you expect a second choice to have all the answers? How do you promote second to first just like that? They might not want to be promoted. They might not be up to it. The sun, struggling to break through the clouds which had it surrounded, finally did so right over the spot where I was sitting. I could feel my forehead burning. I would have liked to have been able to get up and move on, but I couldn't. I could have crawled, but chose to stew in my own humiliation instead. I looked at the gym across the road which was advertising Pilates classes and saw two fifty-year-old women with the bodies of twenty-year-olds emerge from it. One of them had wavy black hair, a narrow forehead and a nose on the large side; the other one was a blonde with small brown eyes and freckles and was so petite that there should be a law obliging her to eat. They saw me and walked past, crossing over to the edge of the pavement, pretending not to have seen me. They carried identical oversized designer sports bags, which maybe they'd bought from the boutique next to the gym where none of the items in the window were priced, the kind of shop that says if you're worried about the price tag, don't come in.

I thought about Emma and her father – what was his name again? – Themis. Yes Themis, that's right. Dead. Perforated with bullet holes. And she had found him! I imagined what it had been like for them before all of this happened: sitting down on pavements, in the squares around the city, the sun burning their heads, the rain piercing their bones. Women with oversized designer bags and well-dressed children walking past them, just like the ones I had just seen here in Neo Psychiko. People who always had something to eat. And men looking at Emma – not yet a teenager – dreaming of kidnapping her like so many kids at the traffic lights who had vanished without trace in recent years. Kidnapping her and doing everything that entered their sick heads. Child molesters. A different species – not human. However many the Avenger managed to get rid of, there would be others. What he didn't seem to able to grasp was that no matter how hard you try, it's never going to be enough. How far is it possible to rid this world of its filth? Somebody needs to make a decision, wake up and see that we're dealing with a genuine seven-headed Hydra here – not the one in the myth but a real, living monster. All the shit inside us, all the shit around us. For each head that you manage to cut off, another two emerge in its place. Invincible, like cockroaches. Perhaps the time had come for me to acknowledge my limitations, quit and save the day for Maria and the baby. Fight the scum by bringing up an amazing child – now, there's a better plan. It was just that I had no idea how to do it. There was so much violence inside me that I really didn't know if I could learn how. I had been doing what I could for years, with success. I did the best I could with what I had. People have their limits: Endurance. Tolerance. Ability. When they try to exceed these limits, they stumble. They fall. They feel like failures.

Two more women emerged from their Pilates classes. Same style, same walk, same heels, same age as the previous two. A man came out at the same time. Young, smiling, toned. Pilate himself, perhaps. On the other side of the gym was an old villa now operating as a café, with a sign outside on the pavement boasting a garden round the back. A mother with twins in a double buggy came out. She was flanked by two bodybuilders, while a third pushed the buggy. This would be an interesting alternative career for Jimmy if Angelino ever fired him. There's always work to be had if you only know where to look.

None of these people tried to talk to me. For them I was probably nothing out of the ordinary – just one more Athenian down on his luck. I made absolutely no impression on them at all. In the words of Seferis himself, *Strange people! They say they're in Attica but they're really nowhere.* Maria worships Seferis. Sometimes when she was able to stay with me a bit longer than usual she would read him to me. She might appreciate the fact that I was now sitting in a street named after him. At least the irony of it. Maybe I'd call her and let her know. Yeah, right. Perhaps not. Man – on bended knee. So many wrong combinations of words. A country that is forced to keep looking down because of all the slaps in the face it gets is not a country fit for people. Right. But was it in the days before the slaps started coming? Only Pilate could perhaps wash his hands in a manner that would answer my question. Unfortunately, he'd already hopped into his BMW and vanished into thin air. I had no intention of vanishing. Where could I go? This place was as good as it got.

Time passed. I took in the people, pigeons, blocks of flats, the pneumatic drill, a couple of trees, some lights left on in someone's living room, pollution, fresh cooking smells, parallel and perpendicular streets but none bearing any names as great as Seferis, as my street did. I was already beginning to feel territorial. The shops that would never feel the effects of the crisis and others which never saw a customer; two ten-year-old boys coming out of school, one chasing the other mercilessly; gestures; faces; cars; motorbikes; flyers dumped in the street; "for rent" signs plastered on the walls of buildings. A violinist busking looked at me arrogantly but decided against taking me on once he realized I was twice his size. He started to walk away. It occurred to me that I had unintentionally stolen his spot. I got to my feet with considerable difficulty and whistled across to him. I gestured to him to come back, and he responded with a bow indicating his gratitude and returned. I had nothing to say to him and left. I had no idea where I was going. And I didn't really care.

# 11

I hadn't walked further than a block before I found myself outside a gym advertising Pilates classes and a shop selling designer handbags that was too expensive to show the prices in the window. I looked up; my head was heavy, but I did see that I was no longer in Seferis Street. That was encouraging; it meant that I was not so drunk that I was going round in circles without realizing it. I looked at the gym and at the handbags. They looked back at me haughtily. This wasn't déjà vu but old-fashioned competition: capitalism in action on a local scale. It was like going back in time to 2008, as though the crisis had happened elsewhere. Neo Psychiko: another country. My phone rang and, faster than I'd ever drawn a pistol, I pulled it out of my pocket. It wasn't Maria's name on the screen. It was Drag's. I thought twice before answering it.

"I've got an idea," he said, not waiting for me to speak first. He was almost excited.

"Unusual and therefore interesting," I answered.

"Are you all right? You sound a bit strange – like you're mixing up your words or something."

"It must be your signal. What idea?" I asked, rubbing my face with my hand, trying to keep my head from drooping under the weight.

"I'm up to my eyeballs here. Spending all my time supposedly securing the safety of the rest of those paedos on that show."

"Supposedly?"

"I use them as bait, set up traps for the Avenger. If he wants to kill them, let him – I'll bring him in later. But we haven't got time to lose. I want to check every detail of this case. So I was thinking, since you're the second most competent investigator in the city ..."

"Who's the most competent?"

Instead of answering, he sighed.

"Are you in pain?" I asked.

"... and because you're going to be investigating the Raptas case anyway, I was thinking perhaps you could look into the connection between his murder and these paedophile murders."

"You're asking me to help the Hellenic police?"

"The Hellenic police never need help. I'm asking you to help *me.*"

"Or maybe you're asking me for another reason – apart from the fact that I'm the best investigator in town?"

"Second best. What other reason?"

"To see if the similarities between the murders are a coincidence. You don't want to waste police resources trying to find out. If they're not just a coincidence, you don't want it to be known inside the force that you've worked it out. Because if one of your lot tells the press, the Avenger will run scared before you've had a chance to bring him in."

"After all these years, you're beginning to learn."

"If it makes you happy, I can call you 'Teacher' too."

"Just not in public, please. I'm just a shy, working-class kid."

"I can tell by the way you dress."

"Any information you need, just say the word. Smart arse," he said before hanging up.

The trick is to always focus on something else. And that something else for me was to make myself useful, which is why exercise didn't help.

When I was a child, whenever my mother used to disappear from home, there was no job around the house I wouldn't turn my hand to. Dusting, mopping, washing the dishes, washing clothes, drying clothes: making myself useful. That way everything would be perfect for when she got back. Give her a reason not to leave again. And that's what my job does for me too. It gives me the sense that I am helping people take a tiny step towards the light. Some people have enough talent to create extra light; I just lift some of the darkness. Of course, I can't defeat the seven-headed Hydra, but I can frustrate it by chopping off its heads as quickly as I can.

It was time to head home.

I fell asleep for about an hour and was woken up by the alarm on my mobile. I had to get ready for my next meeting with Angelino. I started thinking about how happy our childhoods had been, when you could shut off an alarm with a single swat; now you have to fiddle around on your phone looking for the snooze button. Part of me didn't want to wake up at all. Another part of me was *determined* never to get up again. Fortunately, I was in so many pieces that some of the other ones prevailed. I staggered to the bathroom, took a couple of painkillers, had a warm shower and towelled myself not quite dry, the way Maria likes me.

I looked in the fridge and saw I was out of fruit so had to make do with half a litre of supermarket orange juice, the kind that delivers strength, vitality and plenty of sugar. Two cups of black filter coffee later and I was feeling borderline functional. It was getting on for 8.30. Maria was nowhere to be seen. No. Don't think about her. Concentrate on something else: the computer, the case. The similarities between Raptas' murder and the way the paedophiles from the TV show were murdered. Too much of a coincidence – surely? But what did that mean? The mistakes in Raptas' murder had to be deliberate, didn't they? I was getting all my thoughts down on paper as they came to me. I always did that. I write down all the questions I have. If you're not methodical, you won't get anywhere. But you can't get anywhere without evidence, and I had nothing to go on. So instead of speculating about what could be going on, I needed to find something that would lead me to something else, and from there to God knows where. The computer was ready and waiting. I typed "Raptas" into Google Images. Nothing. YouTube: nothing. None of the work he had done while he was working for HighTV. Not a trace. I searched all the other sites I could think of with video content. Same story. In the end all I managed to unearth was a report he'd done for the *Democratic Press* covering a meeting between the then PM and representatives from industry and agriculture, which didn't yield any interesting information. The tone of the report was completely flat. Hadn't Emma said that he had wanted to change the world? It didn't look like he'd done much in that direction. Anyway, how could he change the world? Not with reporting like that. Perhaps that was it; perhaps the reason I couldn't turn anything up on him was that there was nothing on him out there, good or bad.

Then again, it had been eight years since he'd given up his job – but eight years for the Internet is nothing. A recent report on the enormous volume of information in circulation explained that one week these days spawns as much information as the whole of 2002. How could all that information fail to contain even one essential piece of information about the life and work of Raptas? He had worked in the media, after all. Was it really possible that his disappearance, sudden as it was, hadn't moved at least one of those idle online commentators to ask what had happened to him, and that his former colleagues were either completely unaware that he'd been murdered three years ago or, if they had been, had never written about it anywhere?

This was beginning to look less like murder and more like vaporization.

I clicked through the pages with the irrelevant results and then found a video on a news site which included the name Raptas in the credits – but there was nothing by him in the piece. A female war correspondent was narrating. It was about Afghanistan and had attracted seven likes and an avalanche of comments underneath from soccer fans who would chip in now and then with comments on Olympiacos and Panathinaikos, and exchanged insults. There was another comment from someone claiming the report was fixed, everything the reporter was saying was lies invented by enemies of the fatherland, but the truth would out, the nation would triumph, and Smyrna would be Greek again.

In the twenty-seventh page of results I found a number of sites all containing the same statement going back to 2009, the year that Raptas had decided to quit HighTV and move onto the streets with Emma. It was published on a lifestyle site, a piece about journalists under the title "Transfers". It stated that Themis Raptas was ending his long association with HighTV and moving to another chan-nel to take on the role of chief editor. Then two months later there was a follow-up announcement on the same page explaining that Raptas was leaving HighTV to go into business and would resume his journalistic career once he had got his business off the ground, details of which were to follow. Some business, waiting for people to toss their spare change into an upturned hat. I added it to my notes, this time underlining: "Long association with the channel". How is it possible to have a "long association" with a channel and yet leave no trace behind?

In any event, something had clearly happened to Raptas in 2009. Something that forced him to abandon his old life and everything in it – apart from Emma. But five years had elapsed between 2009 and his murder, so perhaps the murder had nothing to do with his old job. I made a note there on the page to probe in that direction too.

Another hour had passed. It was time to get going.

I strapped on the leg holster for my trusty Smith & Wesson 642. It had got me out of some very tricky situations in the past, maybe more even than my favourite Sig Sauer P226.40 S&W, which I usually carried on me in a shoulder holster. I threw on yesterday's jeans, my black boots, a thick blue shirt and my brown leather jacket, not just to conceal my weapon but because the forecast was warning of a sudden drop in temperature and the chill air coming through the only window in the flat confirmed this. For the time being, it was keeping me awake and was the best thing that had happened to me all day.

This time I got to Angelino's house at 11 a.m. and this time instead of Jimmy letting me in, there were two blokes standing guard who looked just like Jimmy, but judging by the look in their eyes were probably more intelligent – not that it would take much. Angelino's security team seemed to be growing by the day. I remembered how even down in Omonia where danger could be lurking anywhere, Angelino was always alone with maybe just one of his people keeping an eye on things at a discreet distance. I couldn't work out why he needed to be so careful here at the house. Why had he suddenly started carrying a gun? It was possible that this had nothing to do with Emma. After all, he did have his fingers in a lot of cases, so it could easily be about something completely unconnected, and simply a coincidence that Emma was in the house. That also might explain why Angelino hadn't mentioned any problems he was having to me. Maybe.

Jimmy then made an appearance from behind the other bodyguards. "See if he's got anything on him," he ordered. The one on the left, a thickhead with long, curly, glossy hair, came up to me.

"Angelino invited me," I said, taking a step back.

"Did he?" said Jimmy with a sly smile, giving the sign to the bodyguard to go ahead with the search.

Technically he was right to do so. That was his job – to disarm anyone who might be dangerous, whether or not they had turned up with an invitation. Only I wasn't a threat to Angelino, and Jimmy knew it. He just wanted to piss me off. And he chose his moment now when he had the numerical advantage.

I had slept, started my investigation and just about regained my equilibrium. I didn't *feel* that I was angry when I arrived at the house. But I was. And I realized I was the minute I picked up on Jimmy's smirk.

I took one step towards him. "OK. Take it," I said, pretending I was about to reach into the left pocket of my leather jacket.

While his eyes moved instinctively to my left hand, I threw out my right, grabbed him from the base of his enormous nose and lifted him off the ground. He was heavy. I was angry enough not to care. His nose snapped in a violent crack which I felt deep inside my fingers. The other two had already drawn, but with Jimmy's back shielding me in such a confined space, they were never going to shoot. Jimmy was helpless, screeching with pain, flapping his arms around comically.

"Not only don't you have any scruples, you don't have any brains." I stole that line from *Detour*, but didn't expect Jimmy to know much about 1940s cinema. "Calm down. I'll let him go now," I said to the other two. I dropped him on the floor, like a sack. The other two then came to take my gun off me. Jimmy was on the floor making noises. I think he was crying. "Please tell Angelino that his next appointment is here," I said.

Emma's performance was over. The only people left in the house were the girl, Angelino and the bodyguards. I gathered from what they were saying to each other that one of them was called Zissis. Zissis was filling Angelino in through the intercom on Jimmy's little accident. He then took me up to Angelino's office on the first floor, knocked discreetly on the door and, hearing Angelino tell him to leave me there and go, left with something approaching a smile on his face. Perhaps he didn't think much of his boss.

Angelino was in his office drinking brandy. "Office" was a bit of a misnomer. There wasn't any office furniture in the room; instead there was a bar heaving with drinks, a few files sitting on the edge, and absolutely nothing else. It felt as though the owner had simply run out of cash before they got to this room. Angelino was sitting down on the wooden floor, his eyes half closed, looking like something halfway between a guru meditating and a guru who couldn't be bothered to meditate because he had already worked out all the answers. His glass was already down to the last third. He had changed back into his famous blue sweatshirt and his fatigues. You can take the home-less man off the streets, but you can't take the streets out of the homeless man. Even if the man is homeless out of choice. He motioned to me to sit down opposite him and offered me a drink. The thought of it made my stomach turn. It had been through enough for one day. I said no.

"How's your friend in the hospital getting on?"

"Oh, yeah. Fine. Great."

From his tone, it wasn't clear whether he was telling the truth, but it was clear that he didn't want to talk about it.

"What about Jimmy?" he asked, sounding almost bored.

"He was forgetting his manners. Again – and for no reason."

"I do pay him, you know. And thanks to you I'll be paying him to recover while he's no use to me at all."

I had nothing to say to that.

"Did Emma tell you all that nonsense about how she'll pay you out of her own money?" he asked, bringing the conversation round to where he wanted it.

I nodded.

"That's rubbish. Whatever you need, you can get it from me. Money and any other kind of help."

"Why are you so interested in Emma?" I asked.

"I've been taking care of her for a while now."

"So she tells me. My question is 'why?'"

"Your question isn't 'why?'." Your question is: am I taking care of her because she's going to bring me in a lot of cash when she gets famous, or I am looking after her because I think she needs looking after?"

"Right. Yes. That is my question."

He tilted his head back a little. I thought I saw a smile form, but Angelino had very thin lips and it was hard to tell when he was smiling and when he was simply pursing them.

"Stratos – we've known each other for years. What's your opinion of me?"

Interesting question. I thought about my mother, and all the times Angelino would help me track her down when she'd get lost in the city and in her mind, and all those times he would sit with her, for hours on end, playing cards with her in the square till I arrived to take her home. I thought about Jordanis, the young Albanian kid he took under his wing when the boy's parents were deported, and who was now thirteen years old and in America on a scholarship. I thought about the information Angelino got for us last year and passed on for free about the contract the Bulgarian mafia had on Drag for 200,000 euros. And it was a rare thing for Angelino to give out information free of charge, and the fact that it was Drag who needed the information made it even more remarkable when you consider that Drag had told Angelino that when he caught him mixed up in anything dirty, he'd have him thrown into Korydallos prison at the first opportunity. Not *if* he caught him – *when* he caught him. And then I started thinking about all those people who had ended up with a bullet in their heads because Angelino had sold the addresses of their hideouts at the right price. A lot of them were inno-cent – or more or less innocent – with wives and children. I remembered his complete indifference when I asked him about it. He just said, "I sell information. Information is like technology; it's neutral. What people decide to do with the information is their business."

Angelino reminded me of Sophocles Street a decade ago when it was home to the stock exchange, where fortunes would be made and lost in the course of a single day, and when nobody knew what the future held. Like the stock market, Angelino could make or break you within a matter of the few seconds it took him to decide whether or not he would pass on a particular piece of information to you – one that could save your life or take it. But despite everything, because of what he'd done for my mother, I looked on him like a brother. And I owed him, something Emma was quick to stress the previous night.

"You think of yourself as a businessman, the kind who has a heart. Usually the businessman has the upper hand, but now and again he lets himself be ruled by his heart," I answered.

"So how does that make me different from you?"

It did. Angelino would just get on with his job and occasionally, when the mood took him, would decide to help people out. As for me, helping people is what I do; it's my function. No matter that I profit from it. When I take on a case after I've looked into it carefully, I know that even if my client is a bastard, my target will be an even bigger bastard who is worth seeing off.

The most ridiculous thing I have ever heard is that people are neither good or bad and that anyone, given the chance and a good enough motive, can do harm. Armchair philosophy. Everybody deep down has their limits, and these limits make them who they are. The urge to do real harm to another human being has got to come from deep in the heart. And it's my job to silence that darkness in their hearts – so long as I'm paid properly.

"What you are is the better businessman," I said, and this time there was no doubt that he was smiling.

"Look, I didn't know Emma – or Themis – very well. I'd seen them doing their Chaplin routine a few times, and at a few rehearsals. I'd always stay and watch them because they kept changing the routine as Emma got older, you know, so it reflected her age. We'd say hello occasionally, that kind of thing. I didn't know that he used to be a journalist, or where they lived, their names, nothing. Just knew them by sight. Fifteen years ago there weren't that many of us on the streets, and we knew everything there was to know about each other. But about the time when Themis turned up with Emma, there were suddenly loads of homeless people and you just couldn't keep track of who everyone was. Even during the years when everyone said that the country was doing well, the number of home-less people was growing; it's just that most of them were immigrants and they weren't included in the official sta-tistics so they weren't officially a problem. If they don't count you, you don't exist. Now there are thousands of them, most of them Greeks. I don't even know them by sight any more."

"But Emma and Themis went on the streets during the good times. There were so many papers and TV channels back then that were so worried about being understaffed that they were fishing students out of journalism courses before they'd even graduated."

"Yeah. I don't really get what happened to him. Something went very badly wrong at work, that's all I know. He didn't want to go back to it."

"And he was successful, isn't that right?"

"Yeah. As far as I know. I didn't watch him on TV or read his stuff in the papers, but when I asked around, everyone said he was really good. So did Emma."

"Any particular successes you heard of?"

He shook his head.

"I don't pay any attention to all of that, no. But I could look into it."

"Let's suppose he was. What sense does it make for a successful journalist and reporter to go and live on the streets with a young child?"

"None. But we've both seen stranger things than that. Sometimes all it takes is a little bit of bad luck."

That much was true. But trying to explain everything that happened to Emma and her father in terms of random events wouldn't get me very far. I was going to work on the assumption that there was a concrete explanation for everything, and I would try to discover what that was.

"Have you found any other homeless people who knew him back then?"

"No one apart from me."

"No witnesses or anyone who knew anything about the murder?"

He shook his head.

"How did it happen?"

"Themis left in the afternoon, and after he'd been away for several hours, Emma started looking for him. You see, he'd never left her on her own for any length of time before. She tripped over him while she was walking around on the hill. She realized it was him from his smell and touch. Her hands are almost supernaturally sensitive. That's how she pulls off all those card tricks. He was already dead."

"And?"

Angelino grimaced, showing that it was a real struggle for him to think about this, let alone talk about it. He got to his feet, picked up the brandy bottle that was on the bar, filled his glass two thirds full, took a deep swig and leaned against the wall as though he needed the support.

"She was clinging on to him. She didn't cry. That was the amazing thing. She was just lying on top of him, silently clinging on to him was she was trying to keep him warm. That's what someone who saw her there said. Some of the homeless people who found her there pulled her off him. Not even Emma can remember how long she spent lying on top of him, whether it was hours or days. They tried to take her with them, but she got away. She disappeared for three months. Took a few clothes from their cave and the money they'd put aside and lived on her own for a bit, like a wild animal. She slept wherever she found a spot on the hill or downtown, in building entrances and on roof terraces and any basements she found unlocked. That's how lots of homeless people live, and if you ask them, they'll tell you it's not too bad. It's when you hear that that you know how hard it is for them to escape it, because once you get used to it you don't even want to return to your old life. Some of my people found her and brought her to me. I'd heard about what had happened and I was looking for her. She was thrashing and flailing about, and wanted to leave. It was three months before she started talking, and she'd cry out in her sleep. I started leaving the square at night and sleeping in the room next to hers so I'd be close by if she needed me. After the first month, she would only stay calm if I was with her – she sort of knew me from the streets. Themis had apparently said nice things to her about me and she recognized my smell. I brought in some specialists to see her, but they scared her. I wasn't always able to get her to calm down. Sometimes I would try to hug her and she'd kick me, keep howling until she exhausted herself and fell asleep again. Sometimes she'd ask me to take her back to the cave or the orphanage, and then other times she would rip into me with her nails, scratching me hard as if she wanted to tear into my flesh. But she never cried."

He took one step forward, detaching himself from the wall. Sometimes, when you've managed to get the words out, you no longer need any support.

"What about the murder? What have you found out about that?"

"Ten bullets, close range. Like they wanted to shred him, body and head. His body was burned by cigarettes. The cops think he was tortured first, so it wasn't some kind of sick ritual. Whoever did it wanted something from him. Money, I'm guessing."

"Did he have any?"

"He had saved quite a lot. For a homeless guy, that is. He'd told Emma that he was going to lend some money to this other homeless guy who needed it to see a doctor.

We found him. He's on his way out. He never saw Themis that day. Cops reckon that someone got to him on the way, either by chance or because they knew he had the money on him, and they tortured him to find out if he had any more hidden away."

That's what I'd read in the file Drag had given me. I was hoping to get a bit more out of Angelino.

"And what do you think?"

He answered immediately. "I think I need to wait to hear from you what happened. Until I do, I don't think anything."

"Angelino, if there's one person who can dig up any information in this city, it's you."

"Mmm …"

"This case involves the homeless – your own people. And as far as I can see, you've got nothing."

"That's right."

"So what makes you think I'll get any further?"

"You've certain things in your favour."

"Like what?"

"Your obsession with investigations. This strange sense of responsibility that pushes you to find out the truth before you act. Attention to detail. Most importantly, you're not known in the homeless community, which means that unlike me, you can use violence to find out the truth. And you don't care about using violence if you think it's in a good cause. I can't use violence against another homeless person. They look on me as family."

I also had access to all of Drag's informers. I'm sure Angelino was thinking the same, though he didn't say it.

"And I've got an idea about how you can get to the information," he said.

"Go on."

"I've got a friend. Antonis Pavlis. Was homeless himself once but now he's an icon painter. I've put a lot of business his way. He still keeps in touch with the community. He can introduce you as a journalist who is doing a piece on the homeless. As you ask them to tell you about their lives, you might be able to find out something important about Themis too. This is his number. Call him and sort out the details. He was out of the country when my people were asking questions about Themis. Now he's back, he'll give you a hand."

He handed me a piece of paper with just a phone number written on it in a beautiful hand. No name. Just a number.

"It won't be easy, you know. Three out of four homeless people who have been on the streets for over a year have reduced mental functioning, even the ones who aren't on drugs. So many of them, but there's no kind of programme or anything to help them. So be warned. A lot of what you'll hear won't make any sense at all."

"But why should they open up to me if they didn't want to talk to you or your people?"

"Two reasons. First of all, we only asked them specifically about Themis. But you can warm them up first. And then because homeless people, just like everyone else, love to have their two minutes of fame. Don't you watch TV or read the papers?"

"I try not to."

"Everyone's interviewing the homeless these days. They all want to share their stories, see their faces on screen, in the papers, online. They're really in at the moment, and they're loving it. It sort of fills the void in their lives – they've lost their homes and feel that they don't belong anywhere."

"Don't you feel like that too? Like you don't belong anywhere?"

"I feel I belong everywhere. This whole city is my home. A house just imprisons you with all its comforts. Comforts are a trap."

"Unless you've got a young girl to take care of."

"Unless you have, yeah. That's when you need them."

"You said earlier that it was all 'in a good cause'. I don't know that yet. I promised Emma that I would look into it. If everything turns out to be the way you say it is, then yes, I'm in. Pro bono. I won't take anything from you. But it will depend on what I find out. You know my rules: I —"

"I don't think you'll end up having to break any of your rules," he interrupted. "But if you do, remember who's asking you to break them." He looked at me. I looked back at him. Neither of us broke the gaze for a long time. Eventually I nodded.

"Oh, and Stratos? To answer your original question – my main interest in this case is to make money. That's why I'm helping the girl, that's why I've rented this building for a year: so I can promote her. Strictly business."

I recalled how he had held her hand the night before, as well as everything Emma had told me about all the things Angelino had done to help her. I recalled his pained face, only minutes before, when he was forced to remember those three months when Emma was traumatized and alone, waking up terrified at night, and when not even he could comfort her. "Strictly business." Yeah, right. He loved her.

"I think I will have that drink after all," I said.

# 12

The kitchen was on the ground floor and the units were all built out of solid wood. The walls were painted in the magnolia of the sitting room. There were too many cupboards for me to count and the white worktops shone with cleanliness under the glare of a chandelier shaped like a train track and weighed down with so much crystal that its price tag must have been something to rival the national debt. I wondered if housekeeping was part of Jimmy's brief.

I had left Angelino's office, and as I came down the stairs I noticed the light on in the kitchen and cooking smells filling the air, which I followed to see who was in there. It was Emma. She had heard my footsteps and turned towards the west door where I was standing. The other door, the north one, led to the bedroom. She was in pink pyjamas and the white cardigan I'd seen her in the day before.

"Hi. It's me, Stratos," I reassured her.

"Hi."

"What are you doing here?"

"What does it look like?"

"You're cooking."

"Is that so strange? Judging by the surprise in your voice, anyone would think you were watching me fly."

After what I had already seen she was capable of, I wouldn't have ruled that out.

"No – it's just that …"

"Angelino and I have been living here for almost a year now. I know exactly where everything is. Please try not to touch anything, will you? Because if you do, I might not be able to find it easily later."

"I won't."

"I never knew much about it before, but there are loads of solutions for the blind. You can put Braille labels on things, or special labels that you can record voice messages onto. And the ovens we have here are so simple – both the regular oven and the microwave. They've got standard functions, so you're soon operating them without thinking about it. But there are still a few things that you can't do. Just a few."

"Like what?"

"Frying. The hot oil spitting up from the pan. Always having to wear long oven gloves so you don't burn your arms on the hob or your wrists when you're taking things out of the oven."

"What are you making?"

"I've finished the feta-stuffed peppers. Now I'm making beef with puréed aubergines. When it's ready I'll call Angelino down to serve. He likes eating late in the evening so he can lend a hand," she smiled.

A regular father–daughter set-up. I thought about my own baby growing inside Maria and suddenly felt very jealous of Angelino.

Emma picked up the very sharp knife she'd left on the side next to what was left of the beef. There were three onions in front of her. With precise movements, she cut them into tiny pieces, scooped them up, tossed them into the saucepan and began stirring.

"Do you want to stay for dinner?"

"Thanks, but …" But what? I had somewhere to be? Someone was expecting me home?

"OK. I'll stay."

"Great. This is one of my specials. But I cook everything. It's a hobby of mine."

"What about the meat? How do you weigh it?"

"Angelino's bought me some electronic scales which read out the weight – just like the electronic thermometer we have for roasts so I can tell when they're nearly done. And then there's the classic method for stews – I just take off the lid and taste."

She picked up a bottle of wine, poured a few drops into the saucepan and went back to her original position by the chopping board she used for cutting lettuce, this time with another small-bladed knife. As she cut up the ingredients, she moved them in little piles to her left so that she could tell them apart.

I stared at her for a while; neither of us spoke.

"Any news?" she asked, her back turned to me. I got the impression that her voice was shaking.

"It's far too early for —"

"Yes, yes, I know. It was only yesterday that we spoke. I know," she said, cutting me off as though embarrassed to seem impatient.

She grated a tomato, put it in a bowl and then threw it into the saucepan together with a whole tin of chopped tomatoes, a generous amount of salt and some pepper. Her body had tensed up completely from the moment she asked me that question.

"What about the recipes?" I asked to relieve the awkwardness.

"A lot of them are mine. Some of them I get from audio books. That's how I've learned some old magic tricks that I'm perfecting. My dad bought me some in Monastiraki a long time ago and Angelino brings me back various things – not just recipes and magic tricks, but novels too. But I can't be bothered with them. They're in English and it's really tiring trying to work out what they're saying. Even the audio books with the recipes often don't help much, 'cause they say things like 'Stir until the colour changes.' So I have to get Angelino to tell me when the colour changes and then make a note of the time it's taken so I'll know for the next time."

She was moving about all the time she was talking to me. Absolute command over the space, hardly ever stopping to think. If you didn't look into her eyes, it would have been impossible to tell that she couldn't see. She took the four large aubergines she'd left to dry by the sink and put them in the oven.

"There's something I want to ask you," I said.

"Yes?"

"What kind of reporter was Themis?"

Before she had a chance to answer me, a series of muted staccato sounds could be heard coming from the direction of the front door. If I didn't recognize the sound, I would have thought someone was letting off cheap fireworks. But these were no fireworks. It was a large gun with a silencer attached to it. The second I heard it my hand automatically reached for my thigh, forgetting that Jimmy's heavies had taken both my guns off me before I went up to see Angelino. Had he heard the noise?

"What was that?" asked Emma. But I was already next to her, my hand covering her mouth.

"Shh … Please – do as I say. Be quiet till I've seen what's going on," I whispered.

This sudden contact scared her even more. Her body spasmed but she did what she was told. I took the two knives from the worktop and two quick paces took me to the west door of the kitchen, which was the one closer to the gunshots. I opened it slightly so that if someone wanted to burst in they would be starting off at a disadvantage, not knowing what to expect on the other side. I peered through the crack in the door left by the hinges. Three masked men in black were crossing the living room and heading towards the kitchen. One of them was holding a big handgun, probably a .45 Colt. The other two were carrying Kalashnikovs with silencers. They looked nothing like Angelino's other investors. His heavies were nowhere to be seen – neither was Jimmy. Given the shots that were fired, the most likely explanation was that they were no longer with us. But I couldn't understand why they had opened the door to strangers, let alone masked gunmen. I wasn't going to work that one out any time soon. In a few seconds they'd be in here.

"What's going on?"

I could hear Angelino's voice but couldn't see him. I reckoned that he was probably at the top of the staircase on the first floor. The two masked gunmen swung round to pepper him with bullets. I watched his body come hurtling down the staircase and land motionless on the floor at the bottom.

"The girl! I'll wait here for the other guy," snarled the third one – possibly their boss – and pointed to the kitchen door.

"The other guy" was probably me. They obviously knew I was here, but didn't seem to want to track me down. They weren't interested in me so long as I didn't get in their way. The same went for Angelino too, it seemed. Their boss didn't even give him a second look. They had come for Emma. In the space of just a few seconds, all the alcohol in my bloodstream had been replaced by adrenalin. And experience. A blessed combination.

I took Emma by the arm and placed her flush against the recess in the wall close to the door on the north side so that she wouldn't be visible from the west. I ran through the options. There weren't many. In any face-to-face encounter, whatever I did, it was three against one and they were much better armed than I was. There was only one way to deal with this. And that would mean putting Emma in danger. But anything was better than waiting here for them to come and kill us.

"Do you know your way around this floor?" I whispered.
She nodded.

"Do you think you can make a run for it into your room and lock the door behind you?"

"Yes."

"OK. When I tell you, run."

I was using her as bait. It was risky, but it was my only real chance. They would see her, if only for a second before the wall opposite would give her cover. If they were very quick, they might be able to shoot in time. That is, if they had been ordered to. I wasn't sure that they had. But one thing was certain – they wouldn't be expecting her to appear from there. They probably didn't even know about the second door to the kitchen and were expecting to do all the work from the other door. The chance that they would hit her in their surprise was close to zero. The risk was small. And I had no choice.

"*Now!*"

She bounded out of the kitchen like a deer, her movements confident and fluent.

"Over there!" came the voice of one of our visitors, followed immediately by the sound of footsteps as they ran after her.

Nobody fired. Either they weren't quick enough, or they had been ordered not to. I let the first one run past me, and the minute the second one appeared I grabbed him from behind and used the long-bladed knife to slice his throat with one clean cut, not letting him fall. Immediately after that I got the first one in the back of the neck. Luckily I'm a better aim with knives than I am with guns. The blade caught him at the base of the neck; in at the back and out the front. He moved briefly, giddily, from left to right, making gurgling sounds like bubbles bursting as he tried to draw breath. He attempted to grab hold of the knife and brush it off him as though it was some kind of annoying insect that was bothering him. And then he collapsed. The man I was still holding on to was well built and proved to be an excellent shield. Before I was completely sure that I had finished off the first killer, their boss had fired three shots at me, all of them landing on my makeshift shield. He didn't have time to fire a fourth. I wrenched the Kalashnikov out of my shield's hand, took aim above his neck to avoid any nasty surprises from bulletproof vests and sent the scum to join his friends in hell, which does not exist.

The entire scene, from the point when Emma ran out of the kitchen, couldn't have lasted longer than half a minute. I rushed over to Angelino. I found a pulse. He was unconscious, but there was a pulse. He was bleeding from the forehead, but the wound was quite a small one, probably caused by the fall. The problem was the bullets lodged inside him. His blue sweatshirt was drenched in blood. I lifted it up to see where they had entered. Four in the chest and ribs, all on the right side. Every breath he took inched him closer to death because the air he was breathing in through the hole in his chest would eventually cause his lungs to collapse. The air compresses the lung, stopping it from inflating normally. His pulse was quickening while his heart tried to maintain a stable arterial pressure. I then remembered seeing a box of cling film on top of the microwave in the kitchen.

I always felt like this after a shoot-out: I was there and I wasn't there. As though one part of me was observing from afar, spectator and perpetrator in one. I ran into the kitchen, grabbed the cling film and wound it round Angelino's chest several times, hoping that way to stop any air from getting into his chest cavity. I turned him onto his side, over from his injured right side, before picking up the phone on the wall and calling an ambulance. I used my mobile to call Drag and hoped that the ambulance would arrive in the next ten minutes. If it didn't, Angelino wasn't likely to make it. There was nothing more that I could do to help him, and I had to get away with Emma before the police found us here. I pulled the masks off the gunmen's faces. I'd never seen them before. Just as I'd suspected, they were all wearing Kevlars underneath their clothes. They were the real deal. Professional hitmen on serious business. I moved towards the front door and saw Jimmy's body lying there next to one of the heavies. What I wasn't expecting to see was the body of the other one, Zissis, apparently unharmed at the top of the staircase with his trousers down, looking like he'd just come out of the toilet. He stared down at his former colleagues and at me, standing over them holding the Kalashnikov. He looked at me in shock and raised his arms in surrender.

"Put your arms down and pull your trousers up, for God's sake!" I shouted. "I didn't kill them."

He did what he was told and came down the stairs, slowly, nervously, as though trying to work out what was going on because he didn't dare ask. As he came closer, I asked myself again how on earth they had got into the place. And why, when they knew Angelino and I were in the house, they hadn't sent anyone after us but had gone straight for Emma. It didn't make sense; they were professionals. Zissis was getting closer, still fiddling with his trousers, which seemed to be causing him some difficulty. Somebody must have been sent to take care of us, to make sure they wouldn't have any trouble getting away. And somebody must have told them where Emma was, that she'd be downstairs. Zissis was now about thirty feet away from me, and was clearly working out what he was going to say. The whole thing reeked of betrayal. Someone had let them in and had gone upstairs to kill me and Angelino but hadn't been quick enough. And now he was putting on this act to catch me off guard. I deliberately lowered the Kalashnikov a little more and leaned my body in towards the small table where the guns they'd taken off me earlier were lying, giving the impression I was relaxed and not expecting to be attacked. Zissis was now fifteen feet away.

"Yes, but —" he started to say and whipped out a gun from his calf, from inside those supposedly awkward trousers.

It all reeked of betrayal, and the traitor himself was now so close he was taking a load of bullets to the face. If he had any next of kin, they would struggle to identify him. I did not spare any expense with the bullets. Two or three of them went straight through his skull, lodging themselves with a dull smack into the door a few feet away. I rushed back to Angelino, who had lousy instincts when it came to hiring staff, however talented he was at sniffing out information. And he was paying for it. His pulse was even weaker now.

I went over to Emma's door and knocked.

"It's Stratos. All clear now," I said as calmly as I could.

She unlocked the door. "What about Angelino?" she asked, her blue eyes fixed on mine, penetrating my soul. How on earth do you tell someone who has already lost so much that they are about to lose their second father too?

"He's hurt. But he'll be fine."

She took my hand. I looked at it. It was steady, and looked three times the size of hers. A death-dealing hand holding the hand with a magic touch.

"You're lying."

*By "magic" they mean legerdemain*, Angelino had told me. Maybe he was wrong. Maybe Emma was a real magician. Maybe she *did* know everything.

"Take me to him."

I took her to him. Time was really tight. We should have already left, but I took her over to him anyway. She fell to the floor next to him, smelled him, caressed him, moving her hand lightly over the cling film I had wrapped round him. I gave her my hand to help her up. She was shaking.

"He's hurt, but he *will be fine*," I said, stressing the last three words of that sentence with an emphasis so strong it resembled shouting, hoping in the process I'd convince myself too.

# 13

"How's Angelino?" I was on the phone to Drag. He had told me the second I answered it that the cybercrime division had no records of Raptas, no evidence of paedophile tendencies or anything else.

I knew Angelino was still in intensive care forty-eight hours after what the media had christened the Chateaubriand Street Massacre. He'd needed nine units of blood before they could operate, and while the transfusion was taking place they had cut open his chest and inserted tubes between his ribs to relieve the air pressure. The worst damage had been caused by a bullet that had entered through his right armpit and travelled a few centimetres lower down before hitting a rib and lodging itself three and a half inches into his right lung. This bullet had proved to be the hardest to remove. When they saw that it was lodged so deep, the doctors even considered leaving it there, and would have done so had they not judged that the risk of future infection from the fibres that had attached themselves to it was greater than the risk of surgery.

But the blow to his head when he fell down the stairs turned out to be much more serious than I had initially thought, and much more serious than the bullets sitting inside him. Angelino's body had responded brilliantly to surgery, but his brain had still not recovered. The doctors were completely unable to give any kind of prognosis – no idea when or if he would come out of his coma.

That much I did know. I also knew the police were trying to find out who had killed the three murderers inside the house and that nobody had left any fingerprints anywhere. That's because I had been careful to wipe the gun and the knife before I left. But I had to find out how Angelino was getting on so I could tell Emma. When I persuaded her to leave the house with me before the police arrived she had made me promise not to lie to her about Angelino's condition. "Not about Angelino, not about anything," I'd told her. I had no intention of keeping my word. I resolved to protect her from absolutely anyone and anything, including the truth if necessary. It hadn't been that hard to persuade her to leave because Angelino had warned her that if anything ever happened to him, she should try to find me, and had given her my phone number. Emma had asked him what kind of thing he imagined might happen to him, and he had been vague and general enough in his reply to stop her from worrying.

It might not have been difficult to get her to leave with me, but it was turning out to be almost impossible to get her to go to sleep until I reassured her after one whole day that Angelino was out of danger and they were keeping him sedated to reduce the pain after the operation.

Drag gave me the lowdown. "It's looking tough for Angelino, but there's hope that he'll pull through. The next few days will be critical. The doctors are saying that he's made of solid stuff and they're hoping his brain will respond."

"Life on the streets makes you strong."

"Hmm. Any idea how we're going to proceed with this case?" he asked me.

"None."

"This tends to happen to us often."

"But we break through in the end."

"Till some day we won't."

"You think that day will come?" I asked him.

"No. But my horoscope tells me to be modest these days. I also have an idea on how to proceed. I'll speak to the girl as soon as you let me know where you're keeping her."

He'd already asked me this and I had replied by asking him in turn about Angelino, knowing full well that he'd get back to the question that was eating him up.

"Which part of 'no' did you not understand the first time?"

"The part that tells me that suddenly you don't trust me any more."

"Don't be stupid."

"No. First you get rid of your transmitter, and then you hide our key witness."

Drag was an excited child around gadgets. He was obsessed with them and always had to buy them. But owning them is not enough for him; he insists on using them as much as possible. A few years ago we both started using a microscopic transmitter, about the size of a chick-pea. We wore them under our arches; they didn't bother our feet and they transmitted our positions to each other. They could also send out an SOS if our footsteps followed a certain pattern. For the past two days mine had been lying in a drawer enjoying a well-earned rest.

"Don't forget I'm a key witness too. And I've told you everything I know, including everything that Emma's told me, which is precisely nothing. She has no idea why anyone would want to kidnap her, or kill her for that matter."

"The more you talk to her, the more likely she is to come out with something useful. Protecting her like this is only harming the case. If we do get to the bottom of this, it will be through interrogations."

"Kostas – you'll get nothing out of her. And you'll probably put your foot in it and say something she shouldn't hear." I hardly ever used his Christian name, and only when there was a reason. This was a reason.

"Me? Put my foot in it?"

"Yes. You. Put your foot in it. You're not the most discreet man alive, and I don't want you talking to her about Themis or about Angelino."

"But she might know something that will unlock all these cases for us – or at least a few of them."

"I don't even want you to try to persuade her to talk. She's been through a hell of a lot – much more than anybody should ever have to. If there's something you want to ask, ask me, and I'll ask her myself if I get the chance."

"If you get the chance! Stratos, Athens is buzzing with this. You've left six dead bodies and one half-dead body behind you. The TV news is playing scenes from *Scarface* and talking about the mafia takeover of the city and the incompetent police force. Do you know I had the Prime Minister on the phone? The Prime Minister! Not his side-kicks. The Prime Minister, telling me how concerned he was and how much faith he had in me. That was just before he made that public statement trying to calm everyone down. He trusts me, even though I've swiped all her things you asked me to rescue from the crime scene and brought them to you. And after all that, are you really *refusing* to let me speak to the only person we have who might actually know something?"

"Yes."

"Yes, what?"

"Yes, I refuse."

"I don't think I've ever once in twenty-five years told you to go to hell," he answered before the line went dead.

# 14

Before the phone really started ringing, Teri had answered it.

"Teri Berry. Speed. Reliability. Quality. A very good day to you."

"'Berry' from Berikis?"

"Berry from Berry Berry Good. And from Walter Berry, I always loved that guy, the way he ran around the court. Goofy reincarnated into a basketball player."

"How's Emma?"

My first thought as we left Chateaubriand Street was to take Emma to my flat. Maria was away, so I could sleep up there and Emma could use my bed. It was a pretty safe bet – the security systems I'd installed make it practically impossible for anyone to break into my flat. But there were two serious drawbacks: if Maria came home, I would have to tell her everything, and that would make her feel even more vulnerable about the dangers her relationship with me brought; the second was loneliness. Emma would have to spend big chunks of the day all alone while I was out trying to get to the bottom of who was behind the attack on Angelino, what had happened to Themis and whether the two cases were connected.

My second thought was Teri. That would deal with the problem of loneliness, and as for security, I'd spent the past year turning her two-storey house in Galatsi into a mini fortress. That was after both of us had come within inches of our lives there when those two psychotic bastards came after us. The only real drawback was that Teri couldn't let on to Drag that Emma was there. When we got to her house, while Emma was spending time slowly getting to know her new bedroom, I explained to Teri why Drag must never find out. "As if," she said. "As if I'd let that idiot come round here and upset the girl."

That was a relief, because there was no Plan C as none of my business acquaintances were trustworthy enough; the only people I could trust were my three old school friends: Maria, Drag and Teri. And these days, two out of three of them weren't exactly my biggest fans.

"She wants to see Angelino. And you. She's asleep. It hasn't been long. Since about six this morning. I could hear her tossing and turning all night," came Teri's reply.

"What about you?"

"What about me?"

"Aren't you going to get some sleep?"

"Now that I'm looking after her, no. When this whole thing is over, don't worry, you'll get the bill for all the extra face creams and eye moisturizers I'll need to make myself battle-ready again."

"What battle are you fighting?"

"The battle of my life. In the war against wrinkles."

I hadn't slept either. I had also tossed and turned for hours, and when I finally did drift off, I'd dreamed that a baby was being pursued by two arms, my arms, I swear they were mine, and they were desperate to reach the baby because it was being submerged in pitch-black water; I couldn't work out whether it was a lake or the sea. It was completely dark, the only light guiding me was coming from the baby itself, which seemed to be getting further and further away from me. Some battles you win simply because you can't afford to lose them: I caught up with the baby, took it in my arms and held it as though I had been holding it for years. And slowly, my arms began to lift the baby out of the water. It was a large baby, a girl, with closed eyelids. It was calm and had relaxed into my arms as though it had no sense that it was drowning, as though the water was its natural environment, and the moment that it emerged above the surface, the moment that its eyes opened to look at me for the first time, I woke up and could smell Maria's body lying next to me, and hear her breathing. Of course, she wasn't there. But her presence was so overwhelming I was convinced that I could not have dreamed it. The baby, yes, that was a dream. But now I was fully awake and could still smell Maria next to me, and I even started to think that she had somehow got into the flat and had left again. I ran outside like a madman, leaping up the stairs three at a time, and went into her room. She wasn't there, and there was absolutely no sign that anyone had been there at all. She was probably at her parents' house. With her child. With our child. And miserable. She should be with her parents. She should be with someone. She should be with me, with me beside her. With me, who had got to the point where I was hallucinating about her. I tried her mobile for the hundredth time. Switched off. I did have her parents' number. Yes. That would go well: "Hello, this is Stratos, the caretaker. Yes, that's right – Maria's old school friend. The one who didn't know that the child she's carrying was his. Could I speak to her, please?" I didn't call. When you can't put something right, you have to try to make sure that you don't make it worse. Better to sit up all night waiting for daybreak thinking about how and why you managed to make such a mess of everything.

"Tell Emma I'll be over this evening. And that Angelino is getting stronger by the hour and we'll soon be able to visit him. Is anyone else round there at the moment?"

"Babis, of course."

Babis, also known as Big Babis, has been in love with Teri for years; he would do anything for her, despite the fact that there has never – as far as I know – been anything romantic between them. Teri puts him up occasionally when he's between relationships and needs a shoulder to cry on, which was obviously the case now. I had found him asleep on her sofa when I took Emma round there. Teri says that the best way to cheer him up is to sit and play board games with him until they both drop. Big Babis is a nickname he got because he's the same height as Teri – five foot five – and if he was a wrestler, he'd be in the featherweight category.

A few years back, Teri transitioned, and with that Lefteris became Teri. It took us a while to get used to it. I don't believe that Drag has ever really come to terms with it, even now. For some reason he could deal with a gay Lefteris, a very effeminate gay Lefteris, but the surgery was something he couldn't cope with. He seemed able to accept the vagaries and mistakes in nature, but not any sort of human intervention to correct them. He went to great lengths to avoid using any gender pronouns when talking to or about Teri. If he called me and I said "I'm having coffee with Teri," he would reply, "Say hi," rather than "Say hello to her." Aware as I was of how slowly Drag came round to situations that he didn't naturally feel comfortable with, it was unlikely that he would ever adjust to Teri, not in this lifetime. What had cost him more than her transitioning was that we hardly ever got together any more, the three of us, to play cards and have all those petty arguments they used to have when they were friends of the same sex. That familiar cycle of getting together, fighting and making up, helped them feel that nothing had essentially changed since they were teenagers, and that the passing of all those years hadn't touched them at all. They were immortal. Indestructible. Even I'd fallen for it.

"How come you're up at this hour?" she asked.

"I thought we could go for a coffee. Lock Emma's door, and if she wakes up and wants something, tell Babis to give us a ring."

"One of those silent coffees?"

"They're not silent. You talk. Non-stop," I said.

"Ah. That hurt. If I didn't open that sweet, sensual mouth of mine occasionally, even the flies in that café would drop dead from boredom. What time?"

"What are you doing now?"

"I was going to wash my hair."

"How long will that take?"

"Shampoo. Conditioner. Then a long soak. Shall we say three hours?"

"We'll say one hour."

"Tyrant. Come and pick me up from the Varvakeio market. I need five minutes with Miltos."

Teri's five minutes never approximate to anyone else's concept of five minutes. People are always so excited to see her and have such a good time with her that they don't let her leave – to be fair, she doesn't try very hard either. I suspect that some people there wanted to do more than talk to her, but the community inside the covered market is a small one and it's very hard to get away with much more than flirting inside there. It was particularly tricky trying to get away from Miltos in his canteen. Miltos was drowning in debt – he hadn't paid any rent to the municipality since 2013 – but that was the least of his problems. Teri went down there as often as she could and gave him enough money to buy himself a bit of breathing space. It was supposedly a loan. At 0% interest. Because he was a friend, and because he had two small children, and because Teri had the money. Teri had been pretty loaded since her new love interest, a married intellectual, had demanded that she would be his and his alone. If Miltos shared my obsession with noir cinema, perhaps he would have used Robert Mitchum's line in *Angel Face*, "You know something? You're a pretty nice guy, for a girl." But because he didn't share my obsession and because he wanted to show Teri that he was grateful, Miltos would insist on giving her everything on the menu every time she turned up. And crisis or no crisis, he would produce over ten different cooked dishes every day, the first smelling better than the next. All the single men in the neighbourhood swore by Miltos' delicious legendary *bekris mezes* and his moussaka – and by his *tsipouro*. Miltos, with his stomach hanging over his white apron, would brag that his *tsipouro* came straight from Mount Athos, from the same monastery that had first started distilling the drink back in the fourteenth century.

It was ten o'clock by the time Teri decided to leave Miltos. Three young men who had been out all night – students, maybe – were sitting at the table next to ours, putting away their second helping of offal soup, adding healthy doses of chilli flakes to their bowls, the kind that you only ever find in Miltos' restaurant these days. They didn't look like they were in any hurry to leave. One of them shouted out an order for beef stew while stealing a glance at Teri.

"Who's up for another bowl of soup, then?" asked his neighbour, winking and grinning.

"Make that two, Miltos!"

We walked past the rows of fishmongers, greengrocers and grocers until we emerged from the market. I was wearing a woollen sweater and the weather was already ridiculing this choice by flooding the city in sunlight. Teri was in three-inch heels and a fitted red satin crepe dress, chosen apparently because she didn't like to be overdressed so early in the morning.

"Where do you want to go?" I asked her.

"Look, handsome, I was born for Kolonaki."

"And nowhere but Kolonaki."

"Ooh. Do I detect the subtlest note of irony? A small attempt at humour? *Nowhere but* Kolonaki. It's absolutely dead there now. Not that there aren't a lot of people around, and some of the cafés and bars still manage to fill up, sort of, but it just doesn't have that *je ne sais quoi* about it any more. You know, that tacky new-money snobbishness. Feels like most of them are feeling so guilty for having coffee at Da Capo that they resist all malicious gossip. There's a sadness hanging over the Athens of nothing, so much so that it might turn it into something."

"Did you come up with that?"

"Course not. It's one of Hermes' lines. I just deliver it better than he does, and it sounds original, doesn't it?"

Hermes is Teri's intellectual boyfriend. A professor at the Panteion University of Social and Political Sciences. He had once been a customer of hers – she was a very pricey call girl. He fell madly in love with her and stuck with her. Teri liked him, without being crazy about him, because he treated her like a princess. She said to me once, half-jokingly, that as soon as she had saved up enough money, she would hire me to get rid of Hermes' wife so that she could replace her. "And because you've got that thing where you insist on justifying it all to yourself, I'll root out some flaw or sin or whatever and pin it on her so that you'll feel better about the whole thing," she added.

"Nice. Will you please tell me where you want to go?"

"I want us to stay round here, or maybe somewhere in the direction of Monastiraki and go people-watching. There are always people around here. No matter how miserable they are, they'll always come out and try to sell something or buy something at a bargain price. And they even manage to smile occasionally. Smiling isn't taxed, EU scumbags!"

Teri was virulently anti-austerity.

"OK. Let's go to the flea market," I suggested.

"Mmm. You're actually brighter than you look. But then again, how hard can that be with a face like that?"

We set off, walking down the same streets we had crossed hundreds of times since our childhood, streets which if you looked down on them from above would all look the same, just as busy as ever. But the life that filled the streets on our way was a very different life. The lives of people from different races, speaking different languages, would briefly intersect with the lives of Greeks when migrants stood on the street corners selling soap, candles, knock-off designer sunglasses, cheaply made children's toys, pirate CDs, garlic ropes and cinnamon sticks to the locals and the foreigners who crowded round them to see what was on offer and to bargain down the price – many more than went into the local shops these days.

"Do you know when these guys lose out by haggling?" Teri asked me, pointing to one of the African sellers, who had dozens of lighters set out in front of him.

"When?"

"Never! They are all brilliant salesmen. A salesman's talent shows when he's buying, not selling. You see, they pay so little for this stuff; the haggling is just a big act to make the customers feel they've got themselves a real bargain. However low the salesman goes, he's still making a very tidy profit."

"How do you know all this?"

"One of my regulars told me, a couple of years ago."

"OK. OK. Spare me the details."

"You did ask. Anyway, if it was evening, I'd suggest going to Kolokotroni Street. Since nobody has any money any more, all those snooty shops with the designer labels have closed down and a whole world of bars of all sorts has sprung up in their place. Everybody can find enough cash for a drink. Have you been to Piazza, the one that's just opened – with those gorgeous spicy cocktails and the even spicier barman?"

"No."

"Ugh. You've always been such a killjoy – ever since we were young. I can't for the life of me imagine why I love you so much."

I turned and smiled at her.

Abyssinia Square in Monastiraki is one of the loveliest places in Athens. It took its name from the Ethiopians who lived there at one point. What makes it so attractive is the fact that you can enjoy your coffee with uninterrupted views of the Acropolis instead of all those massive high-rises you see from so many other cafés in the city, or you can walk through the side streets hoping to catch a glimpse of the Parthenon from the gaps between the buildings. For decades the square has hosted a Sunday bazaar, known to locals as the *Yousourum,* named after one of the old Jewish second-hand furniture dealers there, one of the first to set up in the square. A clever chap, around thirty years old and an eternal student at the Athens Polytechnic, sick of being supported by his parents, opened the café there, usurping the square's name, and it turned out never to have an empty seat in it. Before we climbed the marble steps leading into the café, we walked round the square, where you can still find used furniture, clothes and shoes, along with the antique shops and stores selling musical instruments. Teri smiled at all the traders, standing there with blankets at the ready in case the heavens opened suddenly in the way they were forecast to do later that afternoon, commenting to me through her teeth that everything looked like a pile of old tat.

"Let's get a balcony table – how romantic is that?" she said teasingly as I sat down at one of the indoor tables, ducking to avoid colliding with one of their dangerously low-slung pendant lights.

She laughed. Teri's laugh sounded like gurgling water, and it was impossible not to smile. I asked the young pregnant waitress to bring me a hot chocolate, and Teri, after giving the matter a great deal of thought, eventually ordered a *freddoccino* special and commented to the waitress on how sexy she found the painting hanging next to us of the nude couple making out in the bathtub. She did manage to keep quiet long enough for us to take in the sight of the Observatory emerging between the cypress trees, and I promised myself that I would visit it one day soon. Till my next visit to the *Yousourum*, when I'd probably make the same promise again.

"Spit it out. In detail. I want the whole story. When you brought Emma over, you effectively told me nothing."

I told her everything. While we were talking, I noticed the rest of the crowd in there – mostly couples, and a group of young men. I thought about how mundane their conversations would be. How normal. How removed from the story I was telling Teri.

"Themis Raptas. I vaguely remember him, by sight, but it's been a while. I can't remember anything in particular about him; I think he'd done a piece on corrupt politicians that had upset a lot of people. Yes, that was him. But I wouldn't stake my life on it. So you're telling me that three years ago they had him killed, this Raptas man, and then for three years, nobody, and then they kill three more in the same way he was murdered?"

"Mmm. And if we suppose that the cases are connected, what links Raptas, with his clean criminal record, and a bunch of paedophiles?"

"But if they are not connected, isn't this a bit too much of a coincidence? Just because someone has a clean record, it doesn't follow that they are innocent. All it means is they've never been caught," she said.

"And then there's Angelino, suddenly bumping up his security since he's had Emma with him, and the attempted kidnapping – or murder – in his house."

"And don't forget Raptas suddenly deciding to disappear and fall off the radar for so many years. One hell of a coincidence. I'm not sorry that all those paedophiles died, but something is going on here."

I nodded.

"Are you sure it was the girl they were after?"

"They weren't interested in Angelino. He was only shot because he got in the way."

"So they might have killed Raptas to get at Emma?"

"I did consider that, but it makes no sense. Raptas and Emma moved around in open public spaces, so if anyone wanted to find her they would have done. But now, with Angelino, she was hidden and protected."

"So the target the first time was Raptas, and now it's Emma?"

"Yes. And because I haven't got a clue as to why, I'm going to need your help."

"Are you telling me you didn't invite me for coffee solely for the pleasure of my company?"

"That's exactly what I mean."

"You filthy dog; what do you want from me?"

"I need to make use of all your contacts in the media."

Five minutes later and Teri had already made me an appointment with a make-up artist friend of hers at HighTV, Raptas' old channel. Teri had worked in make-up herself for many years before reaching the conclusion that she could do a lot better in the oldest profession in the world, and had kept up with a few of her old friends from that time. Though she didn't have any other contacts at the station, and I'd been hoping that she could put me in touch with some bigger players there, she did assure me that Dora, her ex-colleague, was in on all the gossip, and if there was anything to know about Raptas, she would know it.

The waitress brought up our order and slowly moved away. Her belly was already swollen, and the job must have been a struggle for her. I looked at her and thought about Maria and how her belly was growing, and that I wasn't with her, and that she didn't want me to be.

"She's looking a bit like a meatball, that one," said Teri, who was also watching her.

"Yes, yes, she is," I said, deep in thought about Maria.

"Did you know that the female polar bear puts on about four hundred pounds in pregnancy?"

"Oh, you've picked up Drag's little fetish for throwing irrelevant facts into the conversation at the most random moments."

"Of course I have. Each of us carries the other three around inside us. All the time. Which means that somewhere inside you is a very happy, post-surgery woman, even if you don't realize it."

Before I could so much as smile at this, she was off again.

"Maria carries all of us, apart from you, who she's got a double dose of."

I was struggling to breathe.

"Have the two of you spoken at all?" I asked Teri, and I didn't recognize my own voice, the way it emerged from my throat.

She shook her head. She was no longer feeling so chatty. Why hadn't I thought of that? Since Maria couldn't speak to either me or Drag, she would have spoken to Teri.

"Where is she?"

"Oh, drop it, will you? 'Where is she?' If she wanted you to know, she'd have picked up the phone all those times you rang her. She's fine. OK? That is all that I'm licensed to say."

"You don't get how important —"

"Right – I don't get how important it is that she's carrying a child that has become a millstone! I'm that stupid that I don't understand, while the rest of you are pure geniuses! Drag called me as soon as we'd finished talking this morning and asked me if I knew where you were hiding Emma. This is really important to him. So are you saying I should betray your trust and tell him? To hell with the lot of you!"

She was probably right, but I was seeing red. There was no way on earth I was about to leave that café without finding out how Maria was, without Teri picking up her phone and calling her and putting me on to speak to her myself. I felt the darkness descend on my face and Teri must have noticed it too, even though she stayed calm in the conviction that she was right. I have no idea how our coffee would have ended if at that moment a familiar face hadn't sprung up on the screen of the small TV that was suspended at an angle from the wall in the *Yousourum*: it was Drag. And he did not look happy.

# 15

The TV was on mute, so I strode over to the waitresses' station and took the remote. Three or four customers turned round, possibly in irritation, when I turned the sound up, but the second they registered my build they abandoned all hope of complaining and resumed their conversations.

Drag was in his same old trench coat thrown over a yellow sweater, and almost provocatively crumpled. He hadn't combed his hair, which looked in urgent need of a cut, especially now that it was thinning out at the temples, which did nothing to flatter him. He stood in front of a sea of impatient reporters, all waving microphones under his nose. He had the look of a man who would be ten times more comfortable if confronted by the same number of sub-machine guns. The reporters were consumed by hysteria, all shouting at the same time, at an even faster tempo than usual, pushing and shoving each other, and judging by the wobbly picture, the cameramen were as well. They gave the impression that something really important had happened. But what?

What was Drag doing all the way out in Anavyssos at this time of the morning? Assuming that the headline "Anavyssos: Live Now" flashing across the bottom of the screen of the breaking news bulletin was correct on points of time and place.

"Superintendent – would you like to comment on this latest murder?"

"Can you confirm that the victim was also a paedophile?"

"Is the Avenger too clever for you?"

"Superintendent – did they leave a note this time?"

"What are you going to do to protect future victims?"

"Everything," said Drag, ignoring all the questions that preceded it.

"Do you believe that these people are worthy of police protection?"

"Everybody deserves police protection." Drag was quick to reply but did so in the same lugubrious voice I remember him using at school when reciting pages from our history textbook before a test.

"Even paedophiles?"

"The law does not discriminate."

"Even against paedophiles?" asked another.

"Is there an echo here?" asked Drag, looking around him with affected confusion.

"So are we your problem now?" asked the target of his irony.

"Is it true that you're getting a court order to ban the broadcast of *Among Us* again?"

"Yes."

"But there are court decisions permitting it to be aired."

"There are."

"What do you mean?"

"I mean that they exist."

"Superintendent – are you mocking the Hellenic justice system?"

"The Hellenic justice system doesn't need anyone to mock it; it manages just fine on its own."

That's what they were waiting for, as they had briefly lost their rhythm. Like bees synchronizing their wing movements, they erupted into a deafening chorus of "What do you mean?" and "Do you mean to say that the justice system makes a mockery of itself through the judgements that it makes?" and "Is this a direct attack on our judges?"

And with that, Drag had successfully deflected any further questions about the investigation.

"Are you attempting to blame the incompetence of the police on the courts?" shouted one of the drones, managing to be heard above the rest of the swarm.

"The police will solve this case too," said Drag.

"After how many victims?"

"We believe that this will be the last."

"Didn't you believe the same thing before this murder?"

"We did."

"So how can the public have confidence in you now?"

"Because I'm so good-looking."

Utter mayhem. There's no other word for what happened next. The deadpan delivery and the unsmiling face only made it worse.

"Are you mocking us now?"

"Do you consider your behaviour appropriate? Let's go – he's ridiculing us."

"What have you got against the media, Superintendent?"

"Right now you're mocking the Greek taxpayers too, who will be watching and doubting they can expect the full protection of the police."

"No."

"No?"

"I am not making fun of the taxpayer."

"Doesn't your new recommendation to the chief prosecutor to ban the screening of the show amount to an admission that you can't catch this murderer?"

"No."

"Does this not amount to a clear violation of the freedom of the press?"

"No."

"Are you not in breach of the respective judgements?"

"No."

"Then what *are* you doing?"

"Making a recommendation."

"Do you at least have some evidence that gives you cause for optimism?"

"The existence of God," he said, and got to his feet.

"You're now mocking God, as well?" screeched one of the reporters who had yet to speak.

"God doesn't need anyone to mock Him; He manages just fine on his own." And with that Drag marched straight into the crowd of reporters, forcing them to step aside so that he could carve his way through them.

"How do you feel now that our best friend is famous?" asked Teri.

126

"Much better about it than he does, that's for sure."

The image from the breaking news item shifted to the studio where the newsreader was reminding her viewers that the body of the man who had been found the day before in the coastal area of Anavyssos belonged to fifty-year-old Dimosthenes Daniil, one of the paedophiles exposed on the show *Among Us*. He had been arrested for possession and distribution of child pornography online, images involving children up to four years of age. He had successfully used the insanity defence and was serving out his sentence in a psychiatric facility, from which he was released on a regular basis, and had been on his way home yesterday.

I phoned Drag. No answer. It was possible he'd be busy. It was certain he'd be angry. He had been using Daniil as bait, but the Avenger had managed to kill him without falling into Drag's trap. *Defeat* – one of the words Drag despises the most.

My meeting with Antonis Pavlis, Angelino's icon-painter friend, was at two o'clock in Stadiou Street. That left me with over an hour after I said goodbye to Teri. I didn't get the chance to talk her round about Maria because Babis phoned to say that Emma was awake and Teri leapt at the chance to take off. Before she did, she told me that she knew a young girl who had once been forced to do porn films. She knew her from the days when she worked at the support centre for abused children, and was still in touch with her. The girl had suffered a great deal and was willing to share all she knew about her abusers. Teri would ask her if she knew anything about Raptas and the paedophiles to see if she had anything interesting to say. As I had nothing better to do I decided to kill time by walking through Thisseion and Kerameikos, past the ancient Athenian cemetery, the marble-paved squares, the Byzantine Church of the Agioi Asomatoi, the Museum of Islamic Art and the part of the old city walls of Athens down at the Benaki Museum. I nipped into the Museum of the Ancient Agora, housed in the Stoa of Attalos, to see what I could remember from my previous visit to the shopping mall that dominated the lives of Athenians twenty centuries ago. I had to admit that of everything I saw, the only thing that really made an impression on me was a young girl I saw in Thisseion who plunged her arm inside a dustbin searching for something to eat, and I wondered what this rich cultural heritage could possibly mean to her. Perhaps I'm just uncultured.

Further on, a couple of buskers were packing up and leaving. The atmosphere was unsettled – a march was on its way, demonstrating about the death of an illegal immigrant, a street seller, who had been so terrified when the police arrived to arrest him that in his efforts to run away he stumbled, fell onto the railway tracks and was electrocuted. For some reason, none of the protestors were paying any attention to the girl by the bin. She was standing right there next to them. I reckoned that if she actually died, they would very quickly organize a protest march, but help her while she was still alive? No chance.

I decided to turn back in the direction of Stadiou Street, and was outside a place advertising Turkish baths when my phone rang. Maybe it was Maria, sensing my despair. Or feeling desperate herself. Maybe she'd thought the whole thing through and had found the answer that had eluded me. By the time I had pulled the phone out of my back pocket, I had managed to convince myself it was her. But it wasn't. It was Drag.

"Have you heard?"

"Teri and I were admiring you."

"He did a runner. Daniil, the paedo. He got wind of the fact he was being followed and gave our man the slip."

"Well that didn't turn out well for him, did it?"

"Nor for us. Now we'll have to wait for the next attack. There was nothing on the victim's body we can use."

"What about the execution style? The same?"

"Yes. Only this time they chucked the body into the sea."

"They? Plural?"

"That's right. There's no way that the Avenger can be working alone. Our evidence shows there must be two of them. At least."

"Why would they throw the body in the sea?"

"I don't know. For effect? I have no idea."

"But you will have."

"That's the only certainty here. As for those three louts who broke into Angelo's house, I've found past convictions as well as enough witnesses confirming that these characters would kill their own mothers if you threw a bit of cash at them. Pros, but not exactly premier league. I still haven't found out who they were working for. I also had a word with the director of the Happy Home orphanage."

That was the orphanage where Emma spent the first three years of her life.

"And?"

"It seems that for the first time in the history of the orphanage, a file has gone missing."

"Emma's."

"Mmm. And there's no electronic record, either, of who her biological parents were?"

Just as I had begun to think that this case couldn't get any stranger, it did.

"The director promised she would investigate."

"Do you think she'll have any success?"

"I do believe she has no idea what's going on. What about you? What's new?"

"I'm looking into it. I'll let you know tonight."

"I need to speak to Emma."

"Drag …"

"You could be there too."

"No. In her mind, the police are the enemy."

"That's her problem."

"Not just hers."

"Then we won't tell her I'm a policeman."

"I won't lie to her."

That wasn't entirely true. I had already been lying to her about Angelino's condition. Strictly speaking I should have said, "I won't lie to her any more."

"If I don't make a breakthrough soon, I'm going to have to ask you to do this as a favour to me."

"Don't."

"I'll wait to hear from you tonight," he said and hung

up. His tone was the one he used when he spoke to his subordinates. It was as though he felt that the pressure he was under was greater than mine.

This case was beginning to resemble a rodent squeezing through holes wherever it finds them and slyly gnawing away, bit by bit, at my relationships with the only three people I had ever loved in my life.

# 16

Antonis Pavlis was waiting as agreed on the graffiti-filled corner of Stadiou and Korai Street a little further down from the Asty Cinema. He was in a white shirt, grey velvet trousers and black basketball boots. He stood at about five foot eight and was a slender, fit man who couldn't have been over fifty, despite his white hair, which looked even whiter against his tanned skin. He was cleanly shaven, which meant that he didn't mind if people saw the big scar on his left cheek, which looked like it had been slashed by a knife. He'd given me a very accurate description of what he was going to be wearing over the phone, so I knew that this was the man I was looking for. He was standing in front of a wall covered in graffiti. Amongst all those slogans I managed to make out one that said *The Aegean belongs to SpongeBob*.

Ten yards away a group of parents had set up a make-shift open-air school for children with special needs and were holding banners protesting the lack of transport that would enable their children to get to school.

"Stratos?"

We shook hands. I thanked him for his help and couldn't help noticing his aftershave, which was sweet and fruity.

"Anything for Angelino. Any news? I went the day before yesterday, but saw that the police were grilling all his visitors, so I got straight out of there."

"He's getting stronger all the time, but they're keeping him in an induced coma to spare him all that pain," I said, repeating the yarn I had been spinning to Emma. I didn't know how he would react, or whether he would still want to help if I told him the truth about Angelino's condition.

"Shall we go before everything kicks off here?" he asked, pointing in the direction of the riot police who were crossing Stadiou Street and heading for the Ministry of Labour.

"What's going on?"

"A demo on its way. People who've been laid off, demanding to see the minister."

That meant anything was possible, from basic chanting of angry slogans blasting through megaphones to a full-blown riot and tear gas. I turned and looked past the kids who were sitting there drawing and at their parents, who needed to get them out of the way, and quickly. I remembered Teri saying about a month ago, "I worry that I'm beginning to fall out of love with this bloody city."

Pavlis and I headed up the street towards Ianos Books. I explained to him that I was intending to ask around the homeless community in general about their lives and then bring the discussion round to the good times, great moments on the streets, for example the Tramp routines that I'd seen this guy perform with a kid, years ago. That way, if any of those people had already been questioned by Angelino when he was trying to gather information and had stayed quiet, they wouldn't suspect anything. And maybe we would find someone who had more to say than they had told Angelino. Pavlis thought my idea was good and added that we shouldn't tell any of the homeless people we spoke to about the attack on Angelino.

"If they find out, they're not likely to want to open up to us – it will probably spook them even more."

"More than what?"

"More than they already are – they live on the streets. Most of them who have been sleeping rough for a while have got used to it; it suits them, but they don't want any more danger – they've had their fill."

The day Teri had expressed her changing feelings about Athens, Drag had been with us. We were playing stud poker. I was losing and the two of them were splitting the winnings, which is why they were managing not to fight. I remember asking him if he thought we had got so accustomed to danger that we couldn't live without it. That we would feel that something was missing. He didn't know what to say, and Teri answered instead, saying, "It's not so much that you two have got used to it; you could never live without it in the first place." And then she showed me her hand: royal flush. She had annihilated me.

Giannis – that's how he introduced himself to us – apologized for not getting up and coming out of his box. He was wrapped in a red blanket and was shaking. He must have caught a chill somewhere, he said. Must have left the window open. I laughed lamely. He smiled and told me to make sure I used his joke. He talked about himself a lot into the voice recorder I was holding. He whispered that he felt relieved that he didn't have to worry any more about paying the bills, and he was enjoying his new spot because it was next to the bookshop and it helped him remember the time when he used to buy books himself. And he noted that there weren't so many people around any more, since half the shops in Stadiou were boarded up. But he liked that. He liked the fact that even though he was in the centre of the city there were times when it went completely silent. As I listened to him, I thought about this street, the street in which three people including an unborn child had burned to death inside a bank during a petrol-bomb attack without causing much of a reaction. It seemed fair that the shops should die with them. The street had given up its right to life.

Giannis couldn't remember the faces of other homeless people. He said he tried to keep himself to himself. He didn't seem aware of the Chaplin routines. We thanked him and got up to leave. Pavlis left him a bag of food, which judging by Giannis' gaunt frame, would last him a good few days. I offered him my hand. He pulled back in alarm, and then raised it timidly instead of taking mine.

"I thought that he might remember something. He's a relative veteran," said Pavlis apologetically as we walked away.

"I wasn't expecting answers from the first person we spoke to."

He nodded in agreement.

"Let's walk up to Dionysiou Areopagitou Street, and then up towards Filopappou Hill. There's a big crowd up there. We might get more joy out of them," he suggested.

Pavlis, like me, was not big on conversation. He talked just enough to get by. He told me that he had already made some preliminary approaches to some of the homeless who lived up there who wouldn't be able to see us today, but sadly hadn't managed to get anything worthwhile out of them. One of them had told him that he'd seen Themis Raptas summon the devil and the devil had turned up; another one swore that Raptas went around in a space-ship, while a third claimed that he'd seen him under a tree making out with a gorgeous young TV presenter, who was always on, morning and evening. "They show her all the time. I see her when I go inside the electrical shops to beg," he'd explained to Pavlis. Pavlis had spent three hours with the man, bringing up photos of all the well-known female presenters on Greek TV, irrespective of age. But they meant nothing to him. Then, this guy agreed with the other vagrant saying that he, too, had seen Raptas enter the spaceship with the young TV star and both of them turned blue as soon as they entered. Pavlis had warned me that I might get some pretty sur-real responses.

Most of the time we walked in silence. The new Acropolis Museum was looking very bright in the sunlight, which showed no signs of retreating, rather like the rubbish bins that hadn't been emptied for weeks. A politician in his sixties was standing outside the museum. I couldn't remember his name, although I had seen his face often enough on the news because he was in the habit of triggering violent exchanges in parliament. He was making a statement: Athenians should all get out of their houses, enjoy the city and rediscover its myths, visit the museum and rediscover their own identity. His bodyguard was standing beside him holding an umbrella to ensure that the heavily gelled salt-and-pepper hair of the elected representative of the people did not get wet. Yeah, that's right. That's how you get to enjoy the city and have the time to think about its myths. The stray dogs of the area were wisely keeping their distance. I put it down to a sixth sense.

Our second appointment was in front of the statue of Makrygiannis, the hero of the wars of independence, and the young man waiting for us there couldn't be more than twenty. His glasses were damaged and wonky, and he was wearing ripped jeans and an American college T-shirt which hung very loosely from his skinny body. His hair was thin for such a young man, and his bony face was full of spots. He was struggling to keep standing in the same spot, and was very nervous. Pavlis stuffed a few notes into his hand, which seemed to calm him down a little. I'd seen that before with users. The feeling that you've got enough money for your next hit is almost as reassuring as the hit itself. For a while.

"Yeah. I remember him – the Chaplin guy. And the kid." This was encouraging, as up to then he had only given us one-word answers.

"How come? Aren't you too young to have been around then?"

"I ran away from home when I was twelve. Well, I had tried loads of times before that but that was the first time they didn't find me and take me back. My parents, the cops and other pigs."

I knew that if I launched straight into questions about Themis and Emma he might suspect something and start asking questions instead of answering them. So I decided to show more interest in him – just like a real journalist would.

"Why did you want to run away?"

"The beatings. I'd had enough."

"Did it happen a lot?"

"Every two to three days I'd have to stay off school. They'd say I was sick and keep me off so the teachers and the other kids wouldn't see my bruises. I didn't want them to either. I was embarrassed."

"Was it your dad?"

"It was both of them. Whichever one was in a bad mood, I'd get it from them. One day when they were having a really bad argument, I took my chance. I picked up the gun we had in the house and told them if they tried to get me back I'd kill them both in their sleep. They never came looking for me after that."

I shook my head in apparent sympathy. I knew the odds on this being a true story, or of being his story, or of being an amalgamation of many different junkies' stories, were probably even. There aren't many people who open up that easily, and even fewer who open up for money.

"Let's focus on something a bit happier, shall we? Like that Chaplin guy we were talking about before. I've heard that a lot of people, and a lot of homeless people like you, liked him a lot and that he cheered them up."

"Cheered us up? Yeah, right," he said sarcastically.

"What do you remember most about his act?"

"What do I remember?"

He looked over at Pavlis with a sick grin, as though he suddenly realized that he held all the power in this situation and that we needed him.

"Is this all the money?"

"Don't do this," said Pavlis in a stern voice, completely devoid of emotion.

"Do what?"

"You know what. Don't do it."

"I'm not doing anything," he said, realizing that extortion wouldn't get him very far.

"So what do you remember?" I asked, trying to steer the conversation back to Themis.

"I remember … let's see … the kid. A girl, wasn't it? Dressed like a boy."

"Yes."

"They seemed dead close. Like they really loved each other. When they finished their act, I saw them a couple of times going off together, holding hands. I remembered that because it made me jealous that he didn't hit her. But you never know, do you? He might have beaten her when they were alone."

"Anything else?"

"No, not really. Like what?"

He looked uneasily at Pavlis and stuffed the money into his pocket. Perhaps he was worried that Pavlis would take it back because his information wasn't up to much.

"Did they have any friends, for example?"

"Friends? People who live on the streets don't have friends."

"Enemies, then? Did you ever hear about anything? Anyone going after them?"

"No. No. Nothing like that. Can I go now?"

Pavlis looked at me. I nodded, and the lad walked off without saying anything.

We kept walking down Areopagitou Street till we got to a place that means a lot to me, but there's only one person who knows why. That's the way it goes; if more than one person knows something about you, that something probably isn't very important. It was the tiny church of Agios Dimitrios the Bombardier. Tradition has it that the church took its name from an incident that took place hundreds of years ago, when a lightning strike took out the Ottoman powder magazine up on the Acropolis just as they were loading their cannon ready to fire it at the Christian faithful in the church below. A solution of this kind would be very welcome to me now. If all the people who wanted to do harm to Angelino and Emma could gather in one convenient spot, along with whoever it was who killed Themis, and be struck by lightning – now that would be a miracle. That would free up all the time I'm spending charging around the city talking to the homeless to see if anyone remembers a bloke who died three years ago. That would free up the time I needed to destroy my own life at my own pace.

If I was going to lose Maria permanently, I'd have to move away, because practically every corner of the city reminded me of her. It was in this pedestrian area outside the church twenty years ago that we first kissed. We had climbed up the hill to see the sunset and looked at the illuminated Acropolis, which seemed so close that if we only stretched out our hands it would be ours. Not that we needed it. We had each other. After that we had walked back down the hill in silence, both waiting to see who would make the first move. I had no idea what I was supposed to do. The only experience I'd had at that point was with a prostitute who'd refused to let me touch her when I was inside her. When we arrived outside the church, Maria had kissed me, stopped to explore my face with her fingers, and then carried on kissing me. But between then and now were all the years she had been with Drag, while I begged inwardly that of all the intimacies they might have, that she wouldn't touch his face and kiss him like that. I wanted that to be mine, and mine alone.

"We'll be there in a minute. We're not going to talk to them all at once. I thought about gathering them together but decided that one-to-one would be better," Pavlis said.

I turned to look at him almost in surprise. He had fallen so quiet that I had almost forgotten he had been there all the time I had been tormenting myself with memories.

"Why?"

"They aren't good at sharing space. They tolerate each other spread out across the hill, like any neighbourhood, I suppose, but they rarely make friends. Not just because a lot of them will steal anything they can get their hands on, but basically they want to fend for themselves. They're here because they've wanted to get away from other people, not to forge new connections or a community. What did our young friend back there say? 'People who live on the streets don't have friends.'"

Although Pavlis had tried to prepare me for it, words could not begin to describe what I saw there up on the hill. The worst thing was the smell. The stench was overwhelming, and when they opened their mouths to speak, with most of them I really had to struggle to hold the voice recorder close enough to their mouths and resist the urge to step away from them. The ones who drank had slightly better breath – at least it was a vaguely familiar smell. As for the rest of them, it was otherworldly, a combination of rotting food pulled out of rubbish bins and many weeks' build-up of body odour, urine and excrement because they often soil themselves and can't wash it off afterwards.

Next to the smell, it was the sight. A lot of them had let themselves go to the extent that they couldn't even string together a few sentences that made any kind of sense at all. While they were talking to me, their minds would wander and they would either fall silent or make weird noises, as though attempting to clear their heads in the way that the rest of us clear our throats. Some of them started to talk about completely random topics and were incapable of returning to the original question, as though each piece of recent information had been permanently erased. One of them, who was younger than me, looked familiar. He had appeared in a lot of reports and documentaries and his picture had appeared in a number of newspapers because he had dug up his dead wife's body a couple of years ago and kept her at home with him because he couldn't live without her. The Hellenic justice system in its wisdom sentenced him for disrespecting the dead. Then there was the bloke who asked me to make a point of saying he was happy, just in case his son read the article.

Then there were those who were in a slightly better state. They actually seemed to think before they answered my questions about the Chaplin act, but even they had nothing useful to tell me. Apart from Argyris and Sonia, that is. I didn't get their surnames. Nobody up on the hill seemed to have a surname.

Argyris was about sixty, and had a fine head of long silver hair and an even longer beard, which looked pretty well groomed to me. He received us in his home, a construction made of plastic sheeting to keep the rain out. Inside was a threadbare sofa which he had rescued from the rubbish and a makeshift cooker he had built out of a camping gas stove. He told me that he did have a saucepan until fairly recently but someone had stolen it. Theft was a fact of life, and it was only the young ones who still had the will to get into fights over it.

"From where you sleep at night, you can see different shadows inside your space. It's usually just junkies who don't really expect to find anything but are so desperate that they keep looking."

"And you let them?"

"What choice do I have? I'm not going to get up and wrestle with them. If they're carrying a knife, they'll probably kill me. If they're not and I hit them, they'll definitely fall to the ground, and then how do I get rid of them? Most of them can hardly stand up at the best of times. They're like the living dead."

"But doesn't that frighten you? Seeing some stranger come in here at night?"

"No. It's just a shadow. It will leave. It's the other shadows, the ones inside our heads – they never go away. They're full of stories, those ones."

"Your story?"

"Are you asking why I'm here?" he said playing distractedly with the sleeve of his black sweater.

"Yes, I am."

"Do you think your readers are really interested?"

"I hope so."

"Well in that case, I'll tell you. I used to run a hotel on one of the islands. I did very well, but then I went crazy and started spending three times as much as I was making. I owed the banks. They'd all lent me money without seeming to care whether they ever saw it again. All I could think of was money; I'd daydream about it and at night I would dream about it again. Then one day I picked up a book. It was the myth of Daphne and Apollo. He tells her that he is the god of the arts, of medicine and of youth and beauty. He tells her she should be with him, and be his wife. But she doesn't want him. It's all a bit too much for her. She just wants the simple things in life, so she goes to Gaia, her mother, and tells her what's going on, and to help her out Gaia turns her into a bay tree. This makes her one with the earth. Forever. You can't get much simpler than that. And then I realized that was what I wanted too. To be one with nature and nothing else. I came here five years ago and feel like I've been reborn. I look outside morning and night and see the Acropolis. I'm sitting on some of the best real estate in the world."

"You're not wrong there. I used to know someone – he was homeless too – who used to say exactly the same thing as you; that was years ago. He used to perform round the squares and on the streets with a little girl. They had a Chaplin routine."

"Oh, yes. I remember, He was a good guy. I did hear that he was …"

He was trying to avoid the word "murdered". I shook my head.

"Three years ago," I said.

"So what are you looking for? The murderer? Is that why you're here?"

"No. What would be the point? Three years – what could I possibly find out now? Anyway, I'm a social corre-spondent, I don't do crime. The paper has other people for that. I just thought about him when you told me why you'd come here."

"Yeah. Great guy. Don't remember his name, though."

"Themis."

"I don't remember. Maybe he never told me his name. He was always polite. Distant, of course. Didn't talk to many people, but he was always polite. There was this one guy I'd see him talk to quite a lot, but that was it."

"Was he homeless too?"

He thought about it for a while but couldn't be sure. "Oh, no. I don't think so. He'd come up here to see him. I never saw him around any other time."

"Do you remember his name?"

"Never spoke to him. Wait – no. I could probably describe him to you, though."

His description was so general that it could easily match several hundred thousand Greeks. We thanked Argyris for his help and continued on our way.

"I can't imagine you sleeping rough, looking at you now," I said to Pavlis.

He stopped to light a cigarette. We were standing in front of one of those massive pine trees that grow on the hill. It seemed untouched by all the caterpillars that had destroyed so many of the other, smaller trees. A tortoise sloped past a few yards further along without appearing to be in the least bit troubled by the extensive reduction in vegetation up on the hill.

"No. I can't either. Any more. But that's the only sure way you know you've come through – if even you can't imagine yourself going back. Most people end up on the streets because of money, but later the life becomes addictive. Everything inside you goes numb, and everything around you too. You get used to it. You hit rock bottom and discover that it's quite nice, knowing that things can't get any worse. That means you don't have to worry any more. It's over. You get so hungry that in the end you forget you have a stomach. You get colder than it's possible to get. You get beyond scared because you are no longer yourself; instead you look at yourself from the outside so it feels like you're watching someone else's nightmare." As he spoke the smoke from his cigarette wrapped itself around him, assisting him in his attempt to reconnect with the nightmare.

"So how did you escape it?"

"It was tough."

At that moment I felt my phone vibrate in my pocket. For some reason I was sure it couldn't be anybody except Maria. I took it out. Looked at it. It was no one.

After that we had two brief conversations with two more residents of the hill who had essentially nothing to tell us. This went on until we reached the cave where Sonia lived. Pavlis had to go inside and spend at least fifteen minutes trying to persuade her to come out. Before she agreed to start talking, she examined the voice recorder in detail, making sure that there was no camera fitted onto it because there was no way she would speak to a camera. She had her reasons.

"I'll agree to an interview for you. Only for you. Not for Angelino. Not for anyone else. No Angelino ever helped me. When I was in trouble, only you were there for me."

He nodded at her, showing that he knew what she meant. Sonia turned to face me. It was hard to tell how old she was. Could have been anything from forty-five to sixty. Her black hair had started to go grey and she was missing quite a few teeth. She wore a pair of thin black tracksuit bottoms and a grey jacket, which was ripped from the left elbow down to the wrist. Two buttons were missing, but the zip was still functioning enough to help keep her warm.

"I'm not interested in telling the world how we live up here. The world isn't interested either. They'll read what you write over coffee, and they'll shake their heads like they get it. But they don't get it. They never will. They don't need to."

"We can try to explain it to them, though," I said, playing the journalist even though I knew she was right.

"Yes. I suppose some of them might be moved by it and cry. From their eyes."

"From their eyes. What do you mean?"

"The only crying you should take seriously is the sort that comes out of the mouth. The rest is just for people who think they are sensitive. It makes them feel better before they turn to the next page. But I said I would talk for Antonis' sake. So, what do you want to know?"

"Why don't you go to one of the rehabilitation centres?"

"Because I don't want to go to a rehabilitation centre. They have rules there. Up here, I make the rules. Next question."

"Do you like it here?"

"Have I got a choice? Next question."

"Do you live alone?"

"Yes."

Her face hardened when she said this. And she didn't try to move me on to my next question this time. But I did. I asked her a series of anodyne questions of a very general nature before I brought the conversation round to Themis.

"I do remember Themis. Not him exactly, but yes. Details of his face. His eyes. They were very watery. Very human, even though he was living like an animal."

"Do you remember anyone he'd talk to – on a regular basis? A friend? I'm looking for someone who knew him well, so I can talk to them about that routine he had – the Chaplin Tramp one?"

"There was someone who would come and see him. Yes – Vaios was his name. Strange character, but at least he took the trouble to come. Most people here haven't got anyone."

I asked her to describe him for me; her description was just as vague and general and useless as Argyris'. But at least I had a name now.

"I remember the girl too. She would sometimes play with —" She cut herself off, pursing her lips. "Will there be anything else?" she asked, as though she wanted to banish her sadness.

"How long have you been living alone?"

"Since it became necessary." Her answer was sharper than a knife freshly off a whetstone.

"Sonia …," said Antonis, his voice barely audible. Anyone standing at any distance from him wouldn't even have realized he had said anything. Sonia took a deep breath, scratched her face with her chewed fingernails, looked straight through me as though I was no longer visible to her.

"Since it became necessary. Since I took them to the orphanage."

There are some people who you can almost feel breaking down in front of your eyes. They say one thing, and even if they don't start crying, even if they give nothing away, you realize that at that moment they are beginning to evaporate. Just like Sonia was doing now. If you saw them literally melting away, or being burned alive, it would make perfect sense. I felt ashamed for making her go through all this, but I had to stay in role and be the journalist who really wanted the story.

"What do you mean?"

Sonia repositioned me in her field of vision. "Let's get this straight. No details. You can use my name. Sonia's not my real name anyway. But you will not mention the ages of my children; you will not describe me; nothing. You will not put anything in there that could help anyone identify me."

"Agreed."

"It was two years ago. A boy and a girl. Seven and six. I said I was their aunt and that their mother had died and I couldn't take care of them. I had primed them to say the same thing. I went to see them one time after that – from a distance, and made sure they couldn't see me. They looked happy. They were playing and laughing. So I never went back. Some things are just too painful. At first, when we started living on the streets, at the beginning of the crisis, I had them up here with me. I still sent them to school and they never told anyone that we were living in a cave. They kept their distance from the other kids, so no one ever asked. I still had some friends back then who would let them shower at their place in the morning on their way to school so they wouldn't smell. They got them all the books and pencils and things they needed, but they've all left now. Gone abroad to find work. They couldn't keep it together here. In the end the children started fainting from hunger at school. The headmistress found out that the phone number I'd given her didn't exist. She told them to tell me that she would call social services if I didn't go to the school and talk to her. What a bitch. What a cow, I thought back then. I didn't send them in for a week. But then I thought about it and realized she was right. I was keeping them with me without being able to feed them. Why? What kind of love is that? So I made up my mind and took them down to the orphanage. I did all the paperwork too, giving my consent for their adoption if the right people came along. They're lovely kids. They never once complained through all of this. But they begged me not to take them there. They promised they'd never ask for anything, not for food, not for nothing. When I left them there I told them they'd grow up into fine young people, beautiful and strong and that I would visit them all the time. And if I got a job, I would come and get them. I lied. I don't want them to see me again. I want them to forget I ever existed."

# 17

Sitting in the back seat of a taxi on the way back to Galatsi, I tried to come up with answers: answers for Emma, who would want to know when she'd be able to visit Angelino; answers for Drag about what was going on with the paedophile murders; and answers for myself. Who had Themis Raptas been, and who had Angelino been so scared of that he had taken all those security measures to protect himself? And answers for Maria, about our future. I tried to convince myself that I shouldn't let this complete inability to come up with anything worry me too much. The first step was to understand the questions. If you understand the questions, the answers inevitably follow. They *have* to.

The more I listened to homeless people talking, the more convinced I became that taking a young child to live with you up there is not something you'd do out of some romantic notion or other, or some knee-jerk rejection of so-called civilized society or a wish to discover the mean-ing of life. You wouldn't even do it if you were desperate and couldn't find work. You'd only do it to try and escape something. My problem was that the only thing that could possibly explain why Themis Raptas had done what he did was pederasty. We had our suspicions, but not a shred of evidence, and very little chance of finding any.

I arrived at Teri's at eight. Babis opened the door for me, looking uninterested as ever. To be fair, I think he always looked like that, whoever he was with. It was just that when he was with me, he made a real effort to look even more bored, just to make me feel like an intruder. He wasn't happy about my relationship with Teri because he couldn't believe that somebody could be friends with Teri without having an erotic interest in her. In his eyes, she was the ultimate woman, so much so that he, who had never lifted a finger to help anyone in his life, had turned into Teri's man Friday, helping the unaccompanied minors at the detention centre in Amygdaleza. They worked tirelessly trying to get other charitable organizations on board and to get doctors and psychologists involved, seeing that the state had given up and these children were forever trying to escape from the centre. And most of them would end up in prostitution. Twenty of them had already been transferred from Amygdaleza to the newly painted house on the west side of town, thanks mainly to the efforts of Teri and Babis. Babis visited them regularly to check that things were slowly improving for them. After all, these were children who had seen their parents and siblings die in Syria and Pakistan and were often self-harming or refusing to walk. Teri never visited the children who left. She took care of the ones that were still there, in what was supposed to be a refuge but resembled the worst kind of prison: no mattresses, no pillows, no basic toilets or showers – and no hope for the future.

"Teri's in the guest room with the girl," Babis said.

I nodded and went through, after first making sure to leave my shoes in the entrance hall, one of Teri's non-negotiables. She's not an obsessive but hates doing house-work. The living room, like the rest of the place, was covered in fitted carpets, a relic of her grandmother, who had left her the place. As I crossed the living room, which was full of tiny glass sculptures, past Teri's bedroom to the guest room, I felt the exhaustion of the day getting the better of me. I was sweating. My legs were beginning to protest at all the walking they'd been doing that day, and this together with my irritation at how slowly this case was progressing, clouded my judgement to the point where the only thing I didn't want to do – that is, interrogate Emma – seemed to be my only hope.

The door was closed. I knocked gently. There was no answer. I'm completely at home in Teri's house, so it didn't occur to me to walk away. I opened the door and found Teri hugging Emma the way a mother hugs her child.

"It's Stratos, Emma," said Teri to reassure her.

"Er ... yeah," I said, unable to think of anything better.

"Can't you see we're busy here? Go on, shoo! Out!" Emma laughed. She laughed out loud. I had never heard her laugh, even slightly. Hearing her laugh like that, I quickly forgot at least half the tiredness I was feeling, and my guilt over the questioning I was going to subject her to doubled.

One of the reasons why Babis never felt comfortable with me was the fact that I always kept a change of clothes and an old pair of pyjamas at Teri's because I would often crash there after all-nighters, with or without Drag. The long hot soak I had in some of her exotic bubble bath made me feel much better, as did the feeling of clean clothes against my tired body.

Teri was waiting for me outside the bathroom, sitting cross-legged on the pouffe she had in the hall. She was in a pink dressing gown which only just covered her smooth, hairless calves.

"I've explained about Angelino," she said.

"And?"

"I could see how excited she was about visiting him, and I had to put the brakes on it. I told her that we have a mutual friend, this super cop. He's a real diamond, but can be a bit of a shit as well. And that if she goes anywhere near the hospital, he will take her in for questioning and take you in as well. And how on earth would you explain who you are? Everything would be such a mess. So until Angelino gets better, it's not a good idea to visit. That's what I told her."

"Did she understand?"

"Why shouldn't she? She's not stupid. She knows how to listen. That's why we've got two ears and only one mouth. So that we listen more than we speak."

"Is that one of Hermes' too?"

"Zeno. He was an ancient philosopher. I save that explanation for the ignorant. But my Hermes might have mentioned it too."

"Does your Hermes know about Babis? That he's been staying here?"

"Hermes isn't the jealous type. Jealousy is beneath him."

"Yes, but does he know?"

"No, he doesn't. Jealous or not, I'm not going to go looking for trouble."

I smiled.

"Is something funny? So how's your relationship going?" she asked, clearly annoyed.

That was below the belt and completely uncalled for. She realized it too. I could see it in her eyes. But she didn't apologize. So we left it there, exchanging looks for a while, trying to work out what had got into us all recently, but we couldn't.

"So Emma understood? She's fine with it? She's not asking to see him?" I asked, trying to get the conversation back on track.

"Yes. Of course, I did tell her that Angelino would soon recover completely. I know I'm taking the risk of turning out to be a big liar in her eyes, but how much reality can a child take all at once?"

"You were hugging her in there. I saw you."

"Yes. We were having a heart-to-heart. Nothing that you would find useful. I'd tell you."

They were having a heart-to-heart. So Teri had managed in her own unique way to do something that seemed impossible to me. For some reason the first thing that occurred to me as I listened to her was that here was yet more evidence to prove that I would be a terrible father.

"You know, sometimes I really admire you."

"What do you mean 'sometimes'? What do you do the rest of the time?"

"The rest of the time I see you in that robe stepping on the purple carpet and I have my reservations. Can I go and talk to her?"

She nodded, and told me she hadn't been able to track down that teenage girl who'd been in the porn films. Apparently the girl had vanished and her friends feared the worst. Teri went into the living room to chat to Babis, or rather observe him as he gazed at her in adoration. I left them to it and went to see Emma.

I knocked, waited for her to tell me to come in and opened the door to find her on the edge of the bed, in the same spot I'd seen her with Teri a few minutes earlier. She was in a white sweater, blue tracksuit bottoms and slippers and had laid out a deck of cards on the bed next to her. I thought about everything she had been through, what she was still going through. My own adolescence had been tough enough but at least I'd had a home and a mother, whatever her faults had been. I had my terms of reference. Emma didn't. She had been rejected by her own parents the day they left her at the orphanage, she had lost Themis, and now she was fighting to hang on to Angelino. Although she couldn't be with him, I could feel – or I wanted to feel – that they were fighting this together. Suffering. That was the word that came to me. Emma was suffering. Her blindness was the least of her problems. And I could do nothing to take away her pain. That was the problem with this world. You often feel so much anger towards it, but no matter what kind of gun you have at your disposal, you have no idea where to shoot to solve the problem.

"Shall I show you my new trick? Only Angelino's seen it so far, and only once."

"Yes, go on."

She stood up and sat on a high chair at the small desk. "It's called 'Jack Sandwich'. I'll need your help, so pay attention, OK?"

"OK."

She picked up the deck, shuffled the cards, placed them all in her right hand and started to feed them into her left. She told me to stop her whenever I wanted. I let a few seconds go past before giving the signal. She showed me the top card in her left hand, told me to remember it and returned it to the pile. Her movements, as always, gave no sign at all that her beautiful eyes were not guiding her through this. She placed the cards from her right hand on top of the cards from her left and straightened out the deck.

"Now I'm going to move my thumb and forefinger together like you do when you're tapping out the rhythm of a piece of music, and as soon as I do, you will see the card I showed you." She clapped her hands twice and spread out the deck. As she did so, two cards appeared in the middle, face up. They were the two black jacks of the pack.

"Oh no! I'm so sorry. That wasn't your card, was it? Those must be … the two black jacks," she said without even touching them. With her dead eyes wide open, devoid of any expression, she stared at me as though trying to discover something within me.

"That's right," I answered.

"How could I get that wrong? OK. I want to correct this, so I'll send those two jacks to go and find your card."

She took back all the cards that were on top of the jacks and put them at the bottom of the pack. Next she spread out the jacks along with a few other cards from the top which were still face down so that the jacks stood out. She straightened the deck again and with her right hand touched the two black jacks. She cut and then asked me to cut, and cut for a third time. Once I had, she slammed her hand on top of the deck as though giving an order.

"Please spread out the cards slowly, one by one, so that you can see them."

I did what she asked, and in precisely the middle of the deck, the deck I had cut not once but twice, were the two black jacks, face up, yet again. Only this time, sitting in between them, was the card I had been shown, the card I had been asked to remember.

"Good, isn't it? Especially the bit where I pretend to make a mistake."

She tried to force a smile, but instead she burst into tears. When she cried, her eyes became animated; as though they wanted to prove that life meant pain. I took her hand; I didn't feel comfortable hugging her.

"It's my fault," she said.

"Don't be silly."

"It *is* my fault. Whoever takes me under their wing risks getting killed."

"Listen to me. You're fourteen years old, and like most teenagers believe that you're the centre of the universe.

But you're not." Sometimes being a bit harsh can work. If I tried to comfort her; she would probably keep crying, but this way, challenging her like this, made her switch gear for a while. Having started on this tack, I had to keep going. Tears can be cathartic, but they don't bring any comfort in themselves. My job was to get my hands on hard evidence, not to babysit her.

"I still don't know who attacked Angelino or who shot Themis. But from everything I have found out so far, there is nothing, nothing that points to you as the reason in either case."

"So what have you found out?" she asked me, now very serious. The honest answer would have been "almost nothing", but watching the tears stream down her face, I decided against honesty.

"Quite a lot of things – nothing that hangs together yet, but a lot to go on. I do have a few questions for you, and you'd be helping me out a lot if you could answer them."

"OK."

"Did Themis know anyone, have a friend maybe, called Vaios?"

"Yes. What's he got to do with —"

"I don't know yet. Possibly nothing. Like I said, I'm still trying to piece it all together. I need to find this Vaios, talk to him and see what he knows. What do you remember about him?"

"They didn't know each other that well. I don't think Dad had any close friends really, especially after we went to live on the hill. Vaios would come up to see him maybe once a month, something like that. I do remember one time, though. It was September and we had just bought all the books for the school year. Every year Dad would get me all the books they did at school in Braille and teach me. All of it. Then Vaios arrived and Dad went out of the cave to talk to him and they started fighting."

"Do you know why?"

"No. I couldn't hear what they were saying. I would always stay in the cave and play when Vaios came over. I'd imagine the next trick I would learn. That kind of thing. But I did ask him why they were shouting, and he told me that sometimes that kind of thing happens between friends."

"Anything else you remember about him?"

She thought for a while. She was looking extremely serious, something that did not sit well on such a young face, but it made her look even sweeter.

"No."

"You said earlier that your father didn't have any close friends after you went to live on the hill. What about before?"

"While he was a journalist?"

"Yes."

"I was very little. But I do remember that lots of people would come to the house and that it was always filled with voices."

"Angry voices?"

"No. People talking. About his work. But later, up on the hill, it was always quiet. I liked it better like that."

"Were the voices you remember adult voices, or were there children there too?"

"Sometimes his friends would bring their kids over. They always wanted to play games I couldn't join in because I couldn't see anything, so they quickly lost interest in me and played on their own while I played on my own."

"Did they ever come to the house alone – children? Or with their parents who left them and came back later?"

"No. Most of the kids didn't want to come back because we couldn't play together."

"What about Themis' work? Did he write mainly for adults or for children?"

"From what I remember it was all for adults."

There was no way I could come out and ask her directly if she ever suspected that her father was sexually aroused by children. I would have to make do with the answers she had given me, at least for now.

"What kind of things did he write about?"

"What do you mean?"

"I mean, what kind of reporter was he? Did he do politics, culture, sport, social affairs? What was his specialist area?"

"Social issues, maybe. But he didn't limit himself to one thing as far as I can remember. Wherever he sniffed dirt, he would try to expose it. I told you – he wanted to change the world. That was until he decided that he couldn't and walked away from it all."

"When you say 'it all', was he seeing anyone, a woman?"

I thought I saw her blush, but it might just have been my imagination. Then again, this whole thing might be my imagination, this entire case one horrendous dream which I would wake from and find myself lying in Maria's arms, cradling our baby. And Angelino expecting me in Omonia, together with Emma and Themis, alive and well on the hill or somewhere else.

"Er ... when we lived at home I remember there were a couple of women who would leave the house early in the morning, just when I was waking up. So I suppose they must have slept over, you know. Spent the night. But later, on the hill – I don't think so. There were a few times when he would go off on errands, or so he said, but he would always come rushing back because he didn't like leaving me there on my own, so I don't think he could have been seeing someone. We were together almost all the time."

I was wondering what else I could possibly ask her: did Themis like bathing her, or touching her, if there had been anything sexual about their relationship. But questions like that could be potentially very damaging. The most likely thing would be that she would say no, retreat into herself and never trust me again. And there were thousands of reasons to suggest that their relationship was not like that at all. He might not have been a paedophile at all; if he was one, he might have had a preference for boys; he might have liked girls but not Emma – not in that way; he might have kept all his sexual activities separate from his relationship with Emma, which he held sacred, so I told her I didn't have any more questions about the case.

"Did you ever ask Themis about your birth mother and father?"

"No. I didn't care about them. They obviously didn't care about me, so why should I care about them?"

My phone rang. I looked to see who was calling and thought that since it wasn't bringing me any closer to Maria, it was the most useless piece of kit I'd ever owned. It was Pavlis. I apologized to Emma and left the room.

"Hey – I've got some news. One of the homeless guys stole some fish from the market today. He wrapped it up in an old newspaper and smuggled it out. The paper was from a couple of days ago. There was an article in it about the attack on Angelino."

"Right. So they know what happened. They're scared and don't want to give out any more information?"

"Quite the opposite. The paper carried the photos of the two dead guys from the house in Chateaubriand Street. Both Argyris and Sonia recognized the guy in charge of the attack. It was Vaios. Themis' friend – the one who used to visit him up on the hill."

# 18

"Hold on. Can we just run through this one more time, because my little brain is having a hard time with this," said Drag.

"I bet it is."

We were at Papi's and I had just told him what I'd found out about Vaios. I'd run a check on him from the online news outlets and his real name turned out to have been Michalis Vaiopoulos. Drag was sitting next to me, playing Pac-Man in his enormous white trench coat, which looked like it had been made for some six-foot-six-plus NBA player; he had to watch his step so he didn't tread on it. Under it, he had thrown on a pair of white jeans and a white linen shirt and could easily have been mistaken for the neighbourhood milkman out on the tiles. It wasn't cold, but the temperature had dropped four degrees in one day, which was all the excuse he needed. Papi's latest thing, apart from the mouth-burning cocktail, was the installation of vintage 1980s electronic games in the bar. Whether this was in keeping with the general vibe of the bar or not was evidently something that did not worry him unduly. He had brought them in the night before and, like his jukebox, all of these games only took the old nickels, which meant that he had to supply his customers with the right money and make sure everyone was letting everyone else have a fair go. "Everyone" consisted of me, Drag and a guy in his thirties who was sitting at the other end of the bar. He looked like a throwback to the fifties, complete with wide grey suit, white shirt, blue tie, and braces to hold his high-waisted trousers. When he walked into the bar, he removed his grey hat, exposing his short haircut and carefully groomed sideburns. I reckoned that if he didn't change his dress sense quickly, he would spend the rest of his life being that guy who sits on his own in bars.

Drag was on the fifth level of Pac-Man and had just lost one of his three lives from a stupid error, which had left him fuming like one of those cartoon characters that has smoke coming out of its head. Just before that he'd informed me that the song "Pac-Man Fever" had got to number nine in the charts in 1984. For some reason he felt that I needed to know this. Then he went on to tell me that this was unfair and that the song should have done better. That was when he lost the life, trying to eat all the little ghosts instead of finishing the course. He fell silent.

At that moment the 1950s guy put Ella Fitzgerald's version of "Ten Cents a Dance" on the jukebox and Drag quickly abandoned the game.

"Sacred moment," he explained, though there was something in his eyes that told me he felt bad about leaving Pac-Man to the mercy of all those monsters who were closing in on him. I took a sip of the dry white wine I had ordered, still recovering from the coincidence between my order and what Papi brought me. And although it wasn't much of a wine, my palate received it gratefully while Ella admitted for the second time in the chorus that sometimes she thinks she has found her hero but then discovers that it's a queer romance with the men who come to her to learn how to dance, ten cents a time.

"So what you're saying is Themis Raptas' friend, the only person who ever went to see him while he was living on the hill, was a professional killer who, three years after Raptas was killed, broke into Angelino's house with two other pros to kidnap the girl from her new father, killing anyone who got in their way?" asked Drag as soon as the song was over.

"Your little brain's on fire tonight."

"Have you got a logical explanation for all this?"

"No. I was hoping you would have found out who Vaios and his friends were working for."

"Not yet. The focus is on the paedophile murders now. And then we're getting in more requests every day from all these MPs and ministers for protection after every vote they take in parliament, so I just haven't got the manpower for this case at the moment. I've got one man looking into it and he's only part-time. What happened to Angelino is being treated as a settling of accounts, at least for the time being. And you know what the police think of those."

"Yes, yes. Leave them to it. Don't get involved."

"That's right."

"I'll see what I can dig up on Vaios too."

"Good idea."

He paused for a while. I suspected that he wanted to ask me again about interviewing Emma and wondered whether he would send me to the devil again when I said no. He sighed, the words refusing to come out of his mouth. When they eventually did, I understood why.

"Have you heard from Maria?"

"No."

"I phoned her too. She didn't answer."

"She wants to be alone. Did Teri tell you …?"

"She told me that things are bad between the two of you, that she's left. Nothing else. She told me to ask you if I wanted to know more."

"Maria's pregnant."

He froze. He didn't move. He didn't breathe.

"It's mine," I clarified. "And she's taken off because she doesn't know what to do. And neither do I."

Drag rubbed his eyes and took a sip of Papi's cocktail. "Tell me," he said.

"Can I ask you something first?"

"I thought I was the cop here."

"Why did you and Maria split up?"

"Why …? What do you mean? Back then?"

I nodded. He choked. We'd never talked about this, for one good reason. This kind of thing made us both feel uncomfortable. It would be much easier for us to face a bunch of bastards pointing guns at us.

"Didn't she tell you?"

"I never asked," I told him.

"It was because she was still in love with you."

Brilliant timing.

"She loved me too, of course. Which is why she decided it was a mistake to be with either of us. She wanted a break."

"I was under the impression that you'd had a horrible fight. You suddenly stopped even mentioning one another's name."

"I didn't take the break-up very well. It's not easy to know from such an early age that you've lost the love of your life."

Neither of us said anything for a while.

"So tell me: how did you manage to fuck everything up between the two of you?"

I told him everything. He really didn't have much advice to give me, either about Maria or on the subject of the baby.

"Looks like she needs to be alone for a while, so don't put pressure on her. But when she gets back, don't let her out of your sight. Not for Emma, not for Angelino, not for the good Lord himself."

"What if she doesn't come back?"

"Perhaps it's time to stop feeling sorry for yourself and start acting like you're worthy of her."

Drag – the expert in human relationships, with his condescending comments and his biting answers. So he knew what Maria needed, did he? Whatever it was, one thing was certain: she didn't need him. In which case, he might like to shut up. She didn't need me either, it seemed. And I could feel so much anger rising inside me towards my best friend. I didn't send him to the devil, but after a few minutes of silence we agreed that we had a lot to do and needed to get on.

As we walked away from Papi's I decided that I'd go back to Teri's and spend the night there instead. It would help me feel like I belonged somewhere. The house in Psychiko was less welcoming to me than a hotel room. Teri made up the bed in the small bedroom on the first floor. Babis did his best to give me a stern look. It didn't suit him, but I didn't point this out. I asked Teri to lend me her laptop, and she told me that she'd bookmarked some pages from various porn sites, and I should have a look to see if I could learn anything from them. I looked at her, expressionless, until she burst out laughing and said goodnight.

I spent the next two hours trawling the Net, trying to see if I'd missed anything about Themis Raptas. I found nothing. Maybe someone had said to him – like Maria had said to me – that they wished he was "invisible and non-existent" and he had decided to oblige. Or maybe, like Sonia, he'd been so full of guilt that he'd made the decision to disappear. But none of this made any sense; he had loved Emma. He lived with her and then took her into hiding with him. It seemed impossible that while they were living together like tramps on Filopappou he was also erasing his entire digital footprint at the same time.

I needed evidence, and I needed it now. But because I didn't have any I spent the best part of the night coming up with scenarios in my head, trying to make sense of what had happened, none of which stood much scrutiny – but it all helped me get to sleep.

# 19

Teri made me an omelette with four eggs, bacon and feta cheese. The relish with which I devoured it reminded me that I hadn't eaten since the day before. It was 7.30. Babis and Emma were still asleep.

"How long have you had those?" asked Teri, pointing to my beige-and-green striped pyjamas. The top had a yellow dinosaur on it.

"Maria bought them for me in 1999."

"They're so last century."

"I like them."

"Oh, God."

Teri returned to the tea she was drinking, the same herbal tea she had every morning in the hope it would reduce her cholesterol. "She's a good kid, you know."

I nodded.

"She can stay here as long as you like. There's no problem."

"Thanks. I'll tell her," I said, got up to stretch and was about to go and get ready.

"About Maria," she said.

"Yes?" I managed to mumble, hoping that she would at last be able to give me some information.

"Look – I'm not going to tell you two how to live your lives; I'm just telling you to live them together."

"That's what I want too."

"Then be there for her."

"She won't let me." I thought about telling Teri about the "invisible and non-existent" episode but I didn't want to have to listen to the words.

"I think she'll let you in the end. She'll have no choice. But you'll have to support her, whatever decision she takes."

I considered telling her that this all sounded very unfair. *I should support Maria.* I had been doing nothing else ever since I was a teenager. And I fully intended to carry on supporting her, so long as we could find an answer to the question of how we were going to raise our baby. But I said nothing, and just nodded.

"Good. And take it easy with Dora, won't you?" she said, and announced she was off to load the washing machine. Dora was her make-up artist friend. I was due to see her that afternoon.

"I'll try," I said and started to do the washing-up, but something on the small TV screen above the fridge caught my attention. It was the face of the latest paedophile murder victim. I turned the volume up:

"… now bring you this morning a State Television exclusive. A letter arrived at Attica Police Headquarters a short while ago and seems to be signed by the killers of the four child abusers who were exposed on a television programme. The message reads:

"*Paedophiles are not humans – they are monsters. The despicable Hellenic police have decided to provide protection to these* monsters. *Congratulations. We're really happy that we've managed to make a fool of them. We hope that they appreciate what a mistake they're making, because if they don't they'll have us to answer to. Make no mistake, we will go on. Not just the paedophiles from the programme, but all of them. These aren't the first scum we've got rid of. We've done it in the past. We call on the Greek people to join us in celebration of the fact that there is one less monster out there."*

"The statement was signed 'The Executioners'. The Hellenic police are treating the letter as genuine and it is now with forensic teams. Stay tuned for further developments in this case."

I thought I should ring Drag but decided to get dressed first, into the spare change of clothes I kept here. Then, as I was getting ready, I realized that I had no real desire to ring him, and there wasn't much point in doing it either. I knew he'd be feeling the same way about me.

The statement from the Executioners seemed to be trying in every way it could to steer the investigation towards previous unsolved murder cases of this kind – which amounted to precisely one – in case the police had not spotted the similarities between Themis' murder and these other ones. Three years after his murder, someone still had it in for Raptas. And if hunting down the dead wasn't enough for them, they were out to get his daughter too. Unless, of course, we were dealing with two different sets of people. This case was getting more and more complicated – and more difficult to explain.

Teri offered me her car, but I said no. If she had to take Emma anywhere at any point, she would need it.

I went out into the street and hailed a taxi. I told the driver to leave me on Patission Street, by the University of Economics and Business. This would normally take six or seven minutes, but it took us twenty in the morning traffic. The driver, who had long fair hair and something that was trying to be a beard, was playing a CD of heavy-rock songs and was singing along in such a deafening voice that those twenty minutes felt like sixty. It was a muggy day; Athens was clouded over, reflecting the mood of her citizens. Outside the university, a group of street sellers were fighting with some policemen who were trying to move them on. Tempers were high, and things were already threatening to escalate when groups of students gathered round in support of the street sellers. I kept going, examining the marble slabs of the old Athenian pavements. Nowadays most of them were blocked by the kiosks, which sometimes swallowed the entire width of the pavement and would force anyone into the road who wanted to get past. Either that or you were sure to bump into public works of some kind or another which necessitated digging up what was left of the pavement. If you're in a wheelchair, or a mother with a pushchair, you're really taking your life into your own hands by going for a walk on the city's pavements. Then there was the pollution, the stench of uncollected refuse, the ubiquitous graffiti, the filth. The concrete, the abandoned buildings, apartment blocks in disrepair, shuttered-up businesses, padlocks on cafés and bookshops, clothes shops, shoe shops. The unlucky ones have their windows covered in thick layers of posters, one glued on top of the other;

the fortunate ones have been absorbed into the Athenian Arts Circle programme and temporarily converted into small galleries or exhibition centres displaying blown-up sepia photographs of Patission in the old days.

Just before I reached the junction with Marnis Street opposite a two-storey building which had been lying empty for years, I turned right into an old apartment building. I walked straight through the lobby to the back of the building and pushed open the back door, which led onto a garden where, sitting on the bonnet of an old wreck with slashed tyres, smashed-in lights and its doors hanging off, were two men in their twenties. Another two blokes who were a little older were standing in front of them. My reception committee. Each of them was holding a bottle of beer and they were just too well built to look innocent. The guns they had hanging from their belts didn't help either. When they saw me, they went quiet, not quite believing I was there. Their reflexes obviously weren't up to much. The two that were on the bonnet stood up and the two who were already standing put down their bottles. Not much of a greeting. A fifth character appeared from behind the car. He was a bit older still and was holding a Remington 870, one of the guns the Anti-Terrorist Unit uses. From where I was standing, I reckoned it was the 12-gauge MCS model. It looked like it was fresh out of its box, which meant that he would have to fire it a few hundred times to break it in, but after that he would have the best weapon that money could buy. Just in case I didn't understand that he meant business, he also had a Colt Python, the "combat Magnum". But he wasn't pointing either of them at me. Their barrels were pointing up and down respectively as though they couldn't be bothered with me – unless, that is, I gave them cause.

"Something wrong, mate?"

His Greek was good, with just the slightest trace of an accent. He was about five nine with a few extra pounds on him, but they didn't seem out of place because he had such a solid core. His voice was deep and powerful but his question sounded like it emerged almost mechanically from his mouth. He wore an open green shirt over a white vest, his left ear had more piercings than I could count and the enormous rings he had on each hand shone in the light. His head was completely shaven and seemed to have set the style for the rest of them. His friends were uniformly kitted out in black vests, grey tracksuit bottoms and trainers. At the bottom of the garden was a building that seemed separate from the rest of the block.

"I want to speak to Markos," I said.

"No one with that name lives here," said their leader.

"My information says otherwise."

They looked at each other, smiling ironically. They wanted to show me how amusing they found me. Not so much that they didn't keep an eye firmly on me to ensure that I didn't make any sudden movements. When your opponent is obviously stronger than you and all your friends, this can be a worry.

"Look – we told you," said one of the others. "There's no one here with that name. So there's no reason for you to want to talk to him."

"Maybe you'd like to tell Markos that Stratos Gazis is looking for him?"

"Maybe you'd like to get out of here while we're still being friendly?" said their boss.

"OK. I hope Markos will be as friendly when he finds out that because of you lot he's lost a very lucrative contract. I'll be off, then," I said and turned to leave. As I did so I caught them out of the corner of my eye, looking very ruffled, especially the two loudest ones.

"Oi!" shouted the leader.

"Yes?"

"Wait here. The boys will look after you. What did you say your name was?"

"Stratos Gazis. He knows me."

I expected him to walk towards the house at the back, but instead he was coming towards me. He went straight past me and up the stairs. Despite his bulk he was back in less than two minutes. And he had good news.

"Markos wants to see you," he said, before ordering me to stand still so he could take my weapon off me. I then followed him back into the building. The last time I had seen Markos in this block, he was using the small house at the back and had use of the garden. Now it seemed he had taken over the entire building. He had clearly gone up in the world. As we climbed the stairs – apparently the lift was out of order – the top thug made me go in front of him so he could watch my every move. I read the graffiti on the walls. There were various slogans in Arabic. I didn't understand any of them until I saw one which had been helpfully translated into English: *The Arab Spring is Here.*

The penthouse apartment was on the third floor. Markos was waiting for us next to an enormous glass sliding door looking onto the garden. I hadn't seen him for three or four years and the changes in him were not negligible. His appearance had improved along with his status. His previously prominent nose had been reduced by plastic surgery and he had shed around sixty-five of the two hundred and eighty pounds I remembered him as. Unfortunately, he had lost a lot of hair along with the weight and his straight brown locks had been forced into an unintentionally comic comb-over. The retainers he was wearing to straighten his very crooked teeth did little to rescue the overall impression, but his eyes, two tiny deep-set dull green holes, still emanated enough of an aura of rottenness to ensure that any temptation to laugh at him should be resisted. He was sitting behind a good-quality solid wood desk. Three mobile phones were laid out in front of him along with a tablet and a laptop; he was trying hard to give the impression of being a very busy man.

"Stratos. Hi."

"Hi to you."

In every job, there's best and second best. Second best always tries to be as good as best. Markos was second best here, always struggling to be Angelino in the place of Angelino – the best information collector in town. The only problem was that Markos would never be as good as Angelino. To succeed in this line of work took what the Americans call class. And Markos hadn't a clue what that was. He'd started off as a minder for an arms dealer who had taken me on once to sort out a personal situation for him. It hadn't taken Markos long to lose that job, or the two or three he got after that. But instead of seeing these serial failures as a sign of his own incompetence, he saw them as a chance to set up his own personal empire. One of life's great optimists. To be fair, business was quite good, but a far cry from what he had fantasized about. He had a few clients who paid him to get hold of information, but it was nothing as lucrative as he had hoped, so he diversified and started selling drugs as a sideline. A bit of weed, some heroin to begin with, but then he got greedy and moved into coke and E. Why should you make do with 1,300 euros a kilo, or even 10,000 euros a kilo when you can make 80,000 from coke or five euros a pop for a tab of E?

"Johnny here tells me you've got a job for me with a lot of money," he said, motioning with his head in the direction of Johnny. I noticed that Johnny's hand was full of calluses. Calluses were common with people who shoot a lot. They come from loading the magazine with bullets all the time and from pulling the trigger.

"Have you heard about Angelino?" I asked him.

"Sure."

"Do you know who did it?"

"I can't say I've looked into it. I like to keep out of the competition's private business. It's not healthy."

"I want you to look into it."

"What's in it for me?"

"My friendship."

"Yeah, right. What else?"

"I'll owe you."

Markos burst out laughing and then said, "OK."

I had no comeback for that.

"Look – I know you're quite good, but don't you think you're pushing it a bit?" he said, but still in a very good mood.

*Quite good.*

"I mean you come here, stand here in front of me and say that you'll owe me, like I'm meant to jump up and smash a couple of plates because I'm so fucking overjoyed. Why would I need you to owe me? I've got Johnny here and many other boys working for me. I've got it all covered."

"That's what Angelino thought too. That he had it all covered."

That made him think for a moment before he replied, "I'm not Angelino. Now tell me about this job you've got for me."

"OK. But I've got to say, it's a bit strange that you don't want to know who went after Angelino and effectively left the field wide open for you to become number one."

"Stratos – I *am* number one."

"Markos – just between you and me: you're not. You're a failure. Pure scum."

Johnny, who'd been on the alert for a while now, whipped the Python out of its shoulder holster. He was fast, but not fast enough, because I had made sure I was standing very close to him all the time I was talking to Markos. All it took was a sudden whack with my left palm on his carotid artery for the blood supply to his brain to be cut off, and he fell to the floor unconscious. The Python felt relaxing in my hand and I turned to face Markos, who had not managed to react at all.

"Shall I repeat the question?" I asked him.

"Have you got any idea how many of my people there are in this building? All it would take would be one sound from me —"

"If you make a sound, make sure it's a pretty one, because it will be your last. And as for your 'people', don't forget I've seen them. Just like I saw Johnny here. Which is why I'm so scared."

"What exactly do you want?"

His attitude was verging on the blasé, which told me that he had decided to front this one out, even with a gun pointing at him. It wouldn't be the first time that had happened, after all.

"Who gave the order for Angelino?"

"I've no idea."

"No idea," I said moving in on him.

"No. Honest."

I hit him on the side of the head with the handle of the gun. He fell to the floor with a loud thud, giving out a small shriek of pain. When he got back up after a few seconds, there was blood running down from his left eye. He noticed it too and the sight of blood intensified the sense of fear. All the bravado melted away from his face and he started making strange noises, a fusion of pain and sobbing.

"I don't know! Really! I haven't a clue," he repeated, over and over.

"I'll keep hitting you until you lose that eye completely, shall I?" I asked, calmly.

"Please!"

"Was it you? Did you try to have him killed?"

"No! I don't have the right people for that. You saw my boys downstairs. They're my main men. Do you really think they could —"

I raised my free hand to interrupt him and he immediately stopped talking.

"But you know people who do have the right kind of people for that," I said.

"No! I had no reason to. And I don't even know what it was all about, nobody knows, everyone is trying to find out but nobody's talking, it's been how many days now and nobody's heard anything. Angelino was – *is* – a big player, and he has a lot of respect."

"Meaning?"

"Meaning that they're not from this turf. Or they could be older, with a completely closed unit so nothing ever gets out – ever. And I mean ever."

"Anyone in mind?"

"No."

"OK. That brings us back to you. You stood to gain the most with Angelino out of the picture."

"Yes, but I intended to beat him fair and square – take his clients off him. You have to eat wild beasts standing up, alive. That's the only way you get to be one yourself."

Markos was never going to become a "wild beast". Beast, yes. He'd always be a beast, whatever he did. At least his theory was sound. He did know what he would have to do, even though he was incapable of pulling it off. But this was not the time to break it to him. I knelt down on the floor beside him and placed my clenched fist under his jaw, applying an upward pressure to it. He was groaning in agony.

"I am going to find whoever did this to Angelino. And I will kill him. If I find out that it was you…"

"It wasn't!"

"If I find out that it was you, I won't just kill you. I will make sure you suffer – a lot – and then I'll kill you."

"I swear! It wasn't me!"

"Michalis Vaiopoulos."

"What?"

"One of the three who broke into Angelino's house. Their boss. What do you know about him?"

"Nothing. I just saw his picture in the papers."

"He went by the name of Vaios."

"I don't know him."

"You'll find out, though. By tomorrow morning you will have called me and told me who he worked for and anything you can get on him."

"Tomorrow morning? That's imp—"

I made as if to hit him again. He flung his arm into the air defensively, hopelessly, to deflect whatever was coming at him. He started snivelling, snot running down his mouth.

"All right! All right! Tomorrow morning. And if I can't get it by the morning, I'll keep looking. OK?"

What a loser. Even when his life was on the line, there he was, begging for an extension.

"By tomorrow. Call me on this number. If you set your boys on me on my way out, I'll kill all of them for you and then I'll come back and kill you. And if you don't call tomorrow morning, consider yourself dead," I said, scribbling down my phone number on his notepad. I gave him the one my clients and my acquaintances all have. The other I reserve for Maria, Drag and Teri. Lately they'd been using it less and less.

# 20

HighTV's new offices were in Kifissias Avenue, and according to gossip websites which Teri had wasted no time in showing me, were nothing like their old offices in the Tavros district. The station's efforts to win the ratings game by hiring the biggest names in the business and a whole slew of celebrities for their evening slots were reflected in the stratospheric upgrade of its premises, to the joy of everyone who worked there. I had asked Teri if what she was reading counted as news or was the station's own press release. She told me I was a cynic and a whinger.

I'd never been to the old premises so I didn't have a personal opinion, but looking at the five-storey glass structure towering over me, I didn't find it hard to believe that whatever they were in before, this was way better. And it also wasn't difficult to believe that their employees were happier here. Word around Athens was that the staff at HighTV were the only people in the business whose jobs were not under threat. The owner was Lazaros Vayenas, best friend of the previous government and new best friend of this current government, who were planning to issue only a limited number of operating licences for TV channels in the country. Any existing channel that did not succeed in being awarded one of these new licences would be shut down. According to all the pundits, the only licence that was considered a done deal, even before they were open for bids, was HighTV's.

There were three armed guards stationed in the door-way, poised for the outbreak of *War of the Worlds*. They asked me what I was doing there, and tempted though I was, I resisted saying that I had come to breathe the smell of money – that killer line from the vastly under-rated *Force of Evil*. I simply told them I had come to see Dora Landrou.

That was enough to get me through the door. Next stop was the security check and the metal detector. I had taken the precaution of stopping off at home on my way back from Markos to pick up the Peugeot so I could store my weapons in it. Even though the detector didn't pick anything up they spent ages swiping me before sending me to the reception where I was told how to get to Make-Up. My appearance didn't seem to fill them with trust. While they were searching me, I noticed a young girl, twenty years old at the very most, coming in without passing through security at all. She was wearing the tightest pair of white trousers I'd ever seen, and I saw little sign that she was wearing anything underneath them to disguise the per-fectly toned hemispheres inside them. I toyed with the idea of complaining on the grounds of sexual discrimination, but looked at the security guards who had been staring at her as she walked away and suspected that I would not see justice done if I did, so I let them continue.

Stepping out of the lift on the second floor, I found myself standing in front of a door with a metal sign on it reading "Make-Up", which really made the directions the receptionist had given me, as well as his very existence, unnecessary. I knocked and heard a woman shout "One second!" After about half a minute, the main news presenter opened the door and came out, covered in several layers of make-up. He gave me a good look, probably weighing up in his head the possibilities that he knew me, decided he didn't and went on his way without saying anything. Behind him, a few seconds later a smiling girl in her mid-thirties appeared, offering me her hand, saying, "Hi. I'm Dora."

"Stratos," I replied, allowing her to squeeze my hand.

She had a firm grip, assertive, which didn't quite square with her thin, almost weak voice. As soon as she let go of my hand she took a step back so she could get a better look at me. I looked back at her. She had dark hair, a dark complexion, bright if slightly devious eyes, a tiny dimple on her left cheek and a nose that if it had been even a little bit smaller would have failed to give her face its air of strength. She was in good shape and neither her sweater nor her tight trousers did anything to hide the fact. I was beginning to wonder whether this was standard issue for the women who worked here.

"You've got some questions for me, I hear." It felt as though every last pore on her body was flirting with me. And I wasn't sure that I didn't like it.

"That's right."

"Teri mentioned you were good-looking, but not that you were … this!" she said with her eyes glinting playfully.

"This … what?"

"You know – impressive."

"Thank you. You're not so bad yourself," I said in an attempt to seem more sociable than I really am.

"Do me a favour? Let's get out of here and talk over lunch at that fast-food place across the road."

She led the way without really waiting for me to answer. I followed her, watching her sway her body with ease despite the four-inch heels she was wearing.

"You not taking a coat? It's pretty cold outside and it might rain," I said.

"They've been saying that for days. And if I do get cold, I'll have to call on you to warm me up in those big arms of yours – looks like there's plenty of room there!" she said, giving me a big smile which emphasized her dimples. I walked behind her, slowly, waiting to see if she would turn round again to see if I was watching her. She didn't. She was very sure of herself.

"Sorry about this place," she said when we sat down.

"Why did you choose it?"

The fast-food place was sandwiched between a glitzy restaurant and the best crêperie this side of town – maybe in the whole of Athens.

"The pancake guy next door is my ex. In theory we've got an amazing relationship, but at the end of the day, I don't feel comfortable going in there."

"What, with somebody else?"

"No. In general. *Trop compliqué* – you see."

Up to that point, I did see. If she threw any more French at me, though, I would probably need subtitles.

"I understand," I said, sensing she was waiting for an answer to what had not been a question.

"I do miss his Kinder Bueno pancake, a lot, but ..."

"*Trop compliqué?*" I said, helpfully.

"Yeah. And the restaurant on the other side? Forget it. What a rip-off! Forty euros a head without wine. Only the bosses can afford to go there. Anyway, we plebs are only given twenty minutes' break in the afternoon."

We were sitting upstairs in the smoking section. There were three groups of teenagers there with us as well as a young couple who were a bit older and who were kissing like there was no tomorrow. I thought of Drag telling me once in a similar situation that the only other species that kisses with tongues is the white-fronted Amazon parrot. But as soon as the male makes contact with the female's tongue, the male vomits into her mouth.

"There's nothing much wrong with this place; it's just that we're really pushing up the average age."

"Yes, but as long as I can have a cigarette, I don't mind who's with me. Could be aliens for all I care," she said.

Most teenagers smoke with a definite air about them. None of the ones up there could have been more than fifteen. They all had weird haircuts, eyebrow piercings, nose piercings. Two of the girls had neck tattoos, one boy had green hair and another of the girls had such swollen lips that you could bet she'd been injecting them with something. Dora was obviously right. If you wanted to smoke these days, you'd have to be prepared to share the space with aliens.

"Don't you smoke at work?"

"The new laws. It's not allowed any more. Whoever wants to has to nip out onto the balcony. That's fine, but if you're scared of heights like I am you have to go all the way down to the street and go through the security check and all that. Too much hassle. The bastards. The news desk editor smokes like a chimney – but does anyone say anything to him?"

"So far it doesn't sound like you're too happy at the new place?"

"No, I'm not. It's like a military prison in there – but with attractive cells."

I knew better than to trust online news stories. It might seem hard to believe, but most of them do achieve the impossible and are even more unreliable than print journalism.

"So what is it that you want to know?" she asked, play-ing distractedly with the wrapper of the cheeseburger she had ordered but had not touched.

I had told Teri not to give any details about why I wanted to see her and just say that we were friends, that I was an Internet journalist doing research for a piece I was writing about the big TV channels in the city. I wanted to take her by surprise because those first seconds after you tell someone something they're not expecting to hear are the most crucial. You can read a lot into their reaction.

"You've been at HighTV for a long time, haven't you?"

"Wow – yes. More than ten years. I got a job there as soon as I finished my course. The number of faces I've painted …"

"What do you remember about Themis Raptas?"

Her big eyes opened even wider for a moment, her mouth too, enough to reveal a set of perfectly whitened teeth.

"I'm sorry," she said, as though trying to gain time.

"You heard me."

"Themis Raptas! That's a blast from the past."

"I'll explain later. For now just tell me what you know."

"I'd prefer to know why you're asking first."

I noticed that her hand was quite unsteady as she took a long drag on the Marlboro she was smoking. She then crossed her arms like a primary school teacher waiting for one of her pupils to answer her, a teacher worried that she wasn't going to like the answer she'd be given. I also noticed that the skin on her right cheek was showing through under the make-up and was cracked in two or three places. This only made her more sexy.

"Yes, but if I tell you that, it will affect what you tell me."

"Now look, big boy – you might be exactly my type, and if you asked me on a date, say to the expensive restaurant next door, I'd say yes – to everything. But when you go asking me questions about a sensitive topic, I'll answer you if and only if I feel like it, and on my terms. And I want to know why you're asking."

I was impressed. To be able to balance shameless flirting with playing hardball at the same time required talent. And she had plenty of talent.

"I'm doing some research into high-profile individuals who at some point in their lives vanish without trace for no apparent reason."

"In that case, don't waste your time on Themis," she said, almost aggressively.

"Why not?"

"Forget about Themis. From what I've heard, he had his reasons."

"What reasons?"

She turned, looked around and pushed her cheeseburger to one side, drawing deeply on her cigarette. "Themis was charismatic. The word's overused, but in his case it was true. One look from Themis and you felt yourself growing. He wasn't just handsome; he also had depth. Do you know how rare that is in the world of television?"

"Sounds like you were in love with him."

"Who around here wasn't? If he snapped his fingers, they would all fall at his feet. *We* would all fall at his feet. But he never did."

"Was he seeing someone?"

"That was the problem. We didn't know if he was. We tried to find out, really tried ... We heard something about a model from a while back, and someone in advertising, but we never saw him with anyone. Some of the presenters thought he was a closet gay and others said that he was married to the job and worked night and day. Then he went and adopted that little girl and we saw even less of him. That was when he started to cut back his hours after he had been such a workaholic. Before the adoption, when everyone else on his team dropped dead with exhaustion, Themis would keep going. It was around then that the rumours started." She drew on her cigarette again. Her performance came across as quite staged due to her apparent need to pause at regular intervals, but she seemed genuine.

"If the rumours were true, it was just as well he disappeared. If you had asked me back then, I would have sworn under oath that he was innocent – I'd seen him with his daughter. He was so gentle and affectionate with her. The few times that he brought her over to the station, it seemed that she was his world. But then, as I said, the rumours started and he went AWOL and I started to think maybe he was too affectionate with her? God – I can't even bear to think about it."

"Do you mean…?"

"That's right. You say the word; I can't bring myself to."

"That his relationship with his daughter was sexual?"

"I didn't hear anything specifically about his own child. But people said that he liked little children. They were the kind of rumours that people are very careful with. The kind of rumours you make people promise not to repeat but in the end everyone seems to know. And if the rumours were true, where did that leave his own kid?"

"What about evidence?"

"Did anyone have any proof, you mean? No. How would we have got hold of anything like that? I told you – they were rumours. I don't know where they started, but everyone said that there wasn't any doubt. And then of course he disappeared almost immediately after they started. The ground opened and swallowed him up. It might have been a coincidence. I hope it was, because … Anyway. I hope it was. If I could find out that it was all lies, a great weight would be taken off my shoulders. You know, if something like that is happening under your nose, you feel dirty yourself. You do know that …"

*He was murdered*, she wanted to say.

"That's what I'm investigating," I told her.

She shook her head, as though she understood.

"Loukas might know more."

"Who's he?"

"Loukas Sofianos. Journalist. He was one of the people closest to Themis at the station back then."

"They were friends?"

"You could call them that. Themis was always surrounded by people, but he gave the impression of someone who was very much alone, regardless. So I can't really say whether they were friends in the normal way. I know that they used to talk quite a lot and Loukas was Themis' right-hand man."

I asked her to give me Loukas' number, and after telling me a few more things about him she did. She then looked at her watch, and seeing how late it was took a sharp intake of breath, popped her cheeseburger back into its bag, picked it up and got to her feet.

"Have I helped at all?"

"Quite a lot."

"Enough to have earned myself a meal at a nice restaurant?"

"You're a very attractive woman," I said.

"Why does that sound like a 'no'?"

"And I am grateful for your help."

She opened her mouth and passed her tongue lightly over her lips as if to clean them. She did it very quickly but not so quickly that she couldn't be certain that I had seen it. She tilted her head and smiled, as if to say "fine".

"Shall we?" she said.

I followed her to the exit. Two teenagers at the next table, momentarily distracted from their phones, were staring at her. Perhaps they weren't real aliens after all.

We were standing outside the TV building saying good-bye when a giant limousine pulled up outside. It wasn't the Prime Minister who emerged from it, but a blonde woman, a very attractive blonde woman, attractive in that same boring way that most models are attractive.

"Oh no, that's all we need," said Dora, watching her hurry towards the entrance door.

"Who is that?"

"My alter ego. A younger, blonder, sluttier version of me."

"Sorry?"

"She's living the life I never got to live. She's the big boss's girlfriend."

"Vayenas?"

"Who else? You think that limo belongs to her? She's come to see him. He might be planning to use her in more adverts – it's obviously not enough for her that she already presents all the home shopping programmes."

"And you want to be her?"

"If I had really wanted to, I would have been. He suggested it to me a while ago. Said he would put me on anything I wanted: underwear, blinds, herbal slimming teas."

"So why did you pass up such a fantastic opportunity?"

"Going to bed with someone you really like is a big deal," she answered abruptly.

I said nothing.

"Are you with someone?" she asked.

"You could put it like that," I answered.

"OK. But if you ever decide not to put it like that, you know where to find me. You've got my phone number. See you around, green eyes." And with that she walked back into the building with the same sexy wiggle.

# 21

As the day went on, Peiraios Street seemed to be willing
the night to fall and conceal all the filth covering it, all
those catering trailers that remind you of 1950s slums, the
strip clubs which had once been goldmines and were now
closing down one after the other, leaving dingy, dilapidated
buildings behind them.

Loukas Sofianos lived on the ground floor of a small
block between two of the area's successful theatres. When
I phoned and told him I wanted to talk to him about
Themis, he said he was happy to see me. Sofianos was a
veteran journalist. I had to be straight with him – if I tried
to sell him some vague bullshit that I was a journalist who
published online, or how I was just starting out, he could
easily check my credentials, so I told him I was a private
detective. When you can't sell people vague cover stories
you have to be a bit more creative. He opened the door
just as readily as he had agreed to see me. He was pretty
much as I had expected him to be, going on what Dora
had told me. He was in a wheelchair. His face was lined,
his silver hair thin and he looked like he'd had a hard
life, especially considering he couldn't have been more
than fifty-five.

"Stratos?" His gruff voice didn't sound particularly friendly, but it wasn't hostile either. Professional was probably the right word.

"Thanks for agreeing to see me so quickly."

"It's not as if I've got anything else to do. Come in."

I went inside. It was a small flat, not more than a couple of rooms. The smell of takeaways hung in the air. The sitting room we were in was divided into a kitchen area and a sitting area and through the open door at the back I could see the rest of the flat, a bathroom and a bedroom. A bachelor pad. He offered me a drink. I said no. I didn't even take off my leather jacket because I didn't want to give him the impression that I was intending to stay long. Sofianos was fiddling with his wheelchair. He started drinking from a thermos. Judging by his ruddy complexion, I suspected that it was something alcoholic and that this was far from the first thermos of the day. He wasn't very tall, but he was very thin. Too thin, which would make him seem taller if he could stand up. His dark eyes were bright and intelligent, his mouth thin; you could hardly make out his lips.

"Motorbike accident," he said, pointing to the wheelchair.

"How long?"

"Nine years. In my prime."

"There's no operation…?"

"Why do you think I'm sitting in this thing?" He was right, of course. I nodded.

"You said on the phone that you wanted to talk about Themis."

"Yes. I'd just been talking to Dora Landrou in Make-Up and she said that you and Raptas were friends. She gave me your phone number."

"Friends, yes … We were."

His mind began to wander.

"What did you think of Dora?" he asked me.

"Attractive."

"A man of few words."

"OK. Very attractive."

"She likes sex. Loves it."

"I didn't have the chance to confirm that."

"I did. You know, when I could. Still do, once in a blue moon. Before the accident I was a strong bloke. Now it's just out of pity. Maybe she wants to prove that she can raise the dead. What has your investigation got to do with Themis?"

There was no reason to waste time here, so I came straight to the point.

"I'm looking into a case of child abuse." He didn't react. He knew.

"Is this an old case? Themis has been dead for three years now."

"Old. New. All mixed up."

"And what have you heard about Themis?"

"A lot of rumours. Like the ones Dora told me about. I need something more solid."

"You've come to the right place, then."

I said nothing and waited while he took a sip from the thermos.

"The first accusation was from an immigrant. An Iranian. He was the father of an eight-year-old girl. Themis was doing a piece on how our schools were coping with the children of immigrants and he interviewed the girl. Her father then showed up at the station, claiming that Themis had arranged to see her again, for an additional interview, and had raped her. It was me he spoke to. I didn't believe him, not even for a second. My first thought was that this was a set-up.

"We'd worked together for years; he was my idol. When I had the accident, nobody was there for me like Themis was. And that little girl he had adopted." He was on the verge of tears.

"Emma," I said.

"Yes. Do you know her?"

"I know about her from the investigation."

"I loved her like she was my own. I went looking for her when I heard he was dead. Do you know where she is?"

"No. What did you do with the accusation?"

"At first I didn't say anything to Themis. I told the Iranian I would be in touch in a few days and that the station would investigate. I then asked around about him, what sort of lowlife he was and who did he think he was going around making accusations like that about Themis, the best person, the best journalist I'd ever met. You know, there's an old joke among us journalists that even the finest of us has killed his own mother. Themis, on the other hand, was, you know – cut from a different cloth. And Christ, we weren't wrong there. He was cut from a different cloth. But a much worse one than the rest of us. I spoke to convicted paedophiles as well as others who were facing charges. I got to know a lot of them. They said he was one of them. Are you sure? I kept saying, again and again. Yes, they were sure. They'd been sending him material. He'd been sending them material. One of them, who had escaped prison on a technicality, showed me an email Themis had sent him. It was definitely his account – I saw it myself. He showed me all the photographs he'd been sending. Little girls, not even old enough for primary school, with two, three men at the same time. All I wanted to do was kill them all, there on the spot, but Themis first. And then a second father turned up with more accusations – another immigrant."

While Sofianos was talking, I was thinking of Emma and that I was going to have to tell her all this at some point. I was sick to my stomach, which had tied itself up in knots that didn't feel like they would ever go away. I tried to focus. Think logically.

"Since all the men you spoke to were either convicted or facing charges, the cybercrime unit should have confiscated all their files."

"I expect so."

"My sources tell me that they never found anything on Raptas."

"I can't comment on that. All I know is what I saw with my own eyes."

"Did you talk to him? About what you'd found out?"

"What do you think? Even when things hit rock bottom and what we find out makes us feel physically sick, we were old-school, and we always followed the line laid down by our mentors: everyone has the right to defend themselves and give their side of the story. All that old rubbish. I say rubbish because you've already worked out the truth long before you have interviewed every rotten bastard involved. Rubbish, but sacred rubbish nevertheless because without it, we'd be in the jungle. I asked him to meet me, but he said he was too busy. I pressed him and he still refused. It turned out that was the day when he packed everything up and disappeared. I came out with it and told him what was going on. He asked me if I really believed all that about him. I told him that if he was innocent he needed to go to the police and clear his name. He said that it was impossible. And that's when I started to believe it. That he was this monster. My friend. My idol. A monster. I said, 'What did you do to those children?' And he replied, 'I'm only responsible for one child,' and hung up. We never spoke again. His neighbour found his mobile in the bin. But he had already confessed to all intents and purposes. I didn't need anything else."

"What do you think he meant when he said that he was only responsible for one child?"

"How should I know? Apparently it's common when abusers are caught for them to try to make out that their victims are many fewer than they actually are. As if their crime is any less serious if they only destroy one child's life." His rage was palpable. Rage at the crime itself. Rage at the friend who had betrayed him. Rage at his inability to understand who this person who had been his friend for so many years really was.

"How come it never got out?"

"It was the parents of the little girls. They refused to go to the police. When they found out that Themis had done a runner, and days and then weeks and then months went by and there was no sign of life, they began to think of the effect it would have on the girls and they questioned what the point of it was if there was no perpetrator to stand trial. Don't forget these people were foreigners. Their papers were all in order and everything, but they were foreigners nonetheless. They were scared at the thought of the police, of being interrogated in a foreign language. My friend knew what he was doing. But I also knew what I needed to do."

"What do you mean?"

"Have you tried to do an Internet search on Themis?"

"Yes. Many times. There are hardly any traces of him there."

"After a while it became obvious that he wasn't going to turn up, and I started talking to friends and other journalists. Old friends. I told them about the evidence I had. I told them what he'd done. I had a proposition for them – and they went for it. We decided that we would work together to erase all traces of him from the web. We are our digital footprint. If you erase the footprint, you erase the person. We had contacts with the managers of various websites, at newspapers and TV channels. We let them in on it – they were told as much as they needed to know. This was going to be our revenge on Themis. We'd wipe him off the map. You can't find his articles anywhere online. We even erased his name from all those massive scandals he'd been instrumental in exposing. His name disappeared from everything."

"What do you mean 'everything'? What was his most important work?"

"Themis exposed the biggest players in the doping scandal at the Olympics, the cuts the politicians were taking on def— defence contracts. And the illegal trade in, in pharmaceuticals. We all worked together to get rid of it. To be fair, he wasn't interested in taking the credit, but the important work had been his."

The more he talked, the slower his speech became. Some words were a struggle and he needed two attempts to get them out.

"I recently found an old piece announcing that he was going to leave HighTV and go to another channel, and then a later one saying that he was going to go into business."

"He planted all of that himself to explain away his disappearance. He still had a few friends here and there in the press and we … we weren't able to control everything. He still had some friends, the scum."

"So in other words you let him get away?" I asked.

"Some people in the police knew about it and looked for him unofficially and also went after other statements that would incriminate him. But they couldn't open an official investigation. Nobody was pressing charges."

"His emails to the other abusers? Didn't that count as evidence?"

"It wasn't enough. The State Prosecutor would have to fight for years to get him put away on that, even for a short stretch of only a few months. And then he could take himself off to a hospital for psychological support and serve out the rest of his sentence there – and then he'd be out again. We needed more, and we didn't have it. We wanted his scalp."

"Is that the only reason you let him go?"

"What do you mean?"

"Well, if word got out about such a prominent journalist, it would have damaged the reputation of the station and the papers he worked for."

This made him angry. He reddened and the veins in his head started to throb visibly.

"You don't know me. You have no idea who I am. How dare you sit there and talk to me like that? That's not how it works. All of us who knew him, we never played it like that. We didn't give a shit about the reputation of the station – or the newspapers. The man was fucking small children! And you think I was sitting there agonizing about Vayenas or any other media shark?"

He came closer, looking like he wanted to take a swing at me. I stood up. "I'm sorry," I said. Somehow my apology worked like a tranquillizer on him. He stopped in his tracks and for a moment fell silent.

"OK. You're investigating. I get it. I've been there so many times. It doesn't make any difference what line of work you're in. It's all the same. You want to check everything – and you're right to. If you like, go and talk to Anna Kati. She was his oldest colleague. They worked together before I met him. She knows all about it too." He then jotted down her phone number for me and took another swig of the thermos. It seemed to bring him down and pick him up at the same time.

"It still seems unreal, unbelievable to me. Sometimes, that is. I remember the times when we would go drinking together and he'd pour out his soul to me, about how he desperately wanted to get the money together so he could take Emma to the States, to a special school for the blind. He told me all about it, how it got the most out of those kids and sent them on to university, great careers – and left them with no disadvantages to speak of."

I shook my head and said nothing. I didn't want to interrupt him because I didn't want him to lose his flow. I wasn't convinced that he would be able to find it again, and I began to wonder whether Emma or Angelino knew about this opportunity.

"It's in New York, I think. But it cost an absolute fortune. The money we were making back then, even in the really good times, wasn't anything like enough to pay for it. When I heard about Themis and those little girls, that was the first image that entered my head – Themis, all teary, his voice shaking, talking about Emma. I just wanted to grab a gun and kill that moment and all the other times I had spent with him believing he was a good man – not the monster he was."

"Is there any way at all that —" I began.

"That I'm wrong? That the whole thing is a pack of lies or a big misunderstanding? No way at all. If there had been a single ray of light here, believe me, I'd have found it. Pitch-black darkness everywhere. What did you say your name was?"

"Stratos."

"Stratos. That's right. The year before that was when I lost my leg. I swear to God that the pain was nothing compared to what came with the revelations about Themis." He seemed to get a measure of relief from saying all this.

His body relaxed a little into his wheelchair. He held the thermos without drinking from it and looked at me for a while.

"So – have you got enough for your investigation?"

"For now. If I need anything else, I'll be in touch."

"I would have asked you more questions about the details of your investigation if it had been about anything else at all. But in this case, I've already spent many days being sick. Vomiting and crying. When you talk to child abusers you come face to face with *evil*, what we are taught to recognize as evil when we are children. Then as we grow older and get more blasé we dismiss the notion and start to insist that everything is relative, good and evil, both grey areas. That's utter bullshit. Evil *does* exist. It lives inside those monsters, genuine, pure evil. It's unbelievable how you mutate when you listen to them talk. Your mind and your body change, they build up layers of defence and try to convince you that you are safe. But these layers fall off, one after another. I've spoken to murderers. They're completely different. Not the same thing at all as the sense of blood-curdling revulsion you feel when you've been talking to a child abuser. And that feeling never leaves you. You begin to despise your own existence after it has been in contact with theirs. You start to think that the only way you can protect yourself from this evil is by vanishing. They sit there and smile at you and all you can think of doing is beating them to a pulp. And then you get overwhelmed by disgust for not kicking the shit out of them. You come to hate your eyes for having looked at them and all you want to do is wash yourself and get rid of every trace of every second you spent with them. I can't go through it all again. This is a game for younger people like you. Well, I do admire your nerve," he said, raising his flask as though in a toast to me.

He downed the rest in one.

# 22

I fell asleep slumped over my computer, watching *The Kid* for a second time. I wasn't in the mood for real noir. After a strong dose of sad humour, I needed a happy ending. An ending where the kid finishes up surrounded by people who love her instead of discovering that the man she adored is a paedophile. I wanted to turn back the clock a hundred years and hear a note of false hope. The film might have helped, because I hadn't slept as well as I did that night, slumped over my computer, for days.

It was 8 a.m. when I was woken by my phone.

"Stratos. It's Markos." He sounded just as terrified as he'd been when I left him at his HQ. "I've got ... I've got the information you wanted. You see. Pretty quick. You don't get faster than that."

"I'm listening."

"Vaios was working for Fotis Paraschos. Do you know him?"

"No."

"He owns a haulage company, apparently. At least, that's his official line of work."

"And his real one?"

"Black-market medicines. His network covers the Balkans and Turkey as well. Big business. Imports and exports. A lot of people work for him. He's a big name." Markos sounded impressed. "I've worked with him," he said, full of pride.

"Good for you."

"But I never met that Vaios guy. That's how come I didn't know he was Paraschos' man. If I'd known, I'd have told you straight up."

"What kind of people has he got?"

"All sorts. Take your pick: doctors, medical reps and of course people inside the industry who sort all his fake invoices for him so he can get expensive Greek medicines out to Bulgaria, Romania, Albania. Mainly cancer drugs, Viagra – stuff like that. They sell for a lot more abroad."

"Doesn't this lead to a shortage here?"

"Yeah. But you know what it's like. Who's going to go looking for them anyway?"

Not the cancer patients who need them, that's for sure, I thought.

"He brings in drugs from Turkey too. For IVF. Nobody ever checks them. They're much, much cheaper there. He likes me a lot. We're about to make our business relationship more permanent. So when I told him you might be wanting to talk to him, he said yes right away. He might give you a call later on."

"I'll be expecting it," I said.

"And Stratos? Are we OK now – you and me? I've told you everything I know and I've set up a phone interview for you. So we're good, yeah?"

"Yes. We're good," I said and hung up.

It struck me as strange that even a slimeball like Markos should have such a strong submissive streak considering his exaggerated sense of self-importance. As far as Markos was concerned, Markos was a legend. Maybe I had scared him enough.

Much as I had enjoyed sleeping at my computer, my back was protesting. I worked out for an hour, beginning with some basic back extensions and finishing off with sets of twenty one-handed press-ups to make me feel better. After that I spent half an hour in the bathroom, until I had used the last drop of water I had heated with Maria's new boiler. I put on some warm clothes, cut myself two slices of bread and cheese and set off at around half past ten to meet Anna Kati.

From my house to Papagou Town Hall takes ten minutes by car on a normal day. But today two enormous lorries, an almost immobile crane and one woman driver who had caused a pile-up on the way there all conspired with the narrow streets round Papagou to make normal seem like a fantasy and turn the ten minutes into forty. Fortunately, when we had arranged this visit the night before after I'd left Sofianos, Anna hadn't specified a time. She'd just said that she would be at the kindergarten till 3.00 and I could drop by anytime.

I parked behind the town hall and walked the last five minutes, going west, till I reached the entrance to a green building. However fresh the paint, it couldn't conceal the age of the building. It wasn't the only one. This neighbour-hood was one the most built-up of the ones I had driven through, full of single-storey houses more than fifty years old.

The kindergarten principal was at least as old as its building, but her exterior was not as fresh. She looked me up and down, and with no attempt to be subtle asked me what I wanted. She went to get Kati and to sit with Kati's kids while she was out of the classroom. Anna Kati was a tall, thin woman, about my age. She had extremely long hair, dyed red and caught in a ponytail. Her features were stern and there were bags under her eyes, bags of sleeplessness that no amount of make-up could hide.

"Ten minutes. That's it, Anna. I need to leave soon," shouted the principal as she disappeared into Anna's classroom. Anna didn't answer, something which automatically raised my opinion of her. She suggested we sit down on a bench outside the principal's office, which she had surprisingly found the time to lock. Maybe she was worried that I would try to steal something.

"So, you're a private detective?"

I had told Sofianos I was, so I decided to be consistent. "Yes."

"Which firm?"

"Self-employed."

"So you've got your own offices?"

"I'm looking to rent at the moment."

"I'm sorry to ask all these questions. It's a hangover from my years as a journalist." There was a warmth in her voice which almost didn't suit her.

"You're two in one now: journalist and kindergarten teacher."

"No. The journalism is over. Themis made sure of that."

"What do you mean?"

"Loukas told me that you know the basics, so you know the truth about him. But we didn't know. At least I didn't. I'm speaking for myself now. I worked closely with him for fifteen years, give or take, from when I was doing the journalism course, and I didn't have a clue. I was even with him when he interviewed those little immigrant girls he later raped. I was there. When you're there, and you're too blind to see what's going on right in front of you, you're forced to take a long good look in the mirror and make a dramatic career change. After a lot of throwing up."

"Are you a trained kindergarten teacher?"

"Yes, I am. I somehow managed to pass all the modules within the space of ten years. But the main thing was that I wanted to go somewhere where I could make a difference."

"I see."

"Here, with the children, I feel that I'm somehow managing to do something worthwhile. Give something back. Restore some kind of balance after what he did to those other children. I don't know if I'm making any sense."

"I get it. I do."

"There aren't that many jobs left in Greece that leave you feeling human at the end of the day. Most of the time people have to cheat and steal just to survive, whether it's from the state, your colleagues, your employees, your boss – there's always someone. If you don't, you don't survive. But with the kids, you're free of all that."

I nodded and quickly moved on to the next question. After all, we only had ten minutes. "So there's no doubt in your mind that he was guilty?"

"None. Loukas showed me the evidence he found after Themis disappeared. I spoke to the girls' parents afterwards too. Besides, what kind of innocent man with Themis' connections disappears like that? If he was innocent, don't you think he would have stuck around to clear his name? He had fought so many battles to get at the truth as a journalist. Wouldn't he do the same for his own reputation?"

"What do you make of the fact that he spent so many years living like a tramp on the streets with his daughter?"

"Weird."

"Can you rationalize it?"

"I don't know. He might have thought he was doing the right thing – paying for what he'd done. He could be a bit odd sometimes. He'd get hung up on the symbolism of everything – saw it in everything, and if it wasn't there, he would create it. But realistically, he was probably worried he'd get arrested either here or abroad if he decided to try and leave the country."

"But the girls' parents didn't end up filing a complaint."

"Yes, but there was no way he could have known that. He might have thought that they had gone ahead. Or would if he ever showed his face again. He also knew that Loukas and I had found out. The lesson he was always trying to teach us was never to spare anyone guilty. And there was no way we'd spare him. Not over something as sick as this."

"So after he disappeared, did you never hear from him again?"

"Never."

"What about before? Were you working together right up to the end?"

She nodded and her bottom lip came up to her top lip, as if to say that it was a pity. "Yes, we were. We weren't just working together, but were on the verge of – I mean he was on the verge of; I was just helping – breaking the biggest story of his career."

"Which was what?"

"You know that almost all our rivers are polluted by industrial and urban waste?"

I didn't know, but thought it was a given and therefore should have known more about it, so I nodded.

"The only important river that can claim to be clean is the Achelous."

"Isn't it?"

"Ever heard of orphan waste?"

"No."

"Many factories dump their dangerous waste wherever they find a convenient place for it: in wells, rivers, streams, landfill sites – without undertaking any kind of processing at all. We're talking tonnes and tonnes of carcinogenic toxins. They don't even bother to send reports on their waste management to the Ministry and there are no penalties. Everyone is in on it, you see. The Ministry turns a blind eye, especially now with this crisis. They'd say they couldn't possibly justify closing down industries and causing more redundancies at the moment, and they don't have enough qualified manpower to oversee it properly. So what we have in terms of checks and controls is a tiny questionnaire that the factories fill in – if they want to."

"In other words, it's a free-for-all."

"Exactly. Themis found out that there were unnaturally high incidences of cancer in the populations living in villages around all the tributaries of the Achelous, which were close to big factories. He had gathered up medical files from the last thirty years plus. They weren't freely given – we had to steal quite a lot of them. He sent the files to a university in England because he didn't trust the ones here; he was worried that they would fall into the hands of snitches who might blow the whistle on our investigation. His English contacts were going to come over and collect hair and nail samples to test for the presence of heavy metal build-up and to assess the children's physical and intellectual development. Themis was footing the bill for the whole thing – that way he could keep it quiet and would be able to go public with it when he was ready and before the factory owners had time to react. All the evidence in the files suggested a large-scale medical disaster. But we needed more new readings."

"But why aren't the people affected shouting about this?"

"They are. Screaming. Shouting. But they can't get the airtime. If they try to get the papers to publish an announcement, it always gets buried in a tiny column in the back pages. Some of my colleagues – what colleagues? Look at me! I still haven't got used to this. Some of them dismiss them as nutjobs while others suspect that they want to halt the development of the country with all these superstitions, and it goes without saying that the industrial-ists are throwing their weight around too."

"You mean …?"

"I mean that they have the power to do that, and the means."

"What about the evidence from the investigation?"

"I used to have some of it. Themis had all of it, but when he disappeared he took off with everything: computers, notes, everything. And he did something very strange. The evening before he vanished he was working alone in the office and just wiped the whole lot, his hard disk and mine. Everything. He even reformatted my back-up disk."

"How do you explain that?"

"I can't. Not seriously. The only thing I've been able to come up with is that perhaps, in his sick mind, he thought that Loukas had given me everything he had on Themis and he believed that if he erased everything from my computer all that would be wiped as well."

"Yes, but it's not that easy to erase data. Loukas would still have it," I said.

"Of course. I told you, I don't have a good explanation."

Our allotted ten minutes had obviously elapsed, as the lovely principal appeared, cawing to Anna to get back to class. I thanked her and left.

Whatever Themis Raptas was, I would eventually have to tell Emma. But there were still so many gaps. The name of his murderer, for a start. Who was still after him and Emma so many years after his death? Who had attacked Angelino? Was the attack something to do with Emma or not? Before I could answer these questions, I was not intending to say anything; I wasn't going to tell her half the story. That was what I was thinking as I hurried back to my car; the rain, which had been threatening to appear for days now, finally arrived and minute by minute was growing from weak drizzle to heavy drops. Just as I reached my car, my phone rang. The screen showed "Unknown Caller", and my first thought was that it was one of the mobile phone companies touting their latest deals. That's what they were, about eighty per cent of the time. But this wasn't one of them.

"Mr Gazis?" It was a deep, elderly male voice.

"Speaking."

"This is Fotis Paraschos."

The *big name*, according to Markos. I should probably be flattered that he was calling me. I squeezed my swollen ego into the car.

"Hello."

"Before I start, I want you to know that obviously I am not phoning just because Markos has asked me to."

*Obviously.* Interesting.

"Markos mentioned that you work together," I said.

"Markos is a piece of shit. I don't work with shit. He keeps trying to go into business with me."

His voice was a voice of absolute calm, as though he were talking through his shopping list. *Markos is a piece of shit.* So what did that make Paraschos, the pharmaceuticals thief and smuggler for all those cancer patients and hopeful parents?

"In that case, why are you calling?"

"Because I owe you. I'm not doing you any favours. I'm doing it to settle my debt." There was a change in tone.

But that's what debtors did, they tried to be on friendly terms with their creditors.

"But I don't know you."

"Sometimes we end up owing people we don't know."

"Such as?"

"Nikos Dermatas was like a brother to me. His family was like my own."

A few years back, a Russian, Yevgeni, had tried to become the main player in the protection rackets controlling the clubs and bars in the city centre. Nikos Dermatas owned a very profitable bar, and was the first to refuse to pay. One day Yevgeni and his people brought his wife and five-year-old daughter into the bar and forced him to watch for hours as they raped and tortured them before finally killing them. Then they blew up the bar, with Dermatas and all his staff inside. After that, a group of other bar owners in the area hired me to take care of their problem. And I did, with a little help from Drag at a critical moment.

"I spent a lot of time trying to find out who it was who had done what needed to be done," Paraschos said.

"I see. Can I ask you a few questions?"

"First tell me who you're working for on this case."

I could have answered that in many ways: the first answer would have been, "For a fourteen-year-old girl"; the second answer would have been "Angelino". But I gave him a third, one that covered the others.

"For myself."

"OK. Ask away."

"Was Vaios working for you?"

"Not recently. He did work for me for about eight years. Until last year."

"What was his connection to Themis Raptas?"

"He would go and find him once a month, on my behalf. Wherever he was. Filopappou mainly, that's where they used to meet. To give him his monthly payment."

"What monthly payment?"

"Raptas had dug up some information about me during one of his investigations. Instead of going public with it, he decided to blackmail me."

He was amazingly relaxed telling me all this, which convinced me that he was calling from an untraceable number.

"How much?"

"Three grand a month."

"For how long?"

"It started when he gave up journalism and went on until he died. Almost five years."

"What I meant was how long was the agreement for?"

"There was no end date. I don't think he ever intended it to stop. That's why he didn't want me to give him a lump sum."

"Did he have that much on you?"

"He was a good journalist. Irritatingly good. He had connections all over the place, even with people in our circles. They would feed him information – and then there was everything he dug up himself. Unfortunately, there are loose tongues everywhere, especially in my line of work."

"Do you know why he gave up journalism?"

"No. I asked Vaios to find out. Raptas told him to just bring the money and mind his own business."

"Wasn't he frightened of you?"

"He told me from the start that two of his trusted people had all the information on me and that if he turned up in a ditch one day, or if anyone laid a finger on his daughter, the information would go straight to the police. And I believed him. He wasn't bluffing."

"In other words, you had nothing to do with it."

"Not only did I not kill him, but when I heard he'd been murdered, I was prepared for a massive fallout. In the end, one of the two people who had the information, a lawyer, came to see me straight afterwards. I paid him off, he handed over the evidence and left."

"What about the other one?"

"I'm still trying to find them."

"No contact, no blackmailing?"

"Nothing at all."

"So you're worried that it still might all come out?"

"I would really appreciate it if you'd bring it to me if it falls into your hands. I'm always here at our Alimos offices. The fact that nothing has surfaced yet doesn't mean it won't. My competitors aren't exactly fond of me."

"Why did Vaios try to kidnap Themis' daughter?"

"I don't know. Vaios was beginning to get ideas above his station. Long before he left me. He wanted to work for the big bosses, get more money, more action. He thought we were small fry. Inert. At some point, I got rid of him because he was violent to some of our associates for no reason. His behaviour was beginning to hurt business. I don't even know who he'd been working for recently. Or why he tried to kidnap the daughter. Whatever he was doing, it had nothing to do with me."

"Don't you think it's a bit of a coincidence?"

"Athens, Stratos, is a much smaller city than it thinks it is. This is especially true of its underworld. The same old people going round banging their heads against each other, working for different bosses. So no coincidence seems that big to me. Vaios was not sent by me. Whatever he did had nothing to do with me."

"What if he'd wanted to sell you his services? If he found the girl, thought she had the information, found it and brought it to you, maybe you'd take him back?"

"I don't take people back. Ever. Associates, women, nobody. If you leave me, you're gone for good. Everyone knows that."

I thought that another explanation could be that Vaios was after the evidence so that he could blackmail Paraschos himself. But he had no way of knowing whether Emma had it, and the risks – taking on Angelino and his men, me, the police if they got there on time – were too big to be ignored when he had no guarantee that he would find anything.

"Anyone you can think of who could tell me more about Vaios?"

"He was with this singer for years, Tanya … Tanya Gourka. I don't know where she performs these days."

We talked for a while longer, but it was soon clear that Paraschos couldn't tell me anything else. I thanked him and hung up.

On top of all the information about his child abuse, I had just found out that Themis Raptas was using the research he had uncovered in an investigation to blackmail rather than to expose. This was a far cry from the image of the redeeming angel that Emma had of him. To be precise, it was the absolute opposite. It was also a far cry from the image of the great and dedicated investigative journalist his closest associates had. Unless he suffered from a multiple personality disorder, there was something very wrong with the information I was getting. Usually when something like this happens, it's the positive information that bears no relation to reality.

# 23

It was the afternoon and I was at Teri's. I had phoned Drag earlier to brief him about everything I'd found out from Sofianos, Kati, Markos and Fotis Paraschos. I told him we'd have to find out who Vaios was working for now – who had sent him to kidnap or kill Emma.

"I've been listening all this time, wanting to say thanks," he said.

"For what?"

"For going to all this trouble, albeit with a few days' delay, to tell me what you've been up to. I'm truly humbled that you're thinking of me."

I didn't rise to it. I could have mentioned the fact that very often he doesn't tell me what he's doing. He would answer that he does fill me in on the basics, and always on things that I can help him with. And then he'd say that he had the impression that this particular case was one we were supposed to be working on together. There was no point in thrashing all of this out. I listened; he was already wound up. I could just see the vein at the base of his throat pulsating away rhythmically. I also realized that I didn't really care. I hadn't forgotten our conversation about Maria.

"You're taking this case far too personally; you've taken the whole thing on yourself and are shutting me out completely."

It wasn't that he was trying to start an argument – well maybe he would have if I had been too – it was more that he sounded sad, as though I had let him down.

"You're right," I said. Because he was.

"As always," he said before hanging up and going to look into what we had agreed on.

While I was waiting for him to get back to me, I went to Emma's room because she was wanting to show me a new trick and we'd need peace and quiet away from the game of Scrabble Teri and Babis were playing in the sitting room and the noisy disagreements that periodically flared up on the subject of the rules of the game and of the Greek language. When I saw them earlier, Teri had been hitting Babis over the head with an open copy of the Greek dictionary.

Emma was sitting at her desk. She was wearing some baggy sweatpants and a light-blue cardigan, the colour of her eyes. The pink slippers weren't quite the best match, but then again, Teri had bought them and she insisted that there always had to be something pink in every woman's outfit. I should introduce her to Martinos' pink swans and pink circles. She'd love them.

"My hands are really rough. I don't know if they'll be able …" I began.

"Everyone can do this trick. It just takes practice," she answered. Words of encouragement to the beginner.

"Some tricks even benefit from rough hands. Not many, but there are some. The trick is to turn your disadvantages into advantages," she continued as she shuffled the deck. "You know, in my case, being blind is a huge advantage in the work I do."

"Why's that?" I asked her – a serious pupil trying to learn from his experienced teacher.

"People want to feel that what they are seeing is really magic. So if an illusionist starts off with a very complicated trick before the audience has had a chance to warm up, the show is unlikely to go well. You see, they don't want to be impressed by skill and dexterity; they don't want technicians. They want to believe that the laws of nature no longer stand. My dad taught me that. He went and researched it as soon as he realized that I had these special skills with my hands. That's why some jugglers allow some of the balls to drop at the beginning of the show – to keep up the suspense. I don't need to do that. As soon as they realize I'm blind, they think that I have this handicap from the start and that just by virtue of me being me, the laws of nature no longer stand. Whatever I do after that will amaze them, and if I go on to do something a little bit more complicated, they're blown away."

"Angelino told me that your sense of touch is almost supernaturally sensitive."

"Not supernatural. That's going too far. Hypersensitive, yes. Whatever exists and whatever happens in nature is natural, so it can't be supernatural, can it?"

There were probably other things besides card tricks she could teach me. She seemed to know so much more than I did about everything.

"As my eyesight got progressively worse, my sense of touch got more sensitive and I started to register the tiniest of changes in the feel of the objects, which for most people just didn't exist. My fingers are essentially my eyes."

"What do you mean?"

"When I pick up a card" – she picked up half the deck in her left hand and placed it in her right – "I can feel the exact thickness of the card to the nearest millimetre as well as the differences in the humidity of the surface and of the ink used. When I touch a card I can see if it's a picture card and which one it is from tracing the print outline. I'm not saying I don't use all the old tricks that everyone uses to fool an audience; I do. But my sense of touch is what makes all the difference. Angelino bought me a special lotion for my hands to keep them very soft, and I've got much better."

"So why did you do that Tramp routine and not card tricks?"

"My dad … he thought that my gift was very special and that it was too good for the streets. It was meant for greater things, for the future, he used to say."

As she spoke about Raptas, I thought about the time of his death. There was no way he could have carried all that blackmail money he got from Paraschos. From what Paraschos said, he must have collected more than one hundred and fifty thousand euros in total during those years when they were living on the streets. A lot of money. Enough to cover the tuition at a private special school in New York, perhaps? The simplest thing for Raptas to have done when he realized that the net was closing in on him with the child abuse was to take off and leave Emma behind. A blind child doesn't only make it harder for you to get around but also makes it easier to identify you. He did everything he could to keep her with him. It occurred to me that I should examine the case from the opposite perspective: I shouldn't assume that all the negative information I had on Raptas would necessarily unlock the mystery of who he was. Because I had seen so much filth in my life, it was certainly worth considering that a man who brings up a child like Emma might not belong to the dark side, and worth taking the trouble to see if my hunch was right.

OK, I thought. Let's say for argument's sake that Themis was prepared to betray all his principles as a journalist just so that he could get enough money off Paraschos to make his dream for Emma a reality and see her get the education she deserved. Of course, none of this meant that he wasn't a paedophile. That was still an open question. And I still hadn't the faintest idea who killed him.

Drag had already established that there were no accounts held in Raptas' name at any Greek bank. Neither had there been any transfers in his name or Emma's to any bank abroad. Where was all that money? Maybe it was with the evidence he had about Paraschos' dealings. But where? I asked Emma if she and Raptas had any money stashed away in some hiding place. She didn't know. The little cash they did have they'd kept hidden under a rock in their cave, but on the day of the murder Raptas had taken almost all of it to lend that other homeless man who needed it.

"Shall I show you the trick now?"

As if there was any way I would turn her down. She showed me a trick that card sharps use – a classic, she said. They start off dealing from the second card from the top instead of the top card. She demonstrated it five times. I understood it every time but just couldn't pull it off myself, which I thought was quite funny. Emma remained serious, almost offended by the failure of her pupil. After my second failure she took my hand and showed me once more exactly how it was done. I felt the urge to take her hands, kiss them and reassure her that I would sort everything out. That no matter what happened, I would uncover the truth. But I didn't. I kept trying to master the trick and on my twentieth or so attempt, I had just about got it. She then made me promise to practise by myself, and try to improve.

It was 11 p.m. when Drag phoned. He was on his way back from the nightclub on Kifissias Avenue where Vaios' ex, Tania Gourka, was singing. Her name could easily have been Greek, but it wasn't. Tania was Ukrainian; she'd arrived here at the beginning of the last decade as an agency bride sourced for some sixty-year-old from Larissa who was planning a lovely long retirement and old age. As it turned out, his long retirement was cut short and after less than two years Tania was widowed. She would spend half the year in Greece and the other half back with her family in Ukraine. As she confessed to Drag, she kept on drawing the pension of her deceased husband and would send the money back home. She begged him not to report her to the Labour Ministry, who investigated pension fraud, and in return she would tell him everything she knew about Vaios. At some point, because she had always dreamed of becoming a professional singer, she decided to put out some feelers in a nightclub in Larissa, and within two seasons she had become such a huge success on account of her vocal and other talents that a club owner in Athens offered to have her transferred to the capital. The move didn't go that brilliantly for Tania; she never made it as anything like a headline act, she had to share her tiny dressing room with two other women and she was forced to wear next to nothing to keep the customers happy. Her relationship with Vaios was getting worse all the time. He couldn't stomach the fact that she wasn't interested any more and beat the two men she slept with after their break-up to a pulp.

"I won't say that I'm glad he's dead … but the way he was coming after me, I was about to ask for protection," she said to Drag in the dressing room, having chucked out the other two in a volley of abuse.

"Police protection?"

She burst out laughing. "I don't want to be rude, but that kind of thing isn't on offer to the likes of us, my boy."

*My boy.* To Drag. She was lucky to have escaped one of his legendary headbutts.

What he did discover was that in his efforts to get Tania back, Vaios had started to promise her the world. "He didn't go into detail. He just said that he had struck gold with this new job and that very soon we would be very, very rich because he was earning a really good salary, plus all the extras. And if I wanted, he could set me up with connections in TV and I could sing on any show I wanted,

and get the exposure – as long as I got back with him."
Drag was struck by her Greek; there wasn't the slightest
trace of an accent in it.

"Are you surprised?" I asked him. "She's received a
proper Greek education."

"What – in the third-class bouzouki joints?"

"Are you aware of a purer form of contemporary Greek
expression?"

"Yes, gossip."

"I can feel my horizons widening when I talk to you.
Do you think she was telling the truth?"

"She had no reason not to. She didn't kill Vaios, as we
both very well know. So why would she feel the need to
go making up outlandish stories? The point is whether
or not Vaios did have this amazing job and was in a position to make all those promises, or whether he was just
stringing her along."

Drag was right to be cautious. It was quite possible that
Vaios was telling Tania a pack of lies to get her back into
bed. But it was also possible that he wasn't. If he was, we
had no evidence. So we would assume that he wasn't. That's
how investigations work: few leads and a lot of speculation.
And then you just have to hope that one of your theories
will turn out to be right.

"The problem is that even if we take our best scenario,
the one that gives us something to go on, we're still dealing
in very general terms here. Vaios could have been working
for any number of TV executives. What are we supposed
to do? Investigate them all to find out which one he was
working for?"

I could have sworn I heard Drag smiling through the silence on the other end of the line. "You forget who you're talking to. I've already found out. I called an old friend of mine in the National Intelligence Service, who's also a friend of Angelino's. They've got a recent photo of Vaios climbing into the back of a limo with his new boss: Lazaros Vayenas. The owner of HighTV."

# 24

Drag was bouncing up and down on the waterbed. "It's not too bad here," he said.

We were in a massage parlour in Piraeus, in one of the roads off Trikoupi Street. A brothel by any other name, specializing in Asian girls, shift workers. Judging by the takings from wealthy clients all over the country, these girls were very popular with sections of the male population of Athens, Piraeus and beyond.

Drag, apparently without any sense of shame, was wearing a pair of maroon cords, brown leather shoes and a yellow pullover, and had left his white raincoat on the bed. His outfit couldn't have cost more than a single thread of one of the *bokhara* rugs which were covering every square inch of the wooden floors.

"Are you thinking of moving in?" I asked him.

"Not really to my taste," he said, getting down off the bed.

"And without any money in your pocket, I doubt you'd be to theirs either."

"Great. That's my dilemma solved," he replied, and began to examine the whip he'd discovered in one of the drawers together with another sex aid, which, however hard we tried, neither of us could figure out how to work.

Drag was fired up by the fact that we had at last got a serious suspect. This was understandable when you think that the only success he'd had so far in this case was arresting a group of twenty-something gym junkies who had come together to help the Avengers get the job done even though they didn't know them personally. When, on instructions from Drag, the police arrested them, they found them planning the execution of more paedophiles who'd been exposed on that TV show, as well as some local homosexuals. "Paedos and gays? I don't get it. What's the connection?" I asked Drag.

"Don't ask me. Ask them. Ask their local bishop."

He had clearly tired of playing with the whip and started to look at the pictures of semi-naked Asian women covering the walls instead, and when he'd finished with them he returned to the waterbed.

"He's late," he said, looking up at the red clock on the wall above the door, which in the place of numbers bore Chinese characters. Clearly its job was to let the girls know when to get rid of their clients.

"He's here!" I said. Drag leapt off the bed and went across to the window to see Lazaros Vayenas' limo pull into the parking space outside.

We both knew the drill. We'd been rehearsing this for days now: Vayenas, just as he did on all his visits to the parlour, would try to enter the building unnoticed by getting in through the lift round the back. He would then get out on the second floor, which the madam cleared of girls beforehand so that the only person who would actually see him was his beloved Meifeng. Her name meant "beautiful wind" and he was crazy about her. The only difference was that today Meifeng, on her madam's instructions, wouldn't be turning up for work. In her place Vayenas would find me and Drag. Drag had made all the arrangements with the madam, persuading her that if she didn't do what he asked of her, the following day her business would close and she would be left to rot in prison. This had brought the negotiations to a swift conclusion. He'd then instructed her to keep the ground floor functioning as normal so that when Vayenas arrived nothing would arouse his suspicions.

We'd got our information about Vayenas' weakness for Meifeng from that same friend of Drag's and Angelino's in the Intelligence Service. The Service had been following him for some time so that they would be able to intervene in case of a terrorist attack. Vayenas was on the list of the ten richest Greek businessmen. As well as the TV channel, he owned two radio stations, as many newspapers, shares in foreign companies and even more shares in state-owned businesses that had undergone forced privatization by the EU. That was how they became aware of his little trips down to Piraeus. It looked as though Chryssa, the girlfriend I'd seen outside the TV station, wasn't enough for him. Who could blame him? A red-blooded young man like that in his seventies …

Vayenas stepped out of the limo accompanied by two bodyguards who couldn't have looked more different.

One of them, who had also been driving, was even taller than me and twice my size. He had short black hair and walked in the laboured way a hypnotized hippo would. The other guy was small and thin but looked very muscly. Drag stared at him.

"That's Ramon."

"From?"

"Don't know."

"Friend of yours?"

"He's a little piece of shit. Been arrested for five or six murders and we had to let him go each time. Witnesses were either disappearing or changing their stories. I'd lost track of him recently. Didn't know who he was working for."

"Now you know."

"They say he's one of the fastest guns in town. And one of the best shots."

"Better than you?"

"No," he replied, curtly and with his usual modesty.

The two of us hid in the en suite. The madam had warned us that Mei's instructions had been to wait for Vayenas in the bathtub. We left the door ajar and waited.

We heard the bedroom door open and close. From the gap in the door I could see that Vayenas was alone. He always came alone, according to the madam. His thugs were outside.

"Mei!" Vayenas was in a good mood, his voice clear, masculine and metallic.

"I think it's you he wants," whispered Drag.

Vayenas walked into the bathroom to find not Mei but my gun waiting for him, stuck under his nose. He was

236

wearing a blue shirt, red tie and black woollen trousers. His hair was dyed black, raven black. He had very dark skin and a relatively small stomach for his age and size. His small brown eyes opened wide in surprise for a moment, but within a second were back to normal size.

"Who are you?" he asked us, commandingly, as though he was the one holding the gun. Perhaps when you are so used to being in charge, you don't let go, not even to say "good evening". You never relinquish control, not for a second. Without saying a word, I motioned to him to sit down on the toilet seat.

"Who are you?" he repeated, already showing signs of irritation at our insubordination.

"Bennie and Lennie," said Drag.

"I know *you*," replied Vayenas, clearly recognizing Drag from his TV press conferences.

"Yeah. I'm Bennie."

"Sit down," I said.

He took a surreptitious look outside the bathroom door. He was thinking of shouting for his bodyguards, but decided against it. He reckoned that the two doors between him and his men were two too many for them to be able to help him if we decided to kill him. He sat down. The bathroom was a bit of a squeeze for three, but better than the bedroom from where his minders could get wind of something much more easily and enter uninvited.

"We want to tell you a story. Feel free to chip in at any point, fill in some of the blanks," said Drag.

"And if I don't want to?"

"Oh, you will," I said.

He smiled ironically and turned to Drag to avoid meeting my eyes.

"What story?"

"Eight years ago, a journalist working for your station, Themis Raptas, discovered that the Achelous River was experiencing the greatest environmental disaster Greece has ever seen. That thousands of people, children too, living in areas surrounding the river and close to factories were being poisoned on a daily basis."

He made a face, declaring his ignorance.

"Oh, you understand all right," said Drag.

"The disaster is on a par with a radioactive leak into the environment," I said, joining in the conversation. That was the initial assessment made by the team of English scientists Themis had been in touch with after they had examined the evidence he sent them.

"Why should I care about all this?"

"You see, that's just the problem. You don't care. You don't care about the environmental disaster or the people. Just as long as the factories are doing well. Because you're the main shareholder of almost every single factory in the area and now you are building some more there."

"You're insane." Vayenas answered with absolute confidence.

But we knew he was lying. Mimis, one of the six bright young things Drag had put on his team, had been a hacker in a previous life. When he was fifteen he would sit in his bedroom on the island of Samos and hack; he hacked into NASA, but the Americans got wise to this six months after the event. He was arrested, but escaped prison because of his age. When he was a bit older, he decided that he would rather be on the right side of the law than the wrong one. Mimis told Drag that the main shareholders of the industries along the banks of the Achelous were listed as offshore companies. But for someone who can get into NASA, finding the lists of shareholders is child's play. All those labyrinthine journeys through ownership of companies led us to this immensely powerful man who was sitting on a toilet seat in front of us now.

"Insane," he repeated for the sake of clarity.

"You haven't seen me when I'm having one of my bad days," replied Drag.

"Raptas discovered what was going on. But you found out that he had found out," I said.

He continued to avoid meeting my eye. Perhaps Drag seemed more manageable, more familiar. Televisual. Surely two men from the world of television could come to an understanding?

"Raptas wasn't like the protesting residents. You can cut them out, deny them airtime, block all media exposure. But Raptas would have brought it to light, on your channel or another, through the press, the networks, somewhere. He had the power to do that. So you decided to stop him. Is there anything you'd like to add up to this point?"

"That you're both very entertaining, but I am a busy man and don't have time to waste."

"Neither do I," I said and slapped him.

We expected that a man like Vayenas would be quite hard to break, even with a gun pointing at him. Maybe things would have taken a different turn if we had used extensive violence, but Drag had ruled that out on account of his age. Besides, a confession at this point was pointless: if we used a bug, how would Drag be able to justify my presence when the recording on the wire was played back?

What we wanted was for him to find out that we knew and to annoy him enough that he would decide to kill us. If we became targets, we could catch whoever he hired to take us out and get him that way. A lot of ifs, of course. But we had nothing else and still didn't know the truth about a lot of what had happened. So this plan was better than nothing. Drag and I had arranged it so that I would come across as extremely impatient with Vayenas and then hit him on some pretext. When I did, Vayenas changed colour many times before our very eyes. He was not used to being on the wrong end of a beating, except perhaps in the games he played with Meifeng. It probably seemed unconscionable that someone would ever raise a hand to him. He looked at us with deeper hatred than seemed possible to fill sixty square feet. Drag went on talking as though nothing important had happened, as though this was just the first of many that we were willing to give him.

"I got very tired," said Drag.

Vayenas was staring at him fixedly.

"I got very tired trying to work out why Vaios wanted to get hold of Raptas' daughter. But the answer was simple: You wanted to get hold of the evidence from his investigation, the investigation her father hadn't been able to finish – evidence that would leave you burnt. You think the girl has it, and when you discovered all those years later where she was living, you decided to try to get your hands on it. I got really tired of trying to work out what was going on with all those paedophiles. Who the hell suddenly decides to eliminate them all? Then I found out about all those rumours about Raptas. That he was a paedo. And I talked to everybody, one by one, who had talked to his colleagues, making claims against him. First I found the original family who accused Themis of abusing their little girl. Now here's a coincidence: the father, despite having zero education, has been working in a senior management position for years, and even though he's on the payroll, nobody has ever seen him work there. And the other one might be registered unemployed, but he's the flushest man in his neighbourhood. Everyone comes running to him when they're short of cash. He's like the goose that keeps on laying those golden eggs."

"Do you realize that what you're doing is kidnapping and that tomorrow morning you'll be out of the police force?" said Vayenas.

"Are you feeling the cold in here?" Drag asked me. "Or is it just the fear that's giving me this chill?"

"I'll have both of you thrown into jail!" shouted Vayenas, who was about to get to his feet. I was standing over him and pushed him down by the shoulders, forcing him back down onto the toilet seat, groaning. He coughed repeatedly.

"Go on," I told Drag.

"It's assumed that Raptas knew all these other paedophiles. That he shared material with them. Well, I found the emails with the material. The address wasn't his. It looked like it was, but it wasn't. Simple trick. Sofianos, the journalist, fell for it. The paedophiles who supposedly knew Raptas back then are still on trial, after all this time. Their trials keep getting delayed and now they're walking free because eighteen months have passed since they were taken into temporary custody and there's been no trial. It's as if some invisible hand is protecting them. And I intend to prove that that hand belongs to you."

Vayenas coughed again and again, even more loudly. He looked exhausted and was trying to loosen his tie as he coughed. "I need … my pills," he said. "In my jacket; it's on the bed."

Drag stayed with him while I went to get the jacket from the next room. Vayenas searched in the inside pocket, pulled out a pill, and, as he was swallowing it, we heard a loud thud from the bedroom. Vayenas' thugs had just kicked in the door; perhaps Drag and I weren't the only ones wearing transmitters.

I grabbed Vayenas by the collar and watched Drag, who had already burst through into the bedroom. The two heavies were already inside, ready for action, and looked at us both – especially at me, because I was holding their boss.

The lizard-like, less well built one of the two laughed. "Drag," he said.

"Ramon." Drag returned the dry greeting.

Everyone's weapons were already drawn but it would be much trickier for them to shoot, seeing that we had Vayenas. I noticed Ramon was holding a 9 mm Sig Sauer, and was holding it so steadily that he appeared to be frozen.

"Giotis …" he said, motioning to his friend to put down his gun.

And he would have done if Vayenas had not assessed the situation perfectly and said suddenly, "They're not going to shoot me. Kill them."

He was right. That's exactly what Drag and I had agreed, that we'd give him a hard time and then let him go, making sure he wasn't in any danger. He was our main suspect for everything: Raptas' murder, the paedophile executions, the attack on Angelino. We needed him, and we needed him alive.

Before Vayenas even finished his sentence, Ramon had fired a shot at Drag and at that exact same moment Drag had fired one at him. The only difference was that Drag had dropped to his knees to shoot so Ramon's bullet ended up in the wall while Drag's lodged itself between Ramon's eyes. Ramon might have been a very fast and a very good shot, just not fast or good enough.

Of course, I only caught all this out of the corner of my eye, as I had to keep my focus on Giotis. And because he couldn't shoot straight at me without endangering Vayenas, he decided to throw himself on me instead. These guys who look like they have walked off some catch wrestling ring seem to think that the lunge is foolproof. I pushed Vayenas to one side and fired two shots at Giotis, in the sternum, but he kept coming at me as though nothing had happened and then grabbed me by the throat. He was strong as a horse and his grip immediately shut off my breathing. I tried to push him off me with one arm and used the other to shoot at him again, this time in the stomach. It made no difference. No groans, nothing. He must have been wearing a vest, there was no other explanation;

I tried to angle my gun and aim for his neck, but it was impossible. His strength was otherworldly, superhuman. He was choking me and there was nothing I could do about it. I dropped my gun and tried to pull his hands off me with my own but failed, so I landed an uppercut on his chin but not forcefully enough. I heard a noise and saw Drag beating him over the head with his gun. He wasn't going to stop. Giotis was not going to stop. This went on until he suddenly turned and grabbed Drag and they both fell to the floor. I tried to draw some breath as my lungs were desperate for air. Giotis had climbed on top of Drag and had him in some kind of hold. His black sweatshirt was full of blood. He wasn't wearing a vest. I had almost been killed by a man with three bullets inside him. And now he was trying to do the same thing to Drag, only this time his strength was deserting him. He was losing the battle. I spun round, looking for Vayenas. He'd gone. Drag was now holding on to the edge of the bed and kicking Giotis in the face. I ran out. To the right of Meifeng's room was the lift, and a little further along was the staircase. No one was using the lift. I pressed the button and saw that it was still on this floor. Vayenas had chosen the stairs for his escape; they gave him more options. They led to the first floor, where I could hear a lot of shouting going on. It could have been Vayenas causing commotion or it could simply have been panic at the sound of gunfire, making everyone flee the building in their underwear. I turned left after the lift to go after him and a split second before it reached me, I saw a knife coming towards my throat. Instinctively I raised my arm to push it away and felt the blade plunging into me, just below my shoulder. Vayenas was acting shrewdly; he reckoned quite rightly that it would be tricky for him to outrun us, even with a head start. His men had the car keys, so he had no getaway. Instead he had decided to wait on the staircase to surprise the first one of us to come after him. But killing with a knife, unlike a gun, takes technique.

I gave out a small shout of pain and grabbed Vayenas' hand with my right. The knife fell to the floor. I then twisted his arm behind his back and with one upwards thrust dislocated it. The crack was loud but Vayenas' screams were louder. He tried to kick me in the balls. I took a step back and let go of his arm. Despite the pain, he started to run. I caught up with him only a few steps down and hurled him against the pink walls. He really had no idea how unmanageable I was.

"You can start by ..." I said. I picked him up by his collar and his belt and whacked his head against the wall. And then I did it again. And again. "Talking." I was about to slam his head into the wall once more when he raised his hand in weak surrender. "Now," I said.

He sat down on the bottom step of the flight leading to the first floor. His face was full of cuts, and when he first attempted to stand up he fell back down again as though he couldn't work out that he should be using his weight to counteract the fall.

"I must be getting rusty; I used to be in the special forces," he said, spitting blood.

"You were out to get Raptas. From the word go. To stop it all coming out."

He nodded.

"Not like that. Speak!"

"Yes."

"And you concocted the story that he was a paedophile."

"Yes."

"Your idea?"

He nodded.

"So he wouldn't publish his report?"

"He wouldn't listen to reason. Nor to threats. I called him into my office, told him I wanted him to put the brakes on the investigation. I didn't say that the factories belonged to me – just to drop the case. I think his words were 'No way!'"

"And?"

"When someone is about to go to war with you, you have to strike first."

"And you did. You made sure that the false accusation of child abuse did the rounds of all his colleagues so that they could finish him off for you."

"I was one step ahead. He hadn't finished the investigation yet, but I had all my witnesses lined up."

*What kind of innocent man with Themis' connections disappears like that?* I remembered Anna Kati's question. The answer was now clear: an innocent man who is dealing with someone with a thousand times more powerful connections than his, someone who's willing to do whatever it takes to get him out of the way.

"Not witnesses," I said. "False witnesses."

An expression travelled across his mouth which might have been a smile, despite the great pain that any kind of facial movement would have caused him. It looked like he had decided that there was no point in even trying to get up and had made himself comfortable on the floor.

"In the end, the truth is just what most people believe," he said.

Spoken like a true man of the media. It then occurred to me that the police would have been called when the shots were fired. Time was short. And where had Drag got to? I had left him fighting with Giotis.

"Nice theory. Very convenient. So Raptas disappears because he's scared he'll get arrested?"

"Mmm. And that cripple he dragged around with him would have to go back to the orphanage. You know, in war it's not the best side that wins; it's the side with less to lose. If the report had come out, I would have been in and out of court for the next ten years. If the child abuse had come out, Raptas would have lost his daughter; a paedophile, adopting an underage child? I don't think so."

*That cripple he dragged around with him.*

"So even if he had published the evidence, you would have had enough time to destroy his reputation. His report would have been completely discredited and been buried under the noise of the sex scandal."

"You're smart. Do you want to come and work for me?"

"You're doing exactly the same thing now. You're having these paedophiles murdered because you've heard that someone is investigating Raptas' murder. You were worried that this someone has or would get hold of the evidence and publish it. So you started killing paedophiles just like you had Raptas killed so it looked like they were connected."

"You're smart, but I think you take me for an idiot. Raptas was tortured to death. Why would I want to torture him?"

"So he'd give you the evidence he'd gathered against you."

"If I had known he was up on Filopappou, I wouldn't have needed to go to the trouble of torturing him. All I would have had to do was take the girl and he would have handed all of it over."

He was right about that.

"So you're telling me that you didn't know where he was?"

"All I knew was that he was still phoning some of the factory workers occasionally and was still digging around for more evidence, wherever he was."

Raptas remained a true journalist, even when homeless and living on the streets.

"I looked everywhere for him. I preferred to find out what it was that he knew rather than have to resort to neutralizing him. When I hired Vaios years later and he told me all the time I had been looking for Raptas he had been living up on Filopappou and that he'd been seeing him once a month, I thought someone was playing a joke on me."

*Athens, Stratos, is a much smaller city than it thinks it is. This is especially true of its underworld. The same old people going round banging their heads against each other, working for different bosses. So no coincidence seems that big to me.* Paraschos' words.

"I had people turning Athens upside down looking for him but he always eluded them, every time we thought we were getting close. It was as though someone was tipping him off."

While Vayenas was talking, almost on autopilot and defeated, I thought everything he was saying made perfect sense. The paedophile executions were a little different from Raptas', but that was because we were dealing with a different murderer. But then if someone else had murdered Raptas, who was that someone and why had they done it?

Vayenas finally made the decision. He slowly got to his feet, his eyes on me the entire time as he tried to work out what I was going to do to him. I had to keep reminding myself that we needed him alive.

*It was just the two of us. We were a team. "The pack", he used to call us,* Emma had said.

"One more question," I said.

Such was the silence on the staircase that each one of our words sounded like hailstones. Vayenas seemed to be on the point of collapse again. His head was leaning on his shoulder, on the side that had taken the brunt of the wall.

"If Vaios had pulled it off. If you'd managed to get hold of Emma. What would you have done to her?"

"Nothing. We only wanted the evidence," he said, and shrugged in a bid to be more convincing.

*I'm only out for revenge. Justice disappeared the moment he died.* I recalled Emma's words from our first meeting.

Revenge. Even if he was telling the truth and had not killed Themis, Vayenas was single-handedly responsible for the fact that Emma and her father had been forced to leave their home and to live on the streets.

"And then what? After you'd got the evidence?"

There was Angelino too, whose life was in the balance because of Vayenas. I saw my mother's face now. Clear as day, just before she died. With Angelino taking care of her. With her smiling at him. Revenge.

"I'd have let her go," he replied.

"Why am I not convinced?"

I raised my pistol and dispatched him to where he could keep company with Themis Raptas, complete with a bullet in his head.

Drag turned up about a minute later, at about the same time as the first sirens sounded in the distance. His lips were swollen, his eye in a state. Giotis, with the three bullets inside him, had proved to be a real beast of a man before he finally died of internal bleeding.

"What have you done?" asked Drag when he saw Vayenas' corpse. "What have you done?" he repeated, this time noticeably louder. "Get out of here quick," he said, taking my gun out of my hand and slipping it into his holster.

# 25

Back at home and still fully clothed, I collapsed on the bed, exhausted, starving, with my arm in a bandage and slightly drunk – it helps with the pain. I thought about Themis Raptas, a man who was "irritatingly good" at his job, as Paraschos had put it, but in the eyes of his closest colleagues and friends carried a stomach-churning stigma, the stigma of the child abuser. It doesn't get worse than that. A man who knew his life was in danger and at the same time had to fight on the streets on a daily basis for his own survival and for the survival of a blind child. And then to fail, after sacrificing the integrity he prided himself so much on, by blackmailing Paraschos to get money for Emma.

Then I thought about Emma. I closed my eyes and just lay there like that for ages. At one point I thought I saw lights all around me. I got up with a bit of difficulty and staggered into the sitting room. She had to move around the city streets like this, but I was in a flat I knew like the back of my hand. How difficult could it really be? I kept knocking into things – furniture, walls, doors. I feared every step. I put my good hand out in front of me to protect the injured one from further knocks. I had to touch every-thing very carefully to work out what it was. I was scared. I opened my eyes and looked at my watch. Six minutes of blindness. Six minutes. For Emma it had been a lifetime.

I phoned Teri and gave her the briefest of summaries of what had happened. I explained that the police always try to cover for their own but that there were some irregular-ities that were too glaring to cover up. It would be impos-sible to cover up Drag's presence at the massage parlour in Piraeus today where he had left behind three dead bodies, supposedly on his own. And it was also impossible to cover up the fact that one of those dead bodies belonged to Lazaros Vayenas. Drag was now in serious trouble, and it was down to me. We had nothing concrete on Vayenas. I asked Teri not to say a word to Emma and to put her on so I could talk to her.

I was so happy for her. Raptas was clean. But I still hadn't found his murderer. That is, assuming Vayenas had been telling me the truth. But I couldn't share any of this with Emma. This good news was irrelevant to her as she had never for a moment pulled her father down from the pedestal she kept him on, and I didn't feel like discussing my incompetence at catching his killer. I hoped I would be able to correct this, though. Emma had warned me during our first meeting that I would need to be very patient in dealing with this case. At the time I'd had no idea just how patient.

Emma knew nothing about Themis' investigation into the environmental catastrophe. She told me that she was working on a really impressive new trick involving two decks and that she would give me a demonstration when it was ready. She sounded excited. Emma was a professional who derived strength from her work, which was not something I could say about myself lately. I think I managed to say goodnight before I fell asleep.

I dreamed about Themis Raptas. He was dressed as the Tramp and was doing his routine with Emma in one of the Athens squares. But this Tramp wasn't Raptas, it was Chaplin himself. The crowd was ecstatic. Word had got round and the square was filling up with eager and excited crowds dying to watch them. I couldn't get close enough to see; I couldn't get close enough to hear my own voice shouting out to warn them that they were in danger, that their lives were hanging by a thread, that I had come from the future and they needed to listen to me if they wanted to stay together. Themis Chaplin and Emma – happy together wherever they were.

I was jolted awake by the anxiety that they couldn't hear me. I had left the lights on. My head and my arm were in pain, my body was crying out for rest. I got up to take a couple of painkillers and turn off the lights but ended up on the computer instead of back in bed. I went onto YouTube and put on *The Kid*. I remembered Anna Kati saying how much Themis loved the symbolism of everything and that he had loved this film to the point of obsession. All the routines he and Emma performed were taken from it.

A film about two street people who accidentally come together and grow to love each other. Just like Themis and Emma.

A film in which the Tramp gets through despite unbelievable difficulties and brings the Kid up, always with a smile. Just like Themis.

A film which, from start to finish, conveys a melancholy about the mother who abandons the child, just like Emma's mother, who had left her at the orphanage. A film in which bad people try to hurt the Tramp and the Kid but they always manage to escape. Just like Themis and Emma.

A film in which, at the end, the penitent mother reconnects with her child after so many years. She takes both the child and its adoptive father with her, the man who had stood by the child for so long and raised it through all the hard times.

Impossible? Why not?

I kept staring at the last frame, with the door closing behind the three of them, now happily inside their home.

"He loved her!" I said out loud to the nobody who was keeping me company, the nobody who had now permanently taken Maria's place in my life. I thought about it for a while and became even more convinced, partly encouraged by my drunkenness and my exhaustion. When you are sure of something, it is easy to relax: you don't have to bother yourself with alternate scenarios and solutions. Especially when you have run out of alternatives.

"Bloody hell. He loved her. Themis loved Emma's mother!"

I got no reply. I took it as a sign of agreement.

# 26

Drag was struggling. The Chief was livid. He was demanding evidence "here and now". Ministers and MPs were all
leaning on him horribly while the media, TV stations as
well as newspapers, were leaning on them horribly in turn,
and they for their part were under horrendous pressure
of debts and had to find a way of getting a scoop. The
Chief was barking at Drag, telling him that Vayenas' death
needed an immediate and convincing explanation. Ramon
and Giotis were expendable, but a dead Vayenas was a
potential bomb under the Chief's chair. Drag's account of
how he was acting in self-defence when the armed heavies burst into the room was problematic because Drag
would have to explain what he was doing in that room in
the first place. Vayenas' severely disfigured face from all
those blows was something else that had to be explained
away. It was probably unwise for Drag to call me – his
best friend the caretaker – to explain the situation. The
statement made by the immigrant father that Vayenas had
persuaded him to make false accusations against Raptas
to his colleagues did not count against Vayenas, not even
as a misdemeanour. The search the police carried out at

Vayenas' office had turned up nothing that could connect him to the paedophile murders. Everything else that Vayenas had told me was proving awkward to confirm now that he was dead. Drag, despite all this, took it all to the Chief as his own information. Unsubstantiated as it all was, the Chief dismissed it out of hand. He then advised Drag to take extended sick leave until further notice, with immediate effect. Drag slammed the door behind him on the way out and went to instruct his crack team of six to go and find any associate of Vayenas' who knew anything at all about the paedophile executions.

I asked Drag if I could help in any way at all.

"Haven't you done enough?" came the voice down the phone. He was still speaking to me – just – but as some sort of unavoidable irritation. This was the first time I had managed to sabotage one of his cases. He had wanted to arrest Vayenas once he had gathered enough evidence against him. He told me that he was on the way to see Anna Kati, to see if she could remember any of the details of Themis' Achelous investigation and to ask whether it was possible to reconstruct the research.

That wasn't the only evidence we were missing. We still didn't know anything about the identity of Emma's biological parents, and after my idea the previous evening, I absolutely had to know who they were. I phoned the orphanage and told the secretary that I wanted to speak to Hara, their social worker whose surname I had unfortunately forgotten.

"Kyriazi. Hara Kyriazi." She very helpfully supplied it for me.

"Yes, that's it," I answered, and by the time she connected me, I had hung up.

According to her online profile, Hara Kyriazi, social worker at the Happy Home orphanage, who had given Themis so much help with Emma, lived in Michael Boda Street. I got there at two in the afternoon. It was a listed building in the neoclassical style but looked like it was only one step away from dereliction. I had already walked across the front garden and rung the bell, but when no one answered I came back out and stood outside, waiting for her to return. As I had nothing better to do I looked round at all the old buildings in the street, some of which made Kyriazi's house look almost palatial in comparison. I looked at all the acacias on either side of the street, which in about one month's time would flower and fill the pavements with an amazing scent. Many of the people moving around were foreign and looked like they felt foreign too. They were either alone or in twos, wrapped up and bent over, and when they did talk, they did so in whispers. It was not surprising that they were nervous. Just last week two migrants had stabbed the owner of a mini-market on the corner of Boda and Agiou Meletiou Street. A robbery gone badly wrong. The local residents had staged protest marches and formed vigilante groups who had told the media that they were armed and that the useless police were welcome to ask them why, if they dared. Some of them were taking the opportunity to carry out daily attacks on every foreigner who walked around the neighbourhood, smashing the shop windows of all foreign-owned businesses. Children weren't spared either if they had the wrong skin colour.

Hara Kyriazi got home a little before five. She found me outside her house eating a chocolate croissant I had picked up from the nearest kiosk. She had short dark hair, small eyes, an even smaller mouth and a snub nose. She was wearing round glasses and looked about fifty years old.

"Good evening."

She gave me a strange look. Perhaps a little frightened, too. Lots of people get like that when they first see me, and Kyriazi, who can't have weighed more than a hundred pounds, at around five foot two was more than a foot shorter than me. She looked drawn and insubstantial.

"Good evening," she replied, hesitating on the final syllable.

"My name is Stratos Gazis. Private detective. I'd like to talk to you about a case I'm working on – Themis Raptas and his daughter Emma."

I hadn't even got to the end of my sentence before I noticed that she was standing there with her mouth wide open in astonishment.

"What do you want to know?"

"Emma is with me. I'm taking care of her. With some other people. She's fine."

She grabbed hold of my jacket, as though she needed the support. Her head was angled to one side and I couldn't see her face.

"Are you all right?"

She took a step backwards and I saw that she had teared up.

"Come inside," she whispered.

"Hara!" came a voice from behind us.

Kyriazi turned to face the bulky sixty-year-old man who had appeared from the house next door carrying a rifle.

"Minas. Good evening!" she said with a sudden burst of forced enthusiasm, which gave him the necessary encouragement to approach. The rifle was cocked but was pointing to the ground. My right hand was already on the Smith & Wesson in my jacket pocket while I carried on eating my croissant with my left.

"Do you know this gentleman?"

"Yes, yes. He's a friend," she answered as she rummaged in her handbag for a packet of tissues to dry her eyes.

"Are you crying?"

"Oh no, it's just that he's an old friend. I was just really moved to see him again."

"Ah. I noticed him waiting for you. For ages. I wasn't sure if you were in any danger."

"No. Everything's fine."

"Look, I'm sorry. These are strange times we're living in," said Minas.

"Not at all. It's just as well you're around," I told him, releasing the grip on my gun.

Hara shared the neoclassical building with a plump white cat called Zouzou. Zouzou didn't take to me and disappeared the minute I appeared, which meant that Hara had to follow her into the bedroom and stroke her and reassure her. While she was away I took the opportunity to look over the photographs that were plastered from one end to the other of the sparsely furnished sitting room. In every single photo there was Hara, cuddling one child or another. In some of them the children were clearly happy; in others they looked more reserved. Some of the photos included other adults of different ages. They could be the families Hara had helped to adopt. But I didn't really care who they were. I had come for a very specific reason.

"I just went to wash my face, to help me stop crying, but ..." she said when she came back. She was still weepy. "Emma is fine. Emma is fine. I keep telling myself that, ever since you said it." She crossed herself in front of me. "Thanks be to God! Do you believe in God, Stratos?"

"I believe that evil exists. As for whether God exists or not, I'm undecided."

"I left an offering in church – to find out that she was safe, or to see her. If she was OK. Can I see her some time?"

"If she wants to see you."

"Yes, of course, if she wants to. Of course. She's fine! You're still standing. Sit down. She's fine. It's unbelievable. I'm so happy. I left the offering – just so that she'd be OK. To make sure she was OK. Oh, my God!"

Suddenly she was down on her knees praying, with her head touching the floor. Absolute humility. The tears kept coming. I couldn't work out whether it was the shock of the good news or whether this was normal for her. I suspected the latter. I stood there, hoping that she would pull herself together long enough for me to get the information I needed. I waited quietly for her to finish whatever it was she was doing.

As soon as she got to her feet she said, "I killed Emma. I mean, I tried to, I tried to. But because there is a God, I failed," she said, her voice intensifying to a point of near ecstasy. I was at a loss. She was completely insane. Maybe it was she who had scared the cat, not me.

"What do you mean? Emma said that it was down to you that Themis was able to get her out of the orphanage so quickly."

"Yes." She had suddenly slipped into one-word answers. Her eyes were shining and she looked at me without seeing me.

"So …?" I said, trying to keep her going.

"Yes. I did help back then," was all I got.

"Have you got Emma's file, by any chance? It's missing."

"From the Happy Home. Of course it is, because I stole it. And I erased the file on her from our system."

"Why?" I asked, without being at all sure that she was listening.

"Did Emma tell you that she came to find me at the orphanage after Themis was killed?"

I had deliberately avoided asking Emma about the time after the murder when she was alone on the streets. I reckoned that it had no immediate bearing on the case and I was wary of opening old wounds. That had been a mistake. Everything had a bearing on this case. And in all the cases I work on I never let anything go, however trivial it seems. Drag was right. In my efforts to protect Emma, I had damaged the investigation. But if the path to truth intersects with the heart of a child, you either have to stay on the path or blow it to pieces.

"No, we didn't talk about that."

"She did. She had no choice really. She had only ever known us and Themis. I have no idea how she found us in her state, but find us she did. She had walked. Alone. I remember the day and the time very clearly. It was three years ago now. Midday. Boiling hot. So that my sin took place in front of the light of the world. I was standing by the entrance, I remember. I told her we were full and had no beds. Of course, we did have some beds available, but I said we didn't. I told her to come back the next day and in the meantime I would try to find her a space at another orphanage. Naturally, she took off and never came back again. She went straight back to nowhere. Just because I had been paid off. Bribed. It was a lot of money. I was having to help my father pay off his gambling debts at the time. He didn't pay them, of course. However much I gave him, there was never an end to it. He killed himself last year. Not surprising really. I looked down at him in his coffin and said so out loud. All the family were staring at me because I just kept saying it, again and again, 'Why aren't I surprised?' You can't save lives with dirty money. I sent Emma back onto the streets. I, the same woman who had given her to my friend, who had thrown her a lifeline, was now taking it back. You can't know how happy I am to hear that she is well. Nothing else matters. I don't care what punishment I get. I betrayed them, her and Themis. As long as she's all right – that's all that matters."

"Who bribed you?"

The question seemed to scare her. "Shh," she said. "Shh. Don't ask 'who?'. Ask 'what?' Who is for people; what is for monsters. One moment …" She stood up and walked over to a dresser and opened the bottom drawer. She rooted around inside for a while and then pulled out a white document wallet, the kind with ears and a ribbon, and pushed the drawer shut again. "Take a look."

There was a printed label on the outside: *Emmanuela Raptas*. Emma's full name after her adoption. I opened it, and there on the first page was the name of her birth mother, a name I didn't know. Hara was pointing to it. "For monsters," she repeated.

I would normally have paused the reading and asked her what she meant, what it was that made Emma's mother a monster. But I didn't, because I had already seen what was written underneath. There it was in black and white, so there could be absolutely no doubt however many times you read it, however many times you blinked and read it again: the name of her biological father. I looked at it and felt as if I had a heart, because what else but a heart was I feeling sinking to my stomach, looking for a bottom that didn't exist?

Emma's biological father was Themis Raptas.

# 27

Drag and his crack team were working round the clock getting statements from Vayenas' employees across all areas of his business activities. They were trying to establish who was involved in the paedophile executions. They failed. They also failed to uncover any other meaningful evidence. Anna Kati explained to him that it would take months to rebuild the Achelous files from Themis' investigation. She asked him if he had any explanation for why Themis had reformatted her hard drives. Drag passed on the two explanations that I had for it. The romantic view was that Raptas was trying to protect her; by making it impossible for her to continue the investigation, she would not be in any danger from Vayenas. The practical view was that he simply didn't trust her enough and wanted to have full control over the evidence, and this would cement his negotiating position with Vayenas. Take your pick. The dead aren't touchy.

While Drag was suffering and Anna was looking for explanations she would never get, news came through from the hospital. Angelino had come out of his coma and although it was early days, the doctors were optimistic for a full recovery with no lasting damage. Emma was there when he woke up. Angelino insisted that he had woken up not *while* she was there but *because* she was there. Drag didn't waste any time getting over to the hospital to get a statement from him. Angelino explained that the reason he always went around armed before the attack in Chateaubriand Street was that he had noticed some suspicious activity in the neighbourhood. He couldn't be sure at that point whether it was anything to do with his sniffing around the Raptas case, or with another case – Angelino was active on several fronts – so he hadn't said anything to me.

After my conversation with Hara, I badly needed some good news, and Angelino's recovery was a welcome injection of optimism. She had told me the whole story of the passionate but destructive love affair between Nefeli Grigoriou, Emma's mother, and Raptas in great detail. Nefeli was a director at a big advertising company. She had risen quickly in the ranks through sheer determination and hard work. She was impatient with Themis' idealism, not just because he wanted to change the world but because he believed he would. As for children, Nefeli didn't even want to think about it, let alone discuss it. But Themis put a lot of pressure on her, arguing that this would complete their relationship. All she wanted was a glittering career with Themis by her side. That was it.

"Nefeli and I used to talk a lot towards the end – she didn't have any friends and I was the only one who would listen – and I didn't even like her. She'd say, 'Why wasn't I ever enough for him? Why weren't we ever enough for him, the two of us?'"

"So what did Themis have to say about all this?"

"He felt terrible. He thought that it was all his fault."

When Nefeli gave him an ultimatum, saying that she never wanted to have children and that he would have to make a choice between a relationship on her terms or none at all, Themis took off. To make things worse, he started sleeping with her best friend. And about a month later, Nefeli discovered she was pregnant.

"They say that a woman scorned will turn into a monster of one sort or another, but Nefeli was in a class of her own. Even years later, when I met her, she only had to hear his name and her face would change. You felt that she was capable of doing anything, even to you. She told me that it was back then, when they had just split up and she saw him going out with her best friend, that the idea of revenge first occurred to her. Initially she considered having an abortion and only telling him about it afterwards. But as the days went by, and the more she thought about it, this seemed like a very mild form of revenge. So she decided to do the opposite. She'd have the child without telling him. And then she'd leave it in an orphanage, and put down 'father unknown' on the birth certificate. She wouldn't say a word until the child was older, a teenager, whether she was still in the orphanage or had been adopted. The fact that Emma was born functionally blind and the doctors warned that her condition would only deteriorate with time, filled her with joy. She thought about Themis and his instinct to help the disabled, finding out after all those years that he had a daughter with a disability and that he hadn't been around to help her. Stratos, I know how all this must sound, but I did warn you. I told you – she was a monster. A monster created by his betrayal, though."

"How come Themis found out when he did?"

"They'd started sleeping together again. They hooked up at a big party about three years later. They'd both been drinking and ended up leaving together, and spent the next two days in bed. You need to understand that Nefeli was crazy about him. She hated him, of course, but had never stopped wanting him. And she was the love of his life. She just came out with it, there in bed. Themis completely lost it with her. He beat her up badly. She ended up in hospital for a week. He headed straight for the orphanage, on the pretext of some story or other he was working on. I happened to be working there at the time. We knew each other from before, from another story he'd done when he had used me as a source. I was flattered by the trust he showed me and by how honest he was with me. I felt sorry for him too, of course. So I did everything I could to help him get Emma out of there. After he took her away from the orphanage, he didn't know how to tell her that he was her biological father: how do you explain to a child that her parents abandoned her for three years, all alone in utter darkness? Her sight by then had already gone. If he told her the truth he would have to tell her about her mother too, and however furious he was with Nefeli, he couldn't do that. Like I said, he felt very much to blame for everything."

*I'm only responsible for one child.* Themis' words to Loukas Sofianos. He had meant his own child.

"Themis deeply regretted the way he had dealt with Nefeli. What he really wanted was for the three of them to live together as a family. But whenever he tried to discuss it with her, Nefeli would just shut down. In the end she sent him a message telling him and his blind daughter to leave her in peace."

Listening to her talk about Nefeli reminded me of Robert Enke, the German goalie who lost the daughter he loved so much to a rare illness at the age of two.

"What Themis did not know and what I only found out many years later was that Nefeli hadn't been upset by his reaction so much but by the fact that it was confirmation that she would always come second to the child in his eyes. This stoked her fury even more. Finding out that Themis was raising Emma alone, and then that the two of them had disappeared together, made things worse. And then there were all the messages from Themis, saying that he still loved her and that they should try to work things out for the sake of the child. She just couldn't stomach the 'for the sake of the child' part."

"You mean she felt she was in competition with her own child?"

"With the whole world. She wanted Themis completely to herself and she wanted him to feel the same way about her. The two of them against the world. The child was an obstacle. I did ask her once if she felt anything at all towards Emma. She answered, 'Why should I? There are so many children in this world. Too many. I just happened to give birth to that one myself.'"

I thought about Robert Enke again, standing there in

front of that train. He didn't just want to die. He wanted his body to resemble his heart – shattered. And nothing to be left of him.

"After that, when Themis and Emma were missing all that time and she had no news of them, Nefeli couldn't find peace. What she was feeling was completely sick: she was longing to have him and Emma back – simply so that she could reject them both. She even hired a private detective to hunt them down."

"Did she know why they'd gone underground?"

"No. I didn't know either. I still don't."

I promised that I would tell her everything once she told me her whole story.

"Then one day she got a phone call. It must have been roughly two years after they went missing. It was Themis. He said they had to meet because there was something really important he needed to talk to her about. She agreed to see him on condition that he didn't bring Emma, at which point he hung up. And never called again."

"But weren't you *his* friend?"

"Yes, I was. That's why I stole Emma's file. He didn't want her to ever find out that her own mother hated her so much. I didn't know Nefeli until about three years ago, when she phoned me and said she wanted to see me. She didn't say why. I went along anyway, out of curiosity more than anything. She told me they'd found Themis' body and that a friend of hers in the police who knew that they had once been together informed her that Themis had been robbed and killed. She was deathly pale, devastated, but a monster nevertheless. She knew all about my father's gambling problem and his debts; there was nothing she hadn't found out about my family. And she had a proposition for me: if Emma ever turned up at the orphanage again, I was to send her away, back onto the streets. In return, she'd clear my father's debts. That, she said, would be her final revenge on Themis. To destroy the child who had torn them apart."

Up to that moment, all the time Hara was telling this story, it was as though she was repeating something she had heard before, or perhaps the plot of a film she had seen. Something she had no personal involvement in. Even Nefeli's death from an aggressive cancer that had finished her off in the space of only six months was something she covered without the slightest hint of emotion, despite the fact that she was the only person who'd stuck by Nefeli to the last.

There was a long pause.

"To destroy a child. And so help me God, I did," she said, and buried her face in her hands.

# 28

There were no accounts in the name Raptas, no bank transfers. But there was a safe-deposit box in the name Emmanuela Grigoriou. Themis had opened the account for his daughter using the surname of the mother who never wanted her. With Emma's file carefully hidden away at Hara's house, no one would be able to make the connection that would lead to the box. Themis Raptas had been a sharp character; I wish I had met him.

Emma, Drag and I walked into the head office of the Bank of America. Vasilissis Sofias Avenue. America, the continent he'd wanted to send Emma to. Themis' weakness for symbolism had outlived him. We had told Emma that Grigoriou was simply a fake surname that Themis used for her and we had tracked down the account through Themis' name as the depositor. The truth about her mother was one truth she could live without, and I was quite prepared to kill anyone who ever tried to share it with her.

Emma was wearing a black polo neck, a pair of jeans and the elegant black velvet jacket I'd bought her for the occasion. She walked in on my arm. I was in an olive-green suit and white shirt while Drag was wearing a chaotic assortment of the first clothes that had stared back at him when he opened his wardrobe that morning.

The clerk serving us greeted Drag enthusiastically; it doesn't hurt to hang around with a TV star. He greeted me and Emma politely and asked Emma for her ID – "just a formality" – but all the while looked to me to deal with this side of things in view of her condition. Emma reached into her jacket pocket and produced her ID card, which Drag had managed to have processed in just one day, and showed it to him.

"Ahh! Thank you," he said, in that patronizing tone people reserve for children with special needs. Drag shot him a look and I hoped it wasn't about to be followed by one of his classic lines.

"Ahh? What do you mean 'ahh'? She can do everything twice as fast as the rest of us." The world according to Drag. A world in which nothing is said inwardly.

"Yes. Of course," he replied, probably thinking that these TV stars can be really hard on ordinary mortals. And then he just stood there, looking at us.

"Why don't we go and open the box?" I suggested.

"I'm afraid there's a small problem. We only discovered it after Mr Dragas phoned to let us know you were coming."

"What problem is that, big guy?" asked Drag.

He was quite short and a bit of a wimp, so the description "big guy" must have come across as deliberately ironic. This did nothing to improve the atmosphere.

"Mr Themistocles Raptas opened the account on behalf of Miss Grigoriou but he put a condition on it: whoever comes to open the box with Miss Grigoriou has to know the five-digit alphanumeric combination that opens the box. In other words, we cannot open it for you," said the big guy, with a touch of justifiable hostility.

"I can get a court order," Drag said.

"I don't think so."

"You don't think that I can get one?"

"Oh, I'm sure you can get one. But if you can't prove that the contents constitute a terrorist threat, I am afraid that the court order will not be applicable This bank is under American jurisdiction and as such the express written wishes of our client must be respected."

The big guy's expression had changed; he was talking to us through a polite but calm smile, trying not to allow it to turn into a smug little smirk at the man who had insulted him. "However, you are allowed three attempts in case you make a mistake or have trouble remembering."

"What if we can't remember? What then?" I asked.

"I am not authorized to answer that question. If there is anything else I can do for you, please let me know," he said and opened the vault with all the boxes inside. He left us there in our ignorance and closed the heavy steel doors behind us.

Drag and I looked at each other.

"I reckon a nice court order should be enough to get them to open it," he said.

"I'm not so sure. Let's give it a go first and if we don't get anywhere, we won't have any choice. Emma," I said, "any ideas?"

"I don't know. This is all really weird. Dad never mentioned any safe-deposit box."

Maybe he thought he would make it. That he had untangled himself from the past enough not to be in any danger. Or that if he wasn't going to, he would have enough time to explain things to Emma.

"Any favourite numbers you can think of? A date, maybe?" I asked.

"No. Not that I can think of."

"Your birthday? His birthday? Did you celebrate them?"

"His? No, never. Mine – yes."

Emma was born on 6 September 2003. If you cut out the zeros, that made 6903.

"But there are five numbers," added Drag.

I shot a look at him. "Thank you for your contribution. Let's try 'E' for Emma – 6903." Drag typed it in. That wasn't it. Two attempts left.

"Great," he whispered.

"We can leave, and come back with this guy I know who can open up any safe in five minutes. As long as you shoot all the cameras they have inside here. You're a star, they'll forgive you," I told him.

Emma was quiet all this time. She was thinking. We decided to follow her example. The only problem was that we had nothing to work on.

"Let's try 91006. 9 October 2006. That's when he took me home from the orphanage. It was a really important day for both of us. We often talked about it."

Drag tried once more. Nothing.

The box was supposed to contain the blackmail money from Paraschos and the evidence against Paraschos and Vayenas. This was our last chance to prove that I was right.

If we failed, bureaucracy and the courts would hold us back for months without us even knowing if it was worth the effort, or if the box even contained what we thought it did. If we failed, Emma would have to wait even longer to discover why her young life had been caught up in so much violence. She would have to wait even longer to find out what it was that her father had wanted to leave her. As for me, not only would I have failed to find Raptas' murderer, but I would also be responsible for the end of my friend's career. Drag's career was his life.

Drag and Emma said nothing for at least five minutes. I hoped they were thinking something more intelligent than I was. All this time I had been walking in the tracks left by a dead man. Now I would have to become him, and get into his head. But how was I supposed to get into the head of a man I'd never met? A man I'd only come to know through the accounts of the people who had known him? Themis Raptas had dreamed of changing the world. But the world doesn't generally encourage those who try to change it. I remembered that film from the 1950s, *Slightly Scarlet*, when the Chief of Police is talking to the main character, Ben Grace, and says, "You're a dreamer, Ben," and Ben replies, "A man's only as big as his dream." The Chief warns him, "They're gonna pull you out of the river some day." And Ben answers, "That's not part of the dream." Themis wound up just like Ben, except Themis' death was much more violent. Noir cinema is about as close as you can get to real life – but it often pales in comparison to the filth and the stench of real life.

Themis dreamed of changing the world, believed in symbolism, adored Emma, was in a fix with his ex, was obsessed with *The Kid*, in which the professionally fulfilled mother agrees to take back her child in the end. Hadn't Hara said, *What he really wanted was for the three of them to live together as a family?*

"One second," I said.

"Why? What's the hurry? Relax," replied Drag.

I checked my phone for a signal and went onto YouTube, found *The Kid* and pressed Play. I knew the film more or less off by heart and jumped to a point near the end, and then a bit further to the forty-fifth minute. The forty-first second. I hit Pause.

"Can I make a suggestion?"

"It had better be good; this is our last chance."

"It *is* good."

"Go on."

"G6791."

"Are you going to tell us what that is?"

"Some other time," I said motioning towards Emma with a slight incline of my head. To my surprise, Drag seemed to understand.

He took a deep breath.

"G ... 6 ... 7 ... 9 ... 1 ... – And Houdini is your middle name!" he added.

The box opened.

While Drag was examining the evidence, Emma and I went to find the big guy to ask what would have happened if we had failed to open it. It then became clear to me why Raptas had chosen such a complex code. He was trying to cover all eventualities. If Emma had gone to the bank with him or with someone he trusted, they would have known the code. If something happened to him and Emma turned up at the bank with strangers, they wouldn't be able to get into the box, in which event the next condition would have to be met: Emma would be taken to a room to answer a series of questions on her own, things that only she could know the answer to. That was Themis' way of ensuring that whoever turned up at the bank claiming to be Emma really was Emma. If she answered the questions, the bank would be required to call Themis' lawyer so that the box would be opened in his presence and he would then help her manage the money. The same lawyer who had betrayed Themis to Paraschos. I could not have imagined when I told Drag the code just how bad things would have got if I had been wrong.

I didn't want to tell Emma what the code meant, but I had to concoct some sort of explanation. I came up with something that was close enough to the truth. I told her that I was thinking about Themis' obsession with *The Kid* and remembered that there was only one number in the entire film, the number plate of the car that the Tramp chases when it's driving off with the child inside it.

The truth is that G6791 is the number plate of the car in which the mother, craving to be reunited with her child, goes to bring the "Kid" back home.

Symbolism – everywhere – right to the end.

# 29

The problem was that I had believed them all: Fotis Paraschos, Vayenas and Nefeli Grigoriou via Hara. They all had reason to hate Themis – Paraschos because he was worried that his black-market activities would come to light; Vayenas because he too feared exposure and all his attempts to find him had failed; Grigoriou because she loved him in her own sick little way. But none of them had killed him, let alone tortured him to death. This all left me without a suspect. Maybe his death was what everyone had been saying it was all along: a random act – a robbery that had led to murder, and nothing more.

Whatever it was, a month had passed and I still hadn't managed to find the person Emma and Angelino had originally asked me to find. And it didn't look like I was going to either.

Fortunately, nobody seemed to concern themselves with my failure.

Emma and Angelino were just so happy to be together again. Angelino was making a full recovery and Emma was at his bedside night and day at the new house they had rented. She was doubly happy because while Angelino was in this condition, she was able to cover the rent with her own money, the money Themis had put aside for her. I resolved not to allow the slightest shadow to be cast on her joy and kept the truth of the identity of her biological parents from her. Themis had felt too guilty to tell her himself. So did I. There was no reason for her to mourn him all over again. The ashes of her file from the orphanage were now drifting through the Athenian smog.

Drag was far too busy to find time for us to talk about Themis' murder. From the moment he released the evidence against Vayenas that we'd found inside the bank box, media figures, friends and other associates of Vayenas' went to war with the police in general and Drag personally. Other outlets which were owned by the competition or outright enemies of Vayenas' pursued him doggedly, trying to get interviews and statements and in general looking for any excuse to turn him into a hero. They got their chance when Drag managed to get one of Vayenas' advisers to confess everything about the paedophile murders, along with the names of the heavies who had carried out the executions on behalf of the media baron. Two of these self-styled Avengers were Ramon and Giotis, the ones who had tried their luck with us back at the massage parlour.

Teri and Hermes were on holiday in the Maldives, where he was supposed to be attending some kind of symposium. They had already booked their next trip – January in Las Vegas, where Hermes was due to give the opening speech at a conference. "By the way," she said, having called me to say goodbye, "did you know that January gets its name from Janus, the two-headed Roman god: one looking forward to the new year, the other back at the year that just finished?"

She was turning into Drag.

Then suddenly one morning in March, Maria was back.

I was on the balcony, watering her plants.

"Hi," she said.

I felt something resembling a spasm in my throat, as though a scream was trying to escape, and I was desperate not to let it.

During the month that had passed I had made several attempts to find her and had even tried lying in wait outside her parents' house, ringing their doorbell again and again in desperation. I'd called her dozens of times on her permanently switched-off mobile and sent her thousands of messages which remained unread and as many emails, which all went unanswered. And here she was, walking into the house with a simple "Hi".

"Hi yourself," I answered.

"Can we … talk?"

I didn't want to talk. I wanted us to hold each other like the world was ending. To do something that would show the intensity of what we were feeling. Words can't do that. They don't measure up.

We sat down in the kitchen. She was wearing a loose red dress under her black coat, which rode up to her knee when she sat down and crossed her legs. I was tempted to tell her that she shouldn't be crossing her legs in her condition but decided this was not the time.

"I've been thinking a lot about what I said to you."

"That you wished I didn't exist?"

280

"That, yes. And everything else. I think I was being unfair. In part. It wasn't any more your fault than mine. And I couldn't ask you to change for the sake of the child. It's the only work you know – it's who you are – it's who I love. Just as you are. I've loved you since we were kids."

I'd been waiting a lifetime to hear this. I might have known it, felt it, but I really needed to hear it. Except she was looking down as she spoke. As though she had just received a death sentence. Not the way you look when you are telling the person closest to you that you want to try again.

"Everything I said, about the child's safety, about our future as a family, was right. So however long I'd been putting it off, however much I wanted to find an answer that would pull everything together, I knew, I *know* there is no answer."

Her voice cracked.

"I knew I was facing a clear dilemma."

She was still looking down. The longer I listened to her, the more I wanted to look down too, but I held my gaze on her.

"I had to make a choice: to raise a child alone or to stay with you. Without the child."

Her voice cracked even more.

Now it was my turn to receive a death sentence.

"People like you can't have children. And I've made the decision that I want to be with you," she said.

Someone had just plunged something sharp right into my throat. Something long and very sharp. I pointed to her belly, my outstretched finger questioning her. I looked at it in a state of alienation: no part of me could ever ask such a question, would dare ask such a question, could ever bear to ask such a question.

"It's already done," she said.

The blade in my throat began to move up and down rhythmically, digging itself deeper and deeper into my flesh, gouging and gouging, determined not to stop until it had completely hollowed me out. I was happy to go along with it, and work with it. If I had had any voice, I would have told it to keep going.

"It was a girl," she said, and suddenly slipped onto the floor and just lay there, doubled up, buckled and pitiful. I looked at her and could have sworn that I was seeing her for the first time in my life.

She stayed down there on the floor, but she wasn't crying.

So Maria had decided to stay with me. Just like Nefeli had decided to be with Themis. Of course, the two weren't the same. Maria had good reasons for not wanting the child to have me for a father. Of course, it wasn't the same, but at the same time it was. She had denied me the chance to talk her round, to tell her that I would do anything, everything for her and the baby. Even change my life.

I thought of Robert Enke again. I thought about how lucky he was to have had those two years with his daughter. I thought about Themis Raptas, who missed those three years with Emma but after that enjoyed another eight with her, albeit under very difficult circumstances. I would have nothing with my child.

I looked out onto the balcony and thought it was strange that the door had been open all this time as the room was completely airless. I had to get out, quickly, before I suffocated.

"I would never have wanted anything more in life than you and that baby," I said.

It took me an hour to pack my things and leave the house. Maria said nothing. She had stayed there on the floor, doubled up, where I couldn't see her face and couldn't get close to her. I'm not sure if she was even aware that I had left. But I was absolutely sure that there was nothing else I could do.

A month later I was standing next to my Peugeot outside HighTV when Dora approached with her signature walk, which I noted was almost as interesting to observe from the front as the back. "Are you waiting for someone?" she said, the smile she gave promising the world. But that wasn't why I was there.

"I wanted to ask you something," I said, the expression on my face instantly wiping the smile off hers.

"OK."

"Get in," I said.

"I've got my own car."

"Get in." Without another word, she did.

A few hours earlier, alone in my hotel room, I'd been feeling like one of those characters in the comics we used to read when we were kids, with those thought bubbles hanging over their heads and an idea swimming around inside it. But I needed Dora's help to work out if I was right, since Drag and I hadn't spoken after I told him what happened with Maria's return. The way he'd reacted, I no longer recognized the man who had been my best friend for the last twenty-plus years.

# 30

Chryssa Georgala's penthouse flat in Voula, at the address Dora had given me, must have been around fifteen hundred square feet. It had three bedrooms, a living room the size of a rugby pitch, two bathrooms, oak flooring and electronic shutters. The whole place was finished in very bad taste, from the furniture to the vases and candlesticks that decorated every last corner. At least there was a half-decent painting of the Iridanos River, the only surviving of the three rivers that had flowed through Athens in antiquity, the Kifissos and Ilissos having both fallen victims to the contemporary Greeks, who had covered them over as a token of their respect for their ancient heritage.

When Chryssa walked through the door she was in a foul mood, which didn't improve when she saw me sitting in her living room with my gun pointing at her quite pretty face. I had made sure to draw the curtains so that the people in the building opposite wouldn't have to watch us as they swam up and down in their indoor heated pools.

"What! What do you want?" she said, losing the blush in her cheeks.

Compared to the advertisement, where I'd heard her for the first time speaking in a whiny voice, she sounded much raspier, as though she had a cold. She was in a black dress which struggled to reach the top of her thighs. Spring was well and truly here and Chryssa wanted to put on a show for anyone who cared to see, and risking her health seemed a small price to pay.

"Sit down," I said, pointing to a black rocking chair.

"Take it, you can take whatever you want and leave! I've got some money here too. You can have it all!"

She picked up her handbag and was about to open it; I don't know whether she was planning to pull out a purse or a gun and I wasn't going to wait to find out.

"Chryssa! Close your bag. Now," I said and pointed to the chair again. When she heard her name, she went even paler. She went to sit down, coughing loudly.

"I'm not rich, if that's what you think, I —"

"Be quiet. I haven't come for your money. I've got some questions for you. You will answer when I tell you and you will stick to the questions. Got it?"

She nodded and curled up defensively in the chair. Good girl.

"What do you want?" she repeated, a slightly shriller tone overcoming the raspiness.

"I want to talk about Themis Raptas."

This took her by surprise. It was written across her face almost as clearly as in that ad when her character realizes just how comfortable her new bra is. But then again, it could have been that her range was a bit limited.

"Come again?" she said.

"Not 'come again'. You really don't want me to come again. In fact, you don't want me anywhere near you, so talk."

"I don't know. What do you want to know? What was the name? Themis who? What was the surname? Er —"

The "er" came out when she saw me get up and come striding towards her, and it turned into small cries of pain as I grabbed hold of her with my free hand, pushed her up against the nearest wall, threw her to the floor and pulled her along on her knees by her long blonde hair back to the chair.

"If you scream, if you try to resist, I will kill you. If you carry on pretending that you don't know anything, I will kill you. Your only hope of getting out of here alive is telling me the truth."

"Who are you?" she asked without moving from the chair.

"I'm listening."

"What do you want to know?"

"I have a witness who places you with him on Filopappou Hill."

"Doing what?" she said, and instantly realized that she had given herself away. "I mean, Raptas left HighTV years ago. What do you mean? What hill?"

"I'm running out of patience," I said, raising my gun to the level of her head.

"No, please. Don't! OK. We were together. Is that what you wanted to hear? We were together. We were in a relationship. Sleeping together – how else can I put it?"

In the hotel room where I had been sleeping for the past month in the company of my loneliness, I would occasionally turn on the TV and see that there were a lot of people out there who were in a much worse state than I was – the actors and the presenters, for example. Once when I was looking at an ad for tights on the telemarketing channel I realized that I'd already seen the blonde model they were using in two other advertisements, and then I also realized that not only had I seen her before but I had seen her in person a few days earlier outside HighTV climbing out of Vayenas' limo. And then I remembered the homeless man who had spoken to Antonis Pavlis, the one that both Pavlis and I thought was crazy. He said he had seen Raptas getting it on under a tree with a gorgeous TV presenter, the one who was always on, day and night. *They show her all the time. She's always on,* he'd commented to Pavlis. That's the way it works if you happen to be the owner's girlfriend. They'll put you in everything. And if the owner is an old man you sleep with to advance your career, it's natural that you will satisfy your real needs elsewhere with someone closer in age to you. Someone with charisma, someone who, according to Dora, everyone at the station was in love with. Pavlis had shown the homeless man photos of all the presenters on Greek TV without realizing that the man who was in and out of the shops begging had confused the model he constantly saw with a presenter.

"Lovely. We're beginning to make some progress. What else do you want to tell me?"

"Nothing. Like what? I was in love with him, and at some point it ended."

"It ended?"

"Yes."

"Before he was murdered?"

"Yes, before, of course."

"This flat belongs to you, does it?"

"What? Course not! I rent."

"I've been here inside your home for five hours. I've already found the titles with your name on them."

She said nothing. I said nothing. I was waiting.

"OK. OK. So it is mine."

"Paid for with the sweat of hard labour – on top of Vayenas?"

Her green eyes looked at me with hatred. The little viper was trapped and was looking for a chance to expel its venom.

"I don't get it. Are you from Vice? Are you checking up on my morals? Do you want a list of everyone I've ever slept with?"

"Vayenas was after Raptas. Raptas knew they were looking for him. Vayenas told me himself that it had felt like someone was looking out for Themis, tipping him off."

"Vayenas said that? Did *you* …?" What she meant to ask was if I had killed him.

"You don't ask the questions round here. It was you who used to tip Raptas off about Vayenas, wasn't it?"

I said this with conviction even though I wasn't quite sure. It was the only logical explanation, and I wanted to see if she would deny it. She didn't. She started crying, or pretending to cry in the way that the heroines in TV dramas cry right on cue.

"You did, didn't you?"

"I loved him!" she said.

That bit at least seemed genuine. But through the crocodile tears it was difficult to sort the truth from everything else. Perhaps she had the same difficulty herself.

"But as you said, Raptas had been long gone from the station. And he lived up on the hill with his daughter like a regular homeless person. Where did the two of you go when you wanted to be together?"

"Anywhere. We would wait for the child to fall asleep. Sometimes it would be in the cave, sometimes outside. It didn't happen often. And even less after they started hunting him down."

"How did you feel about it?"

"How was I supposed to feel? Horrible. I wanted to see more of him. It's why we split up."

"You broke it off?"

"Yes, of course."

"But you just said you loved him."

"What good is being in love if you don't ever see the person?"

"You've got lovely hair."

I would change the subject at regular intervals just to confuse her and stop her from getting too comfortable. This last comment threw her; she tensed up even more.

"What are you going to do to me?"

"Not what you think. Are you a natural blonde?"

"Yes. What's that got to do with anything?"

"I've already picked some hairs from your bathtub. Fortunately for you, you're not much of a housekeeper, so I won't have to cut any off. But I will if it comes to it. We're going to pay a friend of mine a visit now. He's a cop.

Some blonde hairs were found on Raptas' body. Something tells me yours might be a match."

I wasn't at all sure if I was right. The hairs that Martinos mentioned could have been anybody's. Could have belonged to a passer-by and attached themselves to Raptas during the scuffle before the murder or when he fell to the ground. But that's what investigations are: minimal evidence and a whole load of speculation. And you work through it all until you find the theory that holds water. Chryssa let out a sharp cry as she attempted to attack me head-on.

"You fucking —"

I threw a punch under her nose and pinned her to the floor. Then I called Drag and told him to come over and speak to her. The call lasted less than a minute as neither of us was in the mood to listen to the other's voice for longer than necessary.

I never did find out who the second person Themis had trusted with his research was – apart from the lawyer. It was possible that there was no second person. Maybe he'd just told Paraschos that to put the fear of God into him. When I went to see Paraschos to deliver the evidence that related to him, he told me that he had taken a liking to me, and once again that he owed me.

It didn't take much for Chryssa to buckle under interrogation. Drag explained to her right away while she was waiting for her lawyer to arrive that if she didn't tell him everything he needed to know, he would let her walk but she should expect me to pay her a visit, wherever she was hiding.

Her confession was one endless j'accuse – how Themis had ruined his life and was about to ruin hers with his obsession for pursuing the pollution scandal. If only he had left well alone, he would never have got the attention of Vayenas and their lives would have been just fine. He did what he wanted with her. Forced her to go up onto the hill at night to see him, to give her a little bit of affection, and even that he would as often as not withhold. He would get the information about Vayenas he needed from her, find out if he was still trying to hunt him down, where he was looking, and then send her off home because he didn't like to leave Emma alone, or else he was scared she would hear them and wake up. He made her feel worthless, just a pawn in a complex game he was playing with the world. He made her feel that if she stopped being useful to him, if she dumped the disgusting old man she could no longer stand, he would drop her like a shot.

She suggested to Themis that they run away together, go abroad. She would sell up and with the money he had put by too they would be able to survive. They would work. They would have love. When she forced the issue he told her it was time for them to split up as they could not go on seeing each other so sporadically; it wasn't fair on her to expect her to waste her life like this, seeing that he was not about to change the way he lived. His focus was on getting the money together to send Emma to America. Then he would worry about what he was going to do. For the moment, he had no idea. And when he saw that Chryssa still insisted on being with him under any circumstances, Themis told her to her face the fact that after six years together, he was not in love with her. That she was punching above her weight, that he was surprised she hadn't realized that herself and that she was deluded if she thought they had a future together. Everything was a blur. She took the gun Vayenas had given her for protection and she emptied the bullets into Themis. The bruises and the burns they found on his body came later. Chryssa had seen a film in which the murderer had got away with it by muddying the case for the police by making them think the victim had been tortured to death. So she decided to do the same and went ahead, leaving signs of horrific brutality on Themis' body.

"You know what? I don't regret it," she said to Drag at the end of her confession.

Remorse is a wonderful concept. Perfect for fairy tales. As long as it's contained within them and does not confuse us as we grow older and start to believe that such a thing actually exists.

"That doesn't matter. You'll have plenty of time for reflection in your cell – years, in fact," he answered. At least that's what he told me later when he gave me a courtesy call to thank me for having caught his murderer.

Themis Raptas had managed to escape all those guilty enemies, who would not have hesitated to kill him, only to be murdered by the very woman he thought he was manipulating.

# 31

Teri phoned as soon as she was back from the Maldives. She wanted to talk about Maria, and I suggested we met for coffee. She refused. Even her voice sounded different.

"There's something I've never told you. Of the three of you, I was always fondest of you. I didn't *love* you any more than the other two, but you were always very special to me."

Past tense.

"And I thought I knew you; that's what you think when you grow up with someone. So I never believed that you would behave like such a heartless, hypocritical, sexist pig. Maria made the ultimate sacrifice to be with you, and you *left*," she said.

"Have you finished?"

"Yes."

I put the phone down.

A few hours before that I'd been at the mall observing a new target. It was only luck that had prevented me from bumping into Maria, who had been there shopping. She hadn't been alone. Drag was with her, and for the few seconds I permitted myself to look at them before I disappeared, they looked to me like they were having a lovely time. Together.

A further eight months went past, bringing two lucrative contracts and only a few awkward phone calls with Teri and Drag, in which we all made sure that Maria's name did not come up.

That afternoon in the studio flat I was now renting, I felt the need to break the silence. I turned on my laptop and within a minute was on YouTube rewatching a video that had only been uploaded a couple of days earlier, but judging from the number of hits underneath, almost four million people had managed to see it. With a quick click I jumped the first twenty minutes of the show in which Fred, the tall, thin, well-turned-out fifty-year-old presenter, is doing his monologue before sitting down at his desk and giving a commentary on various photos and topical video clips. He thinks he's funny, and judging by the audience's laughter from the few seconds that they'd been watching him, they think so too. I had read about him online and how he had been drawing the largest prime-time audiences in America for years. I clicked the twenty-first minute. I was nervous. Nervous about watching a recorded show which I was watching for perhaps the hundredth time.

Twenty-one minutes and seventeen seconds: Fred turns to the audience and announces an exclusive surprise guest. Emma comes into the frame, together with her translator, who is holding her by the hand. In her other hand she is carrying a white stick, supposedly to help her move about. The trick, she'd explained to me, is to make people think you're weaker than you are. What the audience sees is a skinny young blind girl, and not the superhuman magician she keeps hidden inside. Fred asks her how old she is, where she has come from and what she is doing there. Emma answers, "You invited me here." The studio audience, who until that point have been respectful and reserved at the sight of the blind girl, laugh out loud the minute they hear the translation. The camera pans over the faces in the amphitheatre and I briefly catch Angelino's face in the crowd. Fred scratches his head as if to acknowledge that the girl has put one over on him. He explains to the audience that Emma is the gold-medal winner from the most recent Magic Olympics, and asks her to present tonight's audience with her winning tricks.

Emma duly picks out a member of the audience at random and asks him to come to the front and select a card. He does as instructed, and then replaces the card in the deck in a different position, shuffles and cuts. Emma then takes the deck and pulls out the card the man had picked. The judges at the Olympics had described Emma as "simply unbelievable". But this is only the beginning. Once the applause begins to subside, Fred complains to Emma that it has taken so long to persuade her to come onto his show and that he has been begging her for ages.

"But I wanted to be here today; on your lucky day," she says.

"Why especially today?"

"Because if you go to any casinos at all today and play blackjack, you'll win a lot of money."

"That's great, because the money they pay me here ..." replies Fred, and the audience dissolves into more laughter.

The only person present who remains serious is Emma, even when she has the joke translated for her. Fred explains to her that she must be wrong because he has never gambled and won.

"Perhaps your luck is about to change," says Emma.

A stagehand appears with a fresh deck, still wrapped in cellophane. Fred tears it open. The camera zooms in on the cards, showing that they are still in their original order. Emma asks him to shuffle and does not touch the pack. She then asks him to do it once, twice more. Some people in the audience are shouting out, saying that they want to shuffle too. Eventually Fred hands the cards over to Emma. She gives them one final shuffle before asking Fred to cut.

"OK," she says. "What we'll do is this: we'll play blackjack with a single deck and I'll deal." She then deals him four blackjacks in a row.

"No way! No way! What are the odds of that happening? All four aces and the picture cards. I've just been told by the producers that the odds are less than one in ten million!" shouts Fred.

"Shall we have another hand? See if *I* can win for once?" says Emma in a slightly aggrieved tone and looking like butter wouldn't melt in her mouth. The translator duly conveys this to Fred, who is happy to oblige. Emma deals a fifth blackjack even though all the aces have already been played.

"What?" says Fred. Emma just shrugs her shoulders, gathers up all the cards and asks him to count out the aces. Fred counts them one by one as the cameras zoom in, and he only finds four.

The audience gives Emma a standing ovation but, feeling more confident now, she turns to them, raises her arm to silence them and announces that she hasn't finished. More laughter. The translator is lapping up the enthusiasm every time he translates something Emma says.

Emma asks Fred for the deck, cuts it six different ways and shuffles it in as many again, hands it back to Fred to cut, asks him to shuffle it any way he pleases and to cut one last time. She picks the pack up in her right hand and tosses it up in the air. The deck spins round briefly before splitting in two mid-air. One half falls straight down and lands in Emma's open palm and the other lands on Fred's desk with the cards neatly arranged, one on top of the other. A fresh round of applause while Emma takes one pile and places it on top of the other before raising her hand to silence the applause again. Instant silence.

*She's got them. Putty in her hands.*

"OK," she says. "We have shuffled and cut these cards about ten times, so they should be really well mixed now, right?"

Fred looks at her full of scepticism. He knows she is about to pull something on him but can't see what. "Er ... sure," he replies.

Emma turns the deck over to reveal that all the cards are in their original order, by suit and value, just as they had been when they came out of the box. The audience is ecstatic. The translator is now raising his arm too, loving every minute. Fred looks at Emma; he's bowled over and applauds her too. Emma takes a bow.

And for only the second time since I met her all those months ago, in what seems another life, I see her smile.

# ACKNOWLEDGEMENTS

Once again, a gigantic thanks to Peter and Rosie Buckman. Charles Pappas' book *It's a Bitter Little World* (Writer's Digest Books, 2005) was very helpful in double-checking certain movie lines in cases where my memory was reluctant to help.